A haircut was the last thing on Aidan's mind.

He stood abruptly. "No," he said in a clipped tone. "Thanks." He took a step to make his getaway, but Ashley jumped in front of him.

He blinked, shocked. He was even more shocked when she placed her palm on his chest. His top two buttons were undone, and her palm landed partially on his bare skin.

Her eyes widened as if she was shocked at herself, too. At her own audacity.

He stared directly into her eyes. She was shorter than him by a few inches. Her skin was almost translucent and looked as smooth as porcelain, like a doll's. She had long auburn hair pulled back from her forehead. Every emotion played clearly across her dainty features, and at the moment she appeared terrified of him. Her hazel eyes were round, the pupils slightly dilated.

Something about that made him pause. She seemed so vulnerable. He'd thought he was a mess these past months, but she didn't seem as if all was well with her, either.

Dear Reader,

Some of you asked if Ashley LaValley, the heroine's sister from *Out of His League*, would be receiving her own story. Here it is.

When we last left Ashley, she was a single mom returning from alcohol rehab. Her precocious son, Brandon, a cancer survivor and baseball fanatic, was Ashley's whole world.

Now it's four years later. Brandon is twelve and starting a new school year at an elite Boston boarding school in hopes of someday becoming a children's oncologist. Ashley has uprooted her whole life—new hairstylist job in the city, new apartment—so that she can support his dream.

But she's surprised to realize her son is growing up and becoming more independent. She doesn't need to revolve her life around him as much anymore. For the first time in a long time, she can—and indeed must—ask herself what she wants out of her own life.

Especially when intriguing, attractive Dr. Aidan Lowe turns up in her salon chair, bringing a new set of love and challenges into her world.

I hope you enjoy their romance.

All the best,

Cathryn Parry

CATHRYN PARRY

The Good Mom

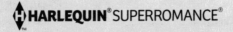
HARLEQUIN® SUPERROMANCE®

Recycling programs
for this product may
not exist in your area.

ISBN-13: 978-0-373-61007-5

The Good Mom

Copyright © 2016 by Cathryn Parry

Printed in U.S.A.

Cathryn Parry is the author of eight Harlequin Superromances. Her books have received such honors as a Booksellers' Best Award, a CataRomance Reviewers' Choice Award and several Reviewers' Choice Award nominations. She lives in Massachusetts with her husband, Lou, and her neighbor's cat, Otis. Please see her website at www.cathrynparry.com for information about upcoming releases or to sign up for her reader newsletter.

Books by Cathryn Parry

HARLEQUIN SUPERROMANCE

Something to Prove
The Long Way Home
Out of His League
The Sweetest Hours
Scotland for Christmas
Secret Garden
The Secret Between Them

Other titles by this author available in ebook format.

To Dee. Thanks for the friendship,
fun and trips to Salem.

CHAPTER ONE

NEW JOB, NEW LIFE, new home.

Today was only her second day on the job. Ashley LaValley still wasn't used to this hair salon's setup. So different from her old life.

She glanced toward the photo of her son, never far from her workstation. There it was—by the sleek bottle of high-end shampoo. A recent photo, Brandon smiled proudly in his newly bought, preppy St. Bartholomew's School blazer. The light of Ashley's life, her son had straight, sandy-blond hair and ruddy skin. Nothing at all like her features.

"Ashley, there's a man here for you," her young coworker Kylie said, approaching Ashley's little corner workstation with a pen in her hand. "He's a walk-in, so he's not on your schedule."

And just like that, a little thrum of worry passed through Ashley. *Ridiculous*, she told herself. *You're doing fine.*

Putting her hand to her stomach, she breathed out slowly. Worrying was the big issue of her life, it seemed. No matter how much she worked and tried and strove, her old fears always resurfaced—usually when she was facing a change. She'd been through enough counseling to recognize what was happening, but this one-day-at-a-time stuff sure did challenge her. And of course she was being challenged—she was dealing with major life upheavals. All the biggies. New apartment. New job. New school for Brandon. New routine.

"You look kind of pale," Kylie remarked, tilting her head. "Are you sure you're okay?"

"I am." Honestly, she needed to pull herself together. She had worked hard to find this job within walking distance of Brandon's new school in Copley Square, Boston, and she couldn't do anything to jeopardize that.

She stuck a smile on her face for Kylie, the young receptionist who controlled the front desk at Perceptions, the sleek salon where Ashley needed to keep working for the next two years, at least until Brandon graduated from his private middle school. "I'm just getting used to my new workstation is all. Let me clean up a bit first." She picked up her broom and began sweeping up snips of blond hair from her last client. "Who's the man I'm taking?" she asked as casually as she could.

"I didn't ask his name." Kylie's brow furrowed, perhaps catching her mistake. Ashley got the distinct impression that Kylie was somewhat new, too. She eyed Ashley's broom. "I don't think you're supposed to do that. We have interns to sweep up hair." Maybe Ashley imagined it, but she thought she saw Kylie roll her eyes ever so slightly, as if Ashley was a hopeless rube.

It was true Ashley had never worked in a salon like this one before. For the hundredth time that morning, she glanced uneasily at the gleaming surfaces of the upscale space, so different from the homey blue-collar haunt where she'd happily worked for the past twelve years. Going to work there had been like being at home. *Where everybody knows your name*, as the old theme song went. Her old boss, Sal, hadn't run a place patronized by intimidating customers who seemed to ooze money and privilege. The lady getting foil highlights in the cubicle next to Ashley's had set down a handbag that cost three thousand dollars. Ashley had noticed it in the window of the boutique next door. That was more than three times the monthly rent in her old neighborhood.

"Ilana specifically asked me to give you this client," Kylie explained. "He came in with his grandmother, and I think she's important. At least, she's in the private treatment room with Ilana now."

Ilana was the owner of Perceptions, and Ashley's new boss. She'd also informed Ashley that for her first two weeks on the job, she was on probation until she proved herself.

"Okay." Ashley blew out her breath and squared her shoulders. *No pressure here.* "I'm on it. Do you know what he wants? A trim and a blow-dry?" she guessed.

"Um, I don't know," Kylie said, "but he *really* needs a haircut. Just wait until you see him."

"Oh, my." One of Ashley's fellow stylists murmured beneath the hum of her blow-dryer. She'd probably been eavesdropping, and was now craning her neck toward the front of the salon. Ashley couldn't see what she was looking at because of the L-shaped placement of the workstations.

As the new girl, Ashley was tucked into the farthest corner, out of view of the waiting area. She was also set back from the spectacular floor-to-ceiling views of bustling Newbury Street, the Fifth Avenue of Boston. That part she didn't mind.

Setting down her broom, Ashley followed Kylie. When they rounded the corner and she had her first unobstructed view of the waiting room, Ashley stopped short.

Her next client looked as out of place in the salon as Ashley felt.

He was tall and broad, almost wild-looking. His handsome face was sunburned, and his wild, dark hair fell to chin level. He seemed gruff and untamed and not at all like the well-groomed city types who usually came in here.

Fascinated, Ashley watched him. While he paced the room, his hands tore through his hair. He wore a drab-colored, collarless, button-up shirt with an olive-toned canvas vest. His cargo pants were utilitarian, and they fit him…very well, she thought with a flush. His shoes were something new to her. Sort of like work boots, made of nice, though somewhat battered, leather. Higher end than she would have expected.

As she watched, wondering what to make of him, he sat in a chair in the far corner. Alone, he leaned his back against the wall and closed his eyes.

The stylist beside her sighed, and Ashley understood why. Even from this distance, her next client exuded a raw sexuality.

With his collarless shirt partially unbuttoned, and his tanned forearms crossed across his wide chest, he appeared completely uncivilized. He gave her the impression of wanting to be outside, free and unbound. His appearance didn't seem important to him at all.

She swallowed. What would it feel like to be so free?

Ashley shook herself. It did her no good—in fact, it was dangerous—to feel curious about any man, even if just physically. She was far too careful in her life to risk doing anything that might negatively affect her son.

"How much time do I have to cut his hair?" she asked Kylie. She was thinking about her probationary status. "Ilana will want me to be finished by the time his grandmother is ready to leave, I assume?"

"Um, yeah." Kylie nodded. "I heard his grandmother tell Ilana they were going out to lunch afterward. She said she hasn't seen her grandson in a year because he was overseas with the Doctor's Aid volunteer group. I think they just came from the airport."

"Wait, he's a doctor?" Ashley asked.

"That's what she said."

Ashley's heart sped up. Her sister was a doctor. Brandon desperately wanted to be one himself. Hence their odyssey to a new, scary life that was so far out of Ashley's league that she felt terrified half the time.

Except maybe she didn't need to feel terrified with this man. She *knew* doctors. Knew what they needed. Knew what they wanted. Understood how they preferred to be treated.

"I'll have him ready in thirty minutes," Ashley said.

"Don't forget our protocol," Kylie murmured.

Ashley tried not to snort. She threaded her way toward him past rows of swivel chairs and stylists' sinks, briefly thinking of her old friends who would have made fun of Perceptions' snooty attitude. *Protocol, indeed.* In Sal's shop, Ashley had had the freedom to use her own personal style. Just a lean against the cabinet in her workspace cubbyhole, with her legs crossed, a casual smile for the client. Easily sliding her feet in and out of her comfortable leather clogs that she'd owned forever. While she encouraged new clients to talk, Ashley would take in the shape of their faces, the forms of their features. With her fingers, a quick, impersonal assessment of the texture and condition of their hair.

Perceptions' rules were different. Lead the new client to the special consultation room. Offer them tea or water. Complete an assessment worksheet. Above all, dress and act the part of a hip, cutting-edge stylist. Ashley felt as if she was dressed for going out clubbing, which she did not do. That young, carefree, confident girl had vanished, years ago, the day she'd discovered she was pregnant and had to make the biggest decision of her young life. Thirteen years later, here she was. Struggling to maintain control.

She stopped at the threshold to the waiting area. As if on cue, the door to the private treatment room opened, and Ilana stuck her nose out.

Ashley clasped her hands and did her best to smile at her perfectionist boss, who was so exacting she often scared her employees—but Ilana just gave her a curt nod in return. Ashley responded with another smile she didn't quite feel. *Fake it until you make it.*

She turned to face her new client, determined to make a success of it. Up close, she saw that her mysterious, handsome client was clearly tired, zonked-out from his long flight.

In fact, he had dozed off into sleep.

AIDAN LOWE HAD fallen into hell. He'd slipped into the fog of the old dream. So real that fragments still haunted him. He could taste it in his mouth.

The grit of the desert. The constant dryness. The heat and the sand perpetually in his eyes. *She* was there, of course, smiling at him. And he walked toward her, as he always did in his dreams. Reached out his hand to touch her...

She turned away from him. Then there was a wave, the concussion of earsplitting silence. A wind that kicked up her blond hair. Her blue eyes focused on his. And then a bright flash of a light, brighter than anything he'd ever before seen.

When he woke up from the dream she was gone.

His whole body shook, and he jerked in his chair. The upheaval, the shock and the pain of the past year flooded back. It never seemed to leave him for long, no matter what he did to chase it away. Maybe if he dropped everything and left...

When he opened his eyes, he wasn't in Afghanistan anymore, but in the brightly lit room where he was waiting for his grandmother.

He rubbed his face. Felt the rasp of razor stubble and a small speck of drool at the corner of his lips. He wiped it away, closed his eyes and wondered what he was going to do next.

He was back in Boston now, but Fleur was dead and it wasn't home to him anymore. He wanted to leave town as soon as he possibly could. As soon as he was satisfied that Gram was okay, that he didn't need to do anything on her behalf. That was his one job this morning. His one small focus on the present reality.

He heard someone softly clear her throat beside him. He opened one eye, just enough to notice a woman sitting to the side of him, so close their knees were almost touching.

"Hello," she said, giving him a bright smile.

He felt himself frown. How long had she been there, her brow creased in concern, watching him?

As he stared at her, she swallowed. A door opened off to his other side, and the woman's gaze flicked nervously in that direction. He turned, too. The woman who owned the place—he was in a salon, he reminded himself, waiting for Gram to get her hair set so he could take her to lunch—stood in the doorway.

She gave the slight woman sitting beside him a short, pointed look—similar to the way that Fleur had communicated with the underlings in her medical practice.

Aidan glanced back to the seated woman, just to see what she would do.

She gave him another nervous smile.

"Can I help you with something?" he asked her.

"I...understand you're here for a haircut."

"Who told you that?" he said, confused.

Her smile faltered. "I assume your grand-mother arranged it with Ilana. My name is Ashley." She smiled again as if under the as-sumption that this so-called haircut would be happening.

He rubbed a hand over his face again. Maybe his father was right—Gram really was slipping. The sooner he solved the answer to his question, the sooner he could leave Boston. "What do you think of my grandmother?" he asked. He'd forgotten the woman's name al-ready, but that didn't matter. "Have you seen a change in her lately?"

"I..." She gave him a blank look.

He shook his head. She obviously had no idea if his grandmother seemed to be suf-fering from dementia or not. She probably didn't even know his grandmother. Gram didn't often talk to people outside her inner circle, especially now that she was in her mid-eighties. He should have realized that to begin with, but his brain was still feeling the effects of the long flight, followed by the shock of re-turning home.

"Never mind," he muttered.

But she didn't take a hint. She actually scooted closer to him, tilting her head and giving him a charming smile, which he hated.

Because since that day nearly a year ago in Afghanistan, when Fleur had been caught up in a war-zone bombing, nothing could melt his heart.

"My sister is a doctor, too," the woman said in a confiding tone. "I know how stressful her life is. I promise not to take long. I'll have you ready before your grandmother even finishes with her appointment."

She didn't get it. A haircut was the last thing on his mind. It was absurd that Gram had even thought to arrange it.

He stood abruptly. "No," he said in a clipped tone. "Thanks," he remembered to say, just to pretend that he was still human. He took a step to make his getaway, but she jumped in front of him.

He blinked, shocked. He was even more shocked when she placed her palm on his chest. His top two buttons were undone, and her palm landed partially on his bare skin.

He stopped short. Her eyes widened as if she was shocked at herself, too. At her own audacity.

He stared directly into her eyes. She was shorter than him by a few inches. Her skin was almost translucent and looked as smooth as porcelain, like a doll's. She had long auburn hair pulled back from her forehead. Every emotion played clearly across her dainty features, and at the moment she appeared terrified of him. Her hazel eyes were round, the pupils slightly dilated.

Something about that made him pause. He wasn't a monster, and...she seemed so vulnerable. He'd thought he was a mess these past months, but she didn't seem as if all was well with her, either.

He gave her some space, waiting for her to speak.

Swallowing, she removed her hand from his chest, but held his gaze. Aidan had been told that he didn't have the best bedside manner in the world. He'd never cared before.

"My son is a cancer survivor," she explained hesitantly. "Childhood leukemia."

She had a son? He didn't know why, but this surprised him.

"What's your name again?" he asked her.

"Ashley."

"And your son?"

She swallowed. "Brandon. He...wants to be a doctor when he grows up."

He crossed his arms. His whole damn life he'd been expected to become a doctor, like the rest of his family. "Okay."

"And..." She bit her lip. Those vulnerable

hazel eyes still desperately latched on to his. "What's your name?"

Dr. Lowe, he almost automatically said. But now that he was home, he wasn't going to be a doctor anymore. "Aidan," he answered.

"Well, Dr. Aidan, my son wants to become a cancer doctor to children—an oncologist—to help other kids the way he's been helped. He still visits the hospital—he wants it so badly. He got the opportunity to attend a private school here in Boston, close by, and we've just uprooted ourselves and relocated to this neighborhood so that he could take advantage of the scholarship. This week is, well... it's his first week in his new school and my first week in a new job."

In his fogged mind, he put two and two together. "You've been ordered to cut my hair, haven't you?"

She had the grace to laugh at their predicament. "Silly, isn't it?"

The fact that his grandmother was ordering people to cut his hair was out of character, for sure. But he didn't think it was a sign of dementia. The fact that he even had to *consider* that his grandmother could have dementia gave him a small moment of sadness.

"I'll take good care of you," Ashley said

quickly. "I promise I'll make it as fast and painless as possible. No chatter." She smiled at him, putting her finger to her lips.

He stared back, determined not to look at those lips. They were tempting, and he didn't want to be tempted.

"I'm sort of debriefing," he said. He felt a sudden wave of anger and pain, and he almost faltered on his feet. He was very much debriefing.

And he doubted that even standing here talking to her was a good idea.

ASHLEY WAS BEFUDDLED as she watched the look on Aidan's face move from wariness and confusion to anger. But there was no mistaking his feelings, because with a grimace of pain and a short shake of his head, he stood and walked away.

Without even pausing. Without even looking back at her.

She froze for a moment, her heart sinking, staring at Aidan's retreating back. With a defiant gesture, he raked his hand once through his wild tangle of dark curls, as if he couldn't have bothered about anyone in the salon, and then he opened the street door and left. Not a backward glance.

Ashley stood, shaking, her mouth opening and closing, debating what she should do. To do nothing was not an option—her new life depended on her doing *something*. Ilana would at some point want an account of what had happened, and if she decided that Ashley had been in the wrong—that she'd angered a client's grandson and failed to sweet-talk him into going along with his grandmother's wishes, then Ashley's employment would be jeopardized, fair or not.

She couldn't let that happen. How to fix it?

Maybe, to start, she should figure out what he'd meant by *debriefing*. That seemed the key to it.

She whirled for someone to ask about him. Kylie was seated at her receptionist station behind the front desk. She wore a headset and a wide-eyed expression, as if she couldn't believe that Ashley had dared to touch a client's chest. Ashley barely believed it herself. The thin cotton shirt he wore was no barrier. His skin had been hot—warm with pulsing blood that beat beneath a layer of muscles. She had been fascinated and scared, but also self-conscious and somewhat horrified that she'd been so tacky as to attempt to physically stop a customer from leaving.

Ashley placed her palms on Kylie's desk. "What do you think is going on with that guy?" she whispered.

Kylie's wide-eyed look came back. "I don't know."

"Maybe something happened before he flew home, at Doctor's Aid? Could we go over everything his grandmother said this afternoon? Each word? Maybe there's a clue."

"Um, okay." Kylie knocked at her teeth with a pen. "Well, his grandmother said that they came directly from the airport. Then they were going to lunch together, at a restaurant by the Aquarium, and she wanted him to get a haircut while she had her regular appointment." Kylie smiled to herself. "I can see why. He really needs it."

"Did she say anything else?" Ashley prodded.

Kylie scratched her head. "Well, Ilana walked over and looked in the appointment app and said, 'Ashley is free.' Then she told me to go get you and tell you that you had a walk-in. And I did." Kylie looked up at Ashley with liquid brown eyes.

Ashley smiled reassuringly at her. "You did well." Honestly, if she owned a salon—her dream business—she would never terrorize her employees. She would be pleasant to them all the time.

Sighing, she ran over her conversation with Aidan again in her mind. "Kylie, he asked if I'd noticed a change in his grandmother. Do you know what he meant by that?"

"Um…" With a bewildered look, Kylie turned to the computer screen that showed their bookings. Ashley gazed over her shoulder.

"Vivian Sharpe!" Ashley exclaimed, reading the entry in the computer. "Aidan's grandmother is Vivian Sharpe?"

"Who's that?" Kylie asked.

Only one of the richest and most influential people in Boston. Ashley groaned. In her more naive days, she'd once attempted to meet Vivian through Brandon and her sister—but the elderly woman had gone to great lengths to keep to her private entourage.

Vivian Sharpe—and her grandson Aidan— were on a whole other rarified level from Ashley. Vivian sat on the board of directors at Wellness Hospital. She had a particular interest in running the Sunshine Club, the cancer charity that Brandon volunteered for. Even worse, she owned the New England Captains, the professional baseball team where

Ashley's brother-in-law used to play, until he was traded to San Francisco. Brandon was over the moon about the Captains.

"Do you know this lady?" Kylie asked.

Ashley sighed. "Not really. I know *of* her, but that's about it."

Ashley communicated with the Sunshine Club office only through intermediaries— usually Susan Vanderbilt, a public relations manager at the hospital. Ashley hadn't understood the etiquette at first, and she'd actually dared to approach Vivian once early on, at a fancy hospital Christmas party that Brandon had been invited to attend. Vivian had barely deigned to speak to her. Ashley's sister had told her not to feel bad—that the elderly philanthropist kept herself aloof from most people, but Ashley had sensed there was more to it than that.

It had seemed personal to her.

Truth was the woman seemed not to approve of her, and that had hit Ashley in her most vulnerable spot—the worry and shame that she was in over her head with Brandon, that she wasn't doing a good enough job at being his mom.

Just great. She felt like weeping, but now wasn't the time or place. Her job and maybe

Brandon's place in his new world were at stake. She wished she could call her sister—ask her if she knew a Dr. Aidan from her time working at Wellness Hospital. Was there anything about him—any commonalities that she might use to appeal to him?

Ashley took out her phone. But her sister didn't live in Boston anymore. She was three time zones away, in San Francisco, and anyway, she was likely in surgery, administering anesthesia.

She could do this. She'd made it this far, hadn't she?

On a whim, Ashley opened up the web browser and typed in an internet search for Doctor's Aid, Boston and Aidan. She found her answer on the first hit.

Dr. Aidan Lowe, that was his name. There was a photo of him—his hair neater, his skin less tanned—posed beside a regal, beautiful, confident-looking woman. Dr. Fleur Sanborne. In the caption she was described not as his wife, not as a fiancée, but as his *partner*.

Life partner, judging by the body language. He obviously adored her.

Ashley clicked on the article. "Friendly Fire Destroys Doctor's Aid Clinic—Hub Doctor Killed."

Hub was the unique word that the local

headline writers used for "city of Boston." Ashley froze reading it, barely able to breathe. Her hands shaking, she could only skim bits of phrases from the newspaper article, dated last October.

Dr. Aidan Lowe, an orthopedic surgeon of this city, escaped injury during an attack that firebombed a volunteer clinic in the war-torn region of southern Afghanistan...

Dr. Fleur Sanborne, also of this city, the chief medical adviser to Doctor's Aid, International, died this morning after succumbing to her injuries...

Gasping, Ashley put down her phone. This was horrible! No wonder poor Dr. Lowe— *Aidan*, he'd asked her to call him—had seemed traumatized. It had nothing to do with her, and everything to do with what he'd been through in Afghanistan.

Trembling, she shook her head. She couldn't even imagine losing someone close to her. And she'd been so worried about a *haircut*?

She tucked her phone away in her pocket. "I need to go outside," she told Kylie. "I'll be right back."

Kylie glanced up from her own phone. "What's going on?"

"I'm not sure yet. I'll keep you posted, though."

"All right." Kylie glanced nervously toward Ilana's private treatment room. "I'll cover for you," she whispered.

Ashley smiled at her. "Thanks. I'll return the favor someday."

On the way outside, she stopped by the beverage cart in the consultation area and grabbed a bottled water. On second thought, she grabbed two bottles, even though it wasn't protocol. She had no idea what she was going to do. She was in too much of a rush, racing the clock, to be nervous about it.

Outside, the balmy air was welcome, and she sucked in great breaths of it. Early September in Boston was the best time of year to be in the city. Crowds of people—college students and tourists and suited financial types—wandered down the sidewalks flanking the wide boulevards lined with trees and flowering bushes. To the right was the small historic church she passed each day on her walk to Brandon's school, but she very much doubted that Aidan had sought refuge there. He seemed angry and disoriented, wanting to leave rather than receive comfort. She didn't know much about leaving—she'd never quite been able to find the courage to pick up and do that—but Ashley knew everything about giving comfort. It was the story of her life, and at the moment, this was the only gift she could think of to offer him.

She walked straight ahead and found Aidan sitting on a bench in the midst of a small courtyard-size garden where she'd noticed office workers gathering to eat their midday lunches. At the moment, most of the benches were deserted. The tended garden plots they faced were beautiful, yellow roses and purple flowering lavender plants scented the air. In the middle of the courtyard was a multi-tiered fountain that streamed soothing plumes of water.

Aidan, however, faced a completely dead plot, with spaded-up earth as desolate as a grave.

She felt sorry for him. Carefully, she headed over to his bench. The cold water bottles were sweating in her palms, and he glanced up at her as she sat.

She had no idea what to say or even how to begin talking to him. But now that she saw him in person, deeply grieving, she decided to just speak from her heart, and see where things went from there.

AIDAN STARED AT the pale, auburn-haired waif who'd had the nerve to follow him outside. "You tracked me down here for a haircut?" he said, incredulous.

"No." She smiled brightly at him. "I'm not giving you a haircut today. I'm just bringing some water while we wait." She handed him a cold water bottle—which he really was dying for—and he gladly accepted it.

In spite of himself he laughed. It seemed that this Ashley woman was good at surprising him.

She smiled wistfully and cracked open her own water bottle, then took a long drink. Sighing, she pressed her hand to her lips. "Don't tell anyone I just did that," she confided. "Staff aren't supposed to drink the Evians and Perriers. That's protocol."

"That doesn't seem fair."

"Maybe. But life isn't always fair, as they say." She fiddled with the label on her bottle, her eyes lowered to his. "I heard you just came back from overseas," she said softly. In the sunlight her hazel eyes were even more spectacular than he'd noticed. Speckles of copper and green. She had a faint—very faint—smattering of freckles, too. "I'm sure it must be an adjustment for you."

"Did you talk to my grandmother?" he asked.

"No." She smiled winsomely. "I haven't even seen her yet. I…don't keep up with the news as much as I should, so I'm sorry I didn't realize who you were right away. I certainly wouldn't have babbled on about my son like that if I'd known."

"You still want your kid to be a doctor?" he couldn't help saying bitterly.

But she didn't take it wrong. She just smiled gently, as if understanding his anger at his situation and excusing him for it. "It's not about me," she said. "If he wants to be a doctor, then it's my job to help him through his schooling so he can get there."

He glanced sideways at her. "Are you married?" he asked bluntly.

"No," she murmured.

"Divorced?" he asked again, even though he knew it was over the line. Knew he was pushing it with his rudeness.

A small smile came to her lips, as if divorce was, for her, a silly thought. "No," she said.

"Widowed?" He had to ask—he was curious now.

She shook her head, but she had a flush to her cheeks this time. The color just heightened the fact that she was pretty. It didn't matter at all to him that she was a single mother, and he might have told her so, if he didn't think it would embarrass her to hear it.

He opened the water bottle she'd brought him. It was good stuff; he'd been drinking boiled bracken tea for so long in the camp they'd set up that it felt good to have fresh, cold, bubbly water slide down his parched throat.

He couldn't stop drinking. He finished it greedily.

Then he sat and stared at the label on his bottle. He hadn't exactly chosen his situation in life, either, even before Fleur's death. She'd been the driver of the whirlwind, and he had tagged along for the adventure.

In the end, nothing had been what he wanted.

Maybe he and Ashley were in sort of the same boat.

"I never expected this to happen with Fleur," he found himself muttering aloud.

"Losing someone I love would be my worst fear," Ashley agreed.

He squinted at her, the harsh sunlight in his eyes. "You worry about your son, don't you?"

"All the time," she confessed.

She was being honest with him. He got the sense that she wasn't being manipulative as he'd feared. He *hated* manipulative people.

And it really did impress him that she cared so much about her boy.

Aidan wasn't usually sentimental. In fact, at Wellness Hospital, he'd been known as somewhat gruff. He knew what others said of him, and it didn't bother him. Usually.

He sighed. "Yeah, okay. I'll go back to the salon with you. I'll talk to the owner and make sure you don't get in trouble, if that's what you're worried about."

"Actually, I have another suggestion. You see, Aidan, I'm really good at washing hair." She gave him such a sweet smile that he didn't know how he could refuse her. "And this salon has a nice men's shampoo. You could face the world feeling cleaned up and relaxed. You could close your eyes and for fifteen minutes, forget about everyone else in there, including me."

He just stared at her.

"No one will bother you, Aidan. I promise."

It sounded appealing, actually. He was tired. He didn't want to go out to lunch with his grandmother right now, but he'd committed himself.

He stood. "I can't believe I'm going to say this, but okay. Just so you keep your job, so your kid's all right and you don't have to worry about him," he clarified.

She smiled at him. "Thank you. But I really am very good at what I do. I'll take good care of you in there. You'll see."

ASHLEY DID ENJOY taking care of other people. It was what she loved best. And Aidan was a doctor, someone who was doing something important with his life. In her opinion, he deserved to be treated well for it.

Upstairs in the salon, she led him down the narrow aisle to her station in the back. Her six new colleagues subtly or not so subtly turned their clients' chairs in order to be able to observe the rugged man who walked before them. His presence in their salon caused a stir, but she hoped he didn't realize it.

She looked over her shoulder and met his gaze. He kept his eyes trained only on her.

The trick was to do only as much as he was comfortable with while still doing a good enough job to please Ilana. At Ashley's old job, she'd cut men's hair all the time, so the simple task shouldn't be a problem. Usually she spritzed their short hair with a water bottle, then clipped it. But Aidan's situation was different.

Once at her chair in the far corner, she draped a blue plastic cape over him.

He glanced at the cape, then at her.

Smiling gently at him, she turned his chair so that he was facing away from the mirror and couldn't see himself or her. Without him realizing she was scrutinizing him, she touched his hair between her thumb and fingers. The texture was curly. Gorgeous hair, in her opinion, but he'd been washing it with a bar of soap, it appeared. He needed a deep-conditioning treatment, but that would have to wait for another day.

"I'm going to lower the back of the chair now," she said softly.

He gave her a boyish smile that unnerved her. Especially since the rest of him was so manly. Strong, developed arms and shoulders that made his muscles strain against the thin cotton material of his shirt when she dipped the chair back. His top two buttons were open, and dark wisps of hair peeked through. His neck was wide, with a sexy Adam's apple. His chin was strong. He had a faint shadow of a beard. This was a man who could shave in the morning and have that shadow by afternoon. His brows were dark, too, and it gave him a serious expression, except when he smiled.

When he smiled, he was an angel.

Her hands stilled, cupping the back of his head. She'd been lowering him toward the sink and his eyes were open wide, watching her. Contrasting with the tan of his skin and the black of his brows, his eyes were arresting. Clear whites, with irises so deep and seeing, the color of rich chocolate.

She had to get a grip on herself.

"I can give you a choice," she murmured, glancing away. "We have two shampoos. Neither of them smells girlie, as my son would say."

"Give me whichever one he likes." He smiled again, with those arresting eyes crinkling at the corners. "How old is Brandon?"

"Twelve. Almost thirteen." Her hand shook—she felt nervous all of a sudden. "His voice is starting to change."

Aidan chuckled. "Tough days ahead. I remember those."

She inhaled. She'd promised to help him relax, and she was the one who needed to concentrate. Turning on the water, she tested it on her wrist. The salon was warm, so she calibrated the temperature of the spray so it was slightly cooler than normal. Carefully, with one hand shielding his eyes and ears from the spray, she wet his hair.

His eyes drifted closed.

She opened the bottle of moisturizing shampoo she'd chosen for him. The smell was fantastic. With her fingertips, she massaged his scalp, working up a lather.

He sighed. As the moments passed, layers of concern and worry seemed to be dropping from his face.

She couldn't help studying him. From his soft smile and calm breathing, he seemed to be enjoying her ministrations. And giving him pleasure made her feel good, too. It danced along the edge of feeling slightly sexual. A humming in her chest. Slight tingling in the juncture of her legs. She only touched his scalp, and in the presence of other people, so it was a safe feeling.

She could even fantasize a bit without any repercussions. She had no doubt that after today, she would never see him again. Their worlds simply never crossed.

His eyes were still closed. No one came near their space. Just a few short moments together in a bubble with a handsome, presumably decent man. No worries. Not about her son, her job, her insecurities.

Shampooing his hair was a harmless pleasure.

But she couldn't prolong it anymore. With regret, she tested the water again, then rinsed the suds. Sifted through his curls in the swirling water, her fingers tangled in him.

She lifted his chair and patted his wet hair with a fluffy towel. Then shaped his damp curls with her fingers so he could return to the world again. *Time to say goodbye.* He opened his eyes.

She'd barely had time to think of an appropriate farewell when she suddenly realized Ilana was standing beside her chair.

"Oh!" Ashley exclaimed.

"Dr. Lowe's grandmother is waiting for him out front," Ilana said in a businesslike tone.

"Thank you. I...believe we're finished here," Ashley said, rattled by her employer's sudden presence.

Ilana peered critically at Aidan's wet hair. He just stared back at her, as if challenging her assumptions.

"How is my grandmother doing?" Aidan asked Ilana, in a deep tone that rumbled.

"She's wonderful, as always." Ilana smiled at him, then turned to look at Ashley, brow raised again, as if to ask why Aidan hadn't received a haircut.

Aidan stood, and Ashley took off the blue plastic cape.

"Ashley is great," Aidan said quietly to Ilana. "My grandmother will be happy to hear about my shampoo. Definitely the best salon experience I've ever had."

He met her gaze, and Ashley smiled at him, though she was sure she was likely Aidan's *only* salon experience. Ilana seemed mollified, however. Her serious expression toward Ashley cracked, the look replaced by a slight— very slight—smile.

Ashley exhaled. *Whew*, she thought. *I did it. Crisis over.*

But instead of just leaving with Ilana, as she'd expected, Aidan instead faced her shelves and reached out his hand.

The photo of Brandon! Mild alarm coursed through her as Aidan lifted the photo of her son, studying him.

"You didn't tell me he went to St. Bartholomew's School," Aidan remarked.

"How do you know that?" she asked nervously.

"The blue blazer," he explained. "The yellow patch."

Her heart was hammering. His observation brought to mind the outing to buy the blazer, two weeks earlier, when her sister had turned to Ashley and murmured, "He asked me about his father. What do you want me to say to him?" And Ashley had handled it. She always handled it—his biological father was deceased, after all, as was her own—but still it rattled her.

None of this had anything to do with Aidan, though—he had nothing to do with her son's paternity, or her personal anxiety.

Aidan was looking at her quizzically, with unspoken questions she couldn't answer, so she just took the photo from him and quietly replaced it on her shelf. "Is there a problem?" she murmured.

"No." But his gaze looked faraway. Everything about his body language screamed, *"Yes! It's a problem."* She didn't know what to make of it, but the back of her neck tingled.

As Ilana led Aidan off to his grandmother—to Vivian Sharpe—Ashley could only wonder if she'd missed something important.

And worry, as she always did.

AIDAN SHOULD HAVE realized St. Bartholomew's School was so close—only two blocks away from the hair salon. From the windows he could see the distinctive spire of the small chapel, the tiny patch of greenery that was their courtyard in the city.

Likely, that's why Ashley had chosen to work here. She'd told him her life revolved around her son, and he believed her. It made him marvel to think of it. Such a foreign concept to the Sharpe-Lowe family.

He turned back for a moment, watching her

reflection move across the windowpane. He could watch her all day. He felt calm and languid after her attentions. The dust of the desert had been washed down that golden sink of hers. It had felt nice to have her fingers sift through his hair. She was nothing like Fleur. Nothing. If two women could have completely opposite personalities, it was them.

He paid the young receptionist, then approached his grandmother, who was sitting on a sofa in the waiting area. She had a fancy black cane by her side—an antique, it looked like. That was new to him, Gram using a cane. When he'd gotten off the plane and met her at the town car, it had bothered him to see it because he preferred to think of her as forever strong. But now he couldn't help wondering—had she deliberately maneuvered him into meeting Ashley today?

Aidan had gone to St. Bartholomew's School as a boy, too. It was a tiny, elite school with exceedingly high expectations. He knew how difficult a place it could be.

Ashley didn't seem to understand that as well as he did. That was only natural.

You could help her, a voice inside said.

He closed his eyes. *Nope*, he said to the voice. His life was too complicated and messed up as it was. His interest was the last thing Ashley needed as she tried to make a better life for her son. If that was at all in his grandmother's mind, then she could just forget it.

It was too bad, he reflected, on his way out the door and down the stairs. He liked Ashley. Liked her basic kindness.

And he really, really liked the way she'd given him that sexy shampoo.

CHAPTER TWO

ASHLEY THOUGHT ABOUT Aidan long after he left. Long after two more clients—a cut and color and then a set—had come and gone.

She couldn't shake the sense that she'd made a mistake in getting too personal with him. She really didn't know him that well, and what if there were repercussions? He'd recognized Brandon's school jacket, and that had unnerved her.

Her hands shaking, she stepped around Jordan, the young intern who was busily sweeping hair from Ashley's workspace.

"Thanks," she said to Jordan. Maybe if she distracted herself from thinking about Aidan by helping someone else, she'd be okay. "Are you a student?" she asked Jordan.

Jordan flipped her long straight hair over one shoulder and smiled boldly at Ashley. Nothing shy about her. "I graduate in June. I'm hoping Ilana hires me after I pass my state exams."

"That's great." Ashley hesitated a beat. "I'll

help, if you want. I know someone who sat on the state board for years and years."

"No, thanks. I'm good," Jordan said. "Thanks anyway."

"Sure." Ashley nodded, hiding her disappointment and gathering up her purse. She was finished for the day and had no reason to stay longer, other than to try to alleviate the general feeling of uneasiness that she wanted to shake.

"You'll get used to working here," Sandie, the stylist who'd worked at the chair next to Ashley, murmured in her ear, causing Ashley to jump. "You just have to get past Ilana's probationary period, and then it'll get better."

"It's not easy starting over someplace new," Ashley admitted.

"You're very brave," Sandie said. "I saw you earlier with Dr. Lowe."

Had she? And what was brave about washing his hair? "He didn't want a haircut," she explained. "I did what I could."

"Well, you were a hit. I overheard what he said to Ilana. You impressed him, Ashley. He'll probably come back to you as a regular client now."

Ashley froze. She hadn't even considered that could happen. That was…that was…

"How did you get this job, anyway?" Sandie

asked her curiously. "Because Ilana is...particular. Turnover is high at Perceptions, but the stylists who stay—well, we have a good reputation. The pay is great, and the customers are loyal."

Ashley sat reeling, still absorbing the information. "I won an industry award last March," she said, "for styling the models' hair at the Museum of Art's Pompeii exhibition party."

"That's great! But how would a hair stylist get involved with the Pompeii exhibition party?" Sandie asked.

"Through my younger sister." Ashley smiled to herself. "She got me involved with the museum a few years ago. She has a big interest in archaeology." Lisbeth, besides being a doctor, was also a history nerd. A big, lovable history nerd. "I learned to style hair for the Roman period using pictures my sister showed me. The women back then wore really intricate braids and headpieces. It was interesting. Some of the museum members commissioned period costumes for the party, and I designed the hairpieces for their outfits."

"I could see where Ilana would be impressed with you."

"I hope so," Ashley murmured.

"Well..." Sandie glanced back toward her station. "Will I see you tomorrow?"

"Of course."

Feeling uneasy again, Ashley clutched her purse and headed out the door to meet Brandon. As she passed the receptionist station, Kylie nodded at her. "Goodbye, Ashley. Are you coming back tomorrow?"

So uneasy.

OUTSIDE, THE SUN had lowered behind the buildings enough that it wasn't as hot as it had been when Ashley had been outside with Aidan earlier.

She walked past the park where she'd sat with him, but she couldn't think of that right now. Feeling shaky again, she paused to take a breath. She'd been walking so fast, so lost in thought, that she almost bumped into a woman coming toward her on the sidewalk. The woman—with a little dog in tow, pulling on his leash—frowned at Ashley as she passed.

Ashley moved to the other side of the sidewalk. Put her hand over her stomach and took a deeper breath.

Almost home. She was at the building next to theirs, which housed a liquor store on the street level. A "package store," as they were known in New England terms, or at least, as people in her old neighborhood called them. "Packies" for short.

Her gait slowed. She couldn't help glancing in the window at the rows of bottles. Wine, her particular weakness, would be at the back of the store. She was no connoisseur, hadn't cared about vintages or grapes, she'd just sipped now and then to keep the edge off and to help her nerves. Shaky nerves, like she had now after her unsettling day of work. The vague sense of shame that she'd done something wrong, but wasn't quite sure what. The anxiety that she was an inadequate person and didn't quite know how to fix it, other than to do what she had to, which was to take care of her child. The child she'd been blessed with, a most precious person. The one person who always loved her back, and she couldn't screw him up, not like she and her sister had been screwed up by their mom and her alcohol-and-men problems.

Ashley touched the window, her hand trembling. A part of her, so raw and visceral, desperately wanted to go inside that package store. To hear the tinkling of the bell over the door. The cool feel of the bottle in her hand. The crinkling of the brown paper bag that covered it. And then, at home in her kitchen, to pop open the cork and pour the white wine into the large plastic cups that she and Brandon had used back when she'd last tasted a drink.

He'd been eight years old. Four years ago. She'd tossed those cups the day she'd come home from rehab. In her mind, she'd done the worst thing ever—she'd left her eight-year-old son for thirty days in the care of her shy younger sister who'd felt uncomfortable with children—and yet she'd also done the best thing, which had been to address her problems. Ashley had taken the steps she'd needed to take. She was a recovering alcoholic.

But why did her hand still shake? Why did she yearn to go inside?

Closing her eyes, she took a breath. And another. And another. All baby steps. All leading her away from temptation.

The only unwise part of her new life—moving into an apartment near a liquor store. But it couldn't be helped. She'd had to make a choice between Brandon's need to be closer to his new school and her own need to be farther away from her old addiction.

Brandon's needs had won. Brandon's needs would always win. As they must.

AIDAN ATE HIS meal silently, alone. His grandmother had been on her telephone for the past half hour.

First her stockbroker, then her lawyer. Then the general manager of her professional baseball team, the New England Captains. If he was lucky, Aidan thought with amusement, maybe he'd get the trifecta plus one, a ringside seat to her conversation with the head of the board at Wellness Hospital.

Finally, she hung up.

"Eighty-five years old," he said to the legendary Vivian Sharpe. "Don't you think you should relax and enjoy yourself for once?"

She gave him a dark look. "You know better than to say that to me."

He set down his fork on his luncheon plate. They were at a fancy seafood restaurant that just felt odd to him, after nearly a year out of the country and living in the situation he'd been in.

He sighed. Might as well come out and say what he'd been thinking. Delicacy had never been a part of his and Gram's relationship. "Dad mentioned in his last email that he and Mom were worried about you. He asked me to talk to you and give my opinion about the state of your, ah, mental faculties."

And then Aidan softened the blow with the wry, comical smile that he and Gram alone liked to share. She snorted at him. He knew it was good-natured on her part, though the message surely had to sting.

She waved her hand. "I'm restructuring my estate, and William and Jane haven't been happy about that fact. Pay no attention to their insinuations. I don't."

Aidan nodded. William, Aidan's dad, was a world-renowned heart surgeon. He and Jane—Aidan's mother, also a cardiologist—had enough money that they didn't ever need to worry about finances again. Even so, finances were the types of conversation they loved to concern themselves with.

Heart surgeons with no hearts, Aidan thought, and not for the first time. He laughed out loud. It was darkly comical, and since he knew there was nothing he could change about it, dark humor with Gram was a fine way to cope.

"You laugh now," Gram said, a spark in her eyes, "but William spoke to me about you, as well."

"He isn't worried about *my* finances, is he?"

"No." She waved her hand again. But this time she met his gaze seriously. "I'm worried about you, too, Aidan, but I'm worried about your well-being." She leaned forward and peered more closely at him. "You've been through a terrible situation. I wish you had come home last October when it happened. I don't know why you stayed."

No more humor, he thought sadly.

"How are you, Aidan? Honestly?"

"I'm fine, Gram," he insisted.

She shook her head. "I may have been on my phone just now, but I noticed you've been ignoring your text messages. That isn't fine."

His grandmother didn't miss a trick. Surely she'd also caught a glimpse of who the text messages were from—Fleur's parents. Right now, he just wasn't in a good place to speak with them. Eventually he would be. But not yet.

He gazed out the window at the view overlooking the blue Atlantic. Sailboats bobbed in the bay. In the distance was a faint smudge of land—one of the islands in the outer harbor.

"Aidan?"

He glanced at the water glass he'd been idly rubbing his finger around. "Yes, Gram?"

"It *is* nice to have you back. And to see you looking civilized again, even if your hair isn't quite short enough yet." She reached out and touched his hair.

He smiled faintly at her. "You asked them to do that for me. It wasn't my idea."

"Yes, I did ask them. Discreetly of course.

And now you look much better. You look cared for."

Ashley had washed it for him. "Cleaned it up," she'd said. He could turn ninety, and he would never forget the feel of her fingers brushing his scalp. It had been one of the most sensual experiences of his life, and yet they'd both been fully clothed. Her breast near his face. The rustle of her skirt as she'd turned. The soft knock of her heels on the wooden floor. The pads of her fingers as she'd brushed a soap bubble from his brow.

"Aidan?"

Again he snapped to. Hadn't realized he'd been daydreaming. "It's strange to be in Boston," he admitted.

"Home," Gram amended.

Was it? Outside the windows near the street, Boston whizzed by. The buildings were familiar; the shops and restaurants in the same places with some facades and names changed. Always, though, the throngs of students—college kids—at the crosswalks.

"How do you feel?" she asked again.

He closed his eyes, ran his palms over his newly smooth hair.

"Honestly, it doesn't feel like home anymore." He'd spent his childhood here, had gone to college and done his residency here.

Now he'd been gone for a year, and it felt like a foreign country.

Gram rummaged inside her tote and pulled out a stack of mail secured with a rubber band. "Your mail. I suppose now that you're back, I'll no longer need to handle it for you."

She'd done the job well for him. Periodically, he'd received an email from her assistant, detailing bills paid on his behalf, invitations answered and declined. "Thank you," he said.

She waved her hand. "You may stay at my townhouse tonight, if you'd like. I had the guest suite made up for you."

"I still have my condo." The words came out gruffly.

There was a pause. She was being circumspect, his formidable grandmother, who had a big heart and who loved him with all of it. "Yes," she said softly. "Yes, you do, Aidan."

His condo was filled with Fleur's presence, of course. With her things and her memories. He'd toyed with the idea of turning his back on it, selling it as is. Hiring someone to empty it and never going inside again.

"You're welcome to stay with me tonight," Gram said again. "In the morning I'm stopping by St. Bartholomew's School for a meeting of the board. It would be nice if you came along."

He looked at her sharply. Of course, he'd suspected back at the hair salon that there might be some angle with St. Bartholomew's somewhere. With his grandmother, nothing was coincidental.

"Why did you really bring me to that hair salon today?" he asked. "Tell me the truth, Gram."

She smiled at him. "To bring you back into civilization with me. Even if she didn't cut it, Ashley did a nice job."

Gram was lying. Feeling sad, he took his napkin off his lap and placed it on the table. "How do you know Ashley? Be honest."

"I've spoken to her only once before."

"In what capacity?"

Gram folded her hands over her purse and looked him squarely in the eye. "Her son, Brandon, is the best fundraiser for the Sunshine Club we've ever had."

Aidan swallowed his shock. The answer was cold and businesslike, even for her.

Yet the Sunshine Club was his grandmother's pet project—her fundraising arm for children's cancer research. The Sunshine Club was Gram's baby. She'd started it decades ago after her youngest child—an uncle Aidan had never known—had died of childhood leukemia. Gram often said that if Luke had been born today, with all the advances in medicine, then he would have lived.

Few people outside the family even knew of Luke, or of Gram's continuing grief. She kept it that way on purpose. Gram had a soft heart, though she preferred to show the world the sharp, hardened exterior she'd developed through her business and charitable pursuits.

"Did you meet Brandon through the Sunshine Club, as well?" he asked. "I understand he's also a leukemia survivor."

"Initially, yes." Gram paused. "My staff supervises him and handles all communication between his mother and the organization. Prior to Brandon, we'd used baseball stars—from the Captains—as our television fundraisers. But quite by accident, Brandon stepped in. And he proved to be much more effective than any of them were."

"How so?"

She smiled at him. "Brandon is very good on television. He's a natural showman."

Aidan thought of the studious-looking kid in the St. Bartholomew's blazer. Brandon had looked like an average twelve-year-old to Aidan. He shook his head. "I don't know that I would have gone on television and asked people for money at that age," he murmured.

When Ashley had first mentioned Brandon wanting to be a pediatric oncologist, Aidan hadn't really believed her. To his cynical mind, it had seemed like more of a parent's dream than a kid's dream.

"You would have done it for the chance to be a ball boy for the Captains," Gram said matter-of-factly.

Aidan sat up straighter. "Ashley's son is a ball boy for the New England Captains?"

"Oh, yes." His grandmother nodded. "It was the price I paid for keeping him happy."

Aidan completely understood the "happy" part—he would have killed for the opportunity to be a Captains ball boy at Brandon's age. Any kid of Aidan's acquaintance would have.

Rubbing his tired head, Aidan sat back. "So why all the subterfuge? Why didn't you just introduce Ashley and me? Simple and easy. Say, 'Aidan, meet Ashley. Maybe you'd like to give her some advice on her son's school'?"

Gram snorted. "You don't know yourself as well as you think you do, do you?" Then she pulled back. "It's…a delicate situation," she said carefully. "I had to proceed with caution. I do need your help, Aidan. You're the only person I know who can help—the best person—and yet I needed to know that you could work with Ashley on your own terms. If I'd been too early, pushing you to meet her, to sit with her, to talk about her son—do you think you would have lasted five minutes?"

No. Of course he wouldn't have. And he hated to be manipulated.

Yet here he was again, put in that situation by people close to him.

Even Gram. And it hurt.

She leaned over the table and put her hand on his "I know how hard it was for you at St. Bartholomew's. It wasn't a happy place for you, and I did the best I could to give you support there."

Yes, she had. His enrollment had been his parents' insistence.

He raised his head. He had to ask the question, because he had to know. "Did *you* pull strings to get Brandon admitted to St. Bartholomew?"

She sighed. "Yes. Though it pained me to do it." She blotted her lips with her napkin, and put it down on her plate. "His aunt was looking at schools in New Hampshire for him, appealing for scholarships. I couldn't risk losing him at the Sunshine Club."

"St. Bartholomew's is academically rigorous," he said quietly. "Can Brandon handle that?"

She gave him a sad, serious look. "Come with me tomorrow, and we'll find out."

With a sinking heart, Aidan did a quick calculation. The kid would be in his first week of his first year at St. Bartholomew's. Preliminary academic testing results would be coming back soon. Maybe Gram had some inside information.

"Is there a chance Brandon will be asked to leave?" he asked his grandmother.

"My influence is limited." She held up her hands. "I can recommend a student for admission, but I can't keep a failing student enrolled." She shook her head. "You know how it is there."

Aidan did. All too well. The school prided themselves on being academically rigorous, among the best in the world. They would keep a lagging student on for the first term, but then at the winter break, they would show Brandon the door, if necessary.

Ashley would be crushed, he thought.

He sat for a moment, thinking about that. He didn't want to picture how upset she would be.

"There's another reason I keep Ashley La-

Valley at arm's length," Gram said carefully, "You should know this." And Aidan glanced up, suddenly alert.

"She went through alcohol rehabilitation four years ago," his grandmother said grimly. "Her childhood was difficult from what I understand—an alcoholic mother, as well—and in such cases, I find it best to keep a certain distance."

His mouth hung open. He could feel it.

But his shock was soon replaced with anger. Wasn't that narrow-minded of her to think that way?

"You could have mentored Ashley all these years," he pointed out. "Instead of expecting me to mentor Brandon now."

Gram gave him a faint smile. "That's one of the things I love most about you, Aidan. You have a kind heart." She glanced at his phone. "Perhaps now you might return Albert Sanborne's text messages?"

Point taken. "Since you seem to know everything," he said drily, "why don't you tell me what Fleur's father wants?"

"Actually, we're all assuming—hoping—that you'll be staying in town long enough to help organize the one-year memorial service for Fleur."

He shook his head. He hadn't even considered there would be such a thing. She'd passed away last October—eleven months ago. There had been a small, private funeral, of course, and though he hadn't attended—he was still in Afghanistan—Gram had.

He was grateful to her for that even now.

"Aidan? Give the word, and I'll handle it for you."

"No, thank you," he replied.

"It's not a problem for me to do so."

"I said *no*."

"Would you like me to arrange a room for you in one of my vacant apartments?" she pressed.

"No, I have a condo."

"Very well. And if you'd like your position back at the hospital—"

"No," he said icily.

"Or a position consulting with the Captains?"

Gritting his teeth, he stood. He'd just spent a year in a war zone, performing amputations on children; he certainly didn't feel like coming back to tape sprained ankles for professional baseball players.

"Take all the time you need," she said softly. "Think about what I've said."

He didn't need time to think, he needed *space* to think.

As he walked to the men's room, he couldn't help thinking that Gram was perfectly fine. He was the one with the head problems.

Or maybe they were heart problems. He wasn't sure anymore.

IN THE END, Aidan stayed with Gram in her spare bedroom. He'd gone back to his condo, but the doorman had handed him a stack of messages.

One from a reporter. Another from the hospital, his former employer. Yet another from Fleur's father, Albert, writing this time instead of calling "just in case your phone isn't working here yet."

His head pounding, Aidan had left it all and walked out to the street, where he'd hailed a random taxi and directed it to Beacon Hill.

His grandmother opened the door in person. She knew enough to hand him a cup of tea and just let him go to sleep.

The next morning, he was still feeling jet-lagged when his grandmother's housemaid opened the bedroom curtains and brought in a tray of watery coffee and toast.

And then he was stepping into his grandmother's town car again, being driven by

Rocco toward the Back Bay and St. Bartholomew's School.

He'd discovered that he was curious to see
what his grandmother was going to do next.
He had a sinking feeling that it might not be
in Ashley's best interests. Or in his.

CHAPTER THREE

"BRANDON, HURRY UP, we're going to be late!"

If there was one thing Ashley could take heart in, early on this Friday school morning, it was that her almost-thirteen-year-old son wasn't in the bathroom preening. There were no girls in his classes at St. Bartholomew's, unlike in his public school. He seemed to be taking that fact in stride, though. Sometimes nothing appeared to faze her happy-go-lucky kid.

She found him in his bedroom, typing swiftly into his smartphone. He kept a social media account that Ashley monitored as best she could. He shared photos mainly. And his friends commented, in their weird kid-speak that was totally different from the kid-speak that Ashley and her friends had used too many years ago.

She put her hand on her hip. "Brandon, we need to go."

"Okay." He gave her the lopsided grin that was already slaying female hearts from the

North Shore to the Cape—wherever the Sunshine Club donation appeals were broadcast.

Thankfully, though, her scary-smart kid still liked school. Ashley had been a middling student—not like her reclusive genius of a younger sister.

But Brandon was neither reclusive nor middling. No, he'd gotten the best of the LaValley family genes—not that that was saying much. It was as if they'd saved up all the good ones for this amazing kid. God, she was lucky.

Brandon grabbed his backpack. His blazer was looped through the top—it was still warm outside—but every day this week she'd watched as he'd put it on, looking natty, as he entered the school archway.

With a bottle of juice in his hand, he said to her, "You don't have to walk with me."

They'd been through this. "I know I don't *have* to most days," she said, "but today I need to."

He cocked his head. "That note is probably no big deal."

He was referring to the letter that the school had sent home, requesting Ashley's presence at a meeting in the headmaster's office this morning. "It's standard, Mom," Brandon had already explained. "In schools like this, they send notes to parents all the time. All my friends probably got them, too."

Frankly, she trusted his judgment when it came to St. Bartholomew's more than her own. He'd been there a week already, and he came home happier each day.

"I'll see the headmaster and find out what he has to say," she told him.

"I know I'm doing well in my English class. There are, like, these kids in my class, they're from Mexico and Korea, and their English isn't that great yet."

"That's a long way from home," she remarked.

"It is. I wouldn't want to be them. I'm only a few miles from home. I can still see my old friends on weekends."

"True," she murmured, grabbing her purse from the closet she kept it locked in. Old habits. Their previous apartment had been broken into twice, and she'd learned not to leave her valuables out where thieves could see them. Then she motioned Brandon toward their front door and locked it behind them.

"So, what does the headmaster do when he wants to talk to your Korean friend's parent?" she asked as they headed toward the street.

"Cho," Brandon said. "His name is Cho." He ran his hand through his shaggy bangs.

"Okay, Cho. What happens? Do they get his parents on a video call? Or send them an email?"

"Cho's father uses an interpreter from their embassy. I think he's an ambassador, with an office down in Washington. Or something like that."

Not for the first time Ashley marveled at the company her son was keeping. It made her heart swell. She felt weepy with all the opportunities he was getting.

"So this is just a normal check-in with parents," she repeated, for probably the tenth time, wishing she had more experience with private schools.

"Don't be nervous, Mom." Brandon shot her a grin. "We're good."

"Right." She nodded, averting her gaze as they walked past the package store that had made her so nervous yesterday. "Good."

Brandon reached in his backpack to put on his earphones and music, but she grabbed his hand. "Can we just talk, please? It's only a few more feet to walk with your mom." She smiled as easily as she could. "Humor me."

He rolled his eyes in mock good humor. "We're okay, Mom." And then he added something she hadn't heard before. "If something was really bad, they would have called Mrs. Sharpe."

Vivian Sharpe? She eyed her precocious son. "Why would they call her? She's not your mother."

He smiled faintly. "Nope. You are. And everybody knows it." Then he took out his smartphone and skimmed through it. Ashley said nothing because it was what all his friends did.

But his comment still bothered her.

"Has Vivian Sharpe contacted you lately?" she asked.

"No, Mom. You know she hasn't."

Okay. She shouldn't worry, then. Maybe she should make a pact with herself to stop worrying.

They fell into an easy pace while she shook off the bad feeling and tried not to worry any longer. This early in the morning, the streets weren't very busy. Brandon scrolled with his thumb while he walked, one eye on the screen in front of him, one eye on the street.

When they got to the school, Brandon paused and glanced up at her. For a moment, he was her little boy again, instead of this more complicated preteen. Still skinny, with a smattering of acne across his nose, he leaned over and gave her a hug.

"I love you, Mommy," he whispered. Her heart lodged in her throat, and she felt close to tears, wanting to hold on to this moment, wishing it could last longer than it did.

And just as quickly, they were walking on. Up the stone steps, passing a group of four men who seemed to be teachers. They greeted Brandon warmly. One of them—Dr. Prosser—the English teacher—directed her to the corridor where the headmaster's office was located. Ashley hadn't been inside since Brandon's admittance interviews last spring.

The receptionist looked up as Ashley entered. Glancing over the top of her eyeglasses, she, too, smiled warmly.

See, nothing to worry about, she told herself. All these nice people cared about her son's welfare. So why was she so jittery?

She sat, folding her hands and placing her purse on her lap. For the millionth time, she wished her sister was here. This was Lisbeth's world, not hers. But it couldn't be helped. Ashley would have to handle this alone.

AIDAN WASN'T EXACTLY sure what he was doing, standing with his grandmother outside the dining hall at St. Bartholomew's. Curiosity, maybe? Secretly hoping for a glimpse of Ashley, his pretty hairstylist?

He must be nuts. He should be back at his condo, getting it ready for a quick sale.

Ding! Another text message hit his inbox. He glanced at his smartphone.

We would like to call on Saturday. What time is good? the message from Albert Sanborne read.

Saturday was tomorrow. And Gram was right; he needed to deal with this.

Noon, Aidan typed back.

There, it was done. One more step in moving on.

He glanced up and realized that his grandmother was moving on, too, doggedly forging ahead with her cane. He saw that she was having difficulty with the uneven stone floor, so he jogged ahead and gave her his elbow, helping her walk past the open doors that showed morning breakfast session in full swing.

It was the same as he remembered from his time, and it was smaller, too. Back when he'd been twelve, thirteen, fourteen—the age of the boys who attended St. Bartholomew's—this place had been his whole world. Most boys boarded at the school, and Aidan had been no exception. Many of his friends had come from far away—from Europe, from Asia, from Mexico. Many were sons of wealthy families. But even the wealthy couldn't protect their kids from everything.

Failure, for example. This had been the first place where Aidan had failed. He'd never been a studious kid to begin with, had never really cared about following in the family footsteps and being a doctor. He'd wanted freedom, the ability to go off anywhere he felt like, to have an adventure.

Fleur had brought him on adventures, the last one being a war zone halfway around the world. Perhaps that had been the initial attraction between them. But even that had fallen apart.

He'd loved her once, and thought she'd loved him, but in the end, he hadn't been able to fix their relationship.

His grandmother had been the one person in his family who'd expressed reservations about Fleur. On the surface, she'd seemed perfect for him. "She doesn't put you first," Gram had said. He'd thought Gram had been crazy to even think that way. Who in his family did that? And he definitely didn't want someone who fawned and trembled in his presence, depending on him. He'd wanted independence. And freedom. And he'd definitely wanted adventure.

Until he'd had his fill of it.

Swallowing, he paused in the hallway, his hand still on Gram's arm. Honestly, it was crazy that he was even here this morning. But maybe he was looking for something, too. So out of character of him. He was thinking. Brooding. Trying to figure out the next step in his life. Something he'd never, ever worried about before. Normally a man of action, he'd been more like...

Like that kid in the corner of the dining hall. A ring of kids surrounded him—he had them mesmerized. Telling some kind of a joke, showing them something on his phone. They were nodding and smiling. The towheaded kid, the life of the party.

"Aidan, we're here," Gram murmured. They were outside the conference room where Gram was scheduled to meet with the board.

"I'll wait outside," he told her. "Call me when you're finished."

"Yes, Aidan." Gram smiled at a tall, thin man who'd stood to greet them. "Dr. Pingree, I'd like you meet my grandson, Dr. Aidan Lowe. Aidan, this is Dr. Pingree, the headmaster."

Aidan greeted the headmaster and shook his hand.

"I understand you've moved back to Boston," Dr. Pingree said.

"For a short time, yes."

"Thank you for coming back to see us. We love to see returning alumni. Especially those as accomplished as you are, Dr. Lowe."

"Thank you," Aidan said politely.

"Since I have a few minutes before the board meeting starts, would you indulge me and allow me to show you our newest improvements in the facilities? It will take just a few minutes. So often we reach out for donation appeals, but we don't usually get the chance to show some of the capital improvements the funds make."

Gram was quite generous with St. Bart's. But she wasn't going on the short tour, she said. Aidan was well aware she had an angle with him today. He knew how to say no to people very well.

Maybe he should.

"Sure," he said to the good doctor. "Why not?" He left his grandmother and headed back to the dining hall by Dr. Pingree's side.

The boys quieted as Dr. Pingree walked through their midst. These would be the first-year boys. Most were clustered together, wearing their new suit jackets, self-conscious, maybe a little afraid with back-to-a-new-school jitters. Aidan guessed that most came from very wealthy, very busy parents who had high standards for their children. He felt compassion for them. He remembered the feeling, the heavy burden of expectations. The fear of not measuring up. The realization of the investment.

The table that the headmaster was leading him toward was the one that Aidan had observed earlier, as he had walked with his grandmother. The table that seemed to be centered on one boy who kept the attention of the others. The happy-go-lucky kid.

Blond hair. Slight. Skinny, as if he'd just had a massive growth spurt to which the rest of his body hadn't caught up yet.

Aidan paused. "Who is that boy?"

"That's Brandon," the headmaster said.

Brandon. Aidan wasn't at all surprised. He'd thought he'd recognized the kid from the photo in his mom's workstation.

Brandon saw them conferring. When the headmaster gestured for him to come over, he got up from the table without hesitation.

"Brandon, this is Dr. Lowe," the headmaster said. "Dr. Lowe, I'd like to introduce you to one of our first-year students, Brandon LaValley."

"Hi, Dr. Lowe." Brandon confidently stuck out his hand. But his voice cracked, and his cheeks flushed.

Aidan gave the boy an easy grin. Took his outstretched hand and shook it. "Hi, Brandon. Pleased to meet you."

"Dr. Lowe is one of our graduates," Dr. Pingree said. "He's currently an orthopedic surgeon at Wellness Hospital."

Aidan didn't correct him. Technically, Aidan supposed, he still had his position on staff there. Really, he was just grateful that the headmaster hadn't mentioned his posting with Doctor's Aid. Or his relationship to Vivian Sharpe. Or his past affiliation with the New England Captains organization.

Aidan was just about to make an excuse to leave when he caught Brandon's expression. The boy stared at him with big eyes and shaggy hair and skinny arms. Aidan remembered the awkwardness of that age, and he felt some compassion.

"Are you going to help tutor me?" Brandon asked anxiously.

"Why? Do you need a tutor?" Aidan asked, taken aback.

"Um…" Brandon glanced hesitantly at Dr. Pingree. "Some of my friends who board here were assigned tutors last night. I, um, think I probably need one, too."

Aidan stared at Dr. Pingree. "Have you discussed me with him?"

Dr. Pingree shook his head. "No, I haven't."

"I saw you once, Dr. Lowe, when I was eight," Brandon piped up. "You were in the Captains clubhouse with Carlton Martinez. You were treating his elbow. I know who you are."

Aidan had stopped consulting with his grandmother's team at about that time. "I'm sorry I didn't get to meet you back then," he said to Brandon.

"That's okay. We're meeting now." Brandon gave him a smile.

Oh, man. He did want to help the boy. The kid was personable—he could see his grandmother's point about his fundraising value. Aidan could feel himself being sucked in to caring what happened to him.

"What…are your requirements for assigning tutors?" he asked Dr. Pingree. "Just as a hypothetical."

"The student has to feel comfortable with the tutor," Dr. Pingree replied. "As does his parent."

His parent. That would be Ashley.

Brandon vigorously shook his head. "My mom doesn't need to know about this. Please. I'm good." He looked anxiously at the headmaster.

What was going on here?

"Your mother is in the office meeting with your math instructor," Dr. Pingree said gently to Brandon. "We have to let her know the status of your algebra pretesting examination."

Brandon winced. "That means I failed, doesn't it?"

"We'll have this conversation later, in private, after we speak with your mother," Dr. Pingree said.

"I don't want her to worry," Brandon mumbled. "She's gonna worry about me."

Oh, man. Aidan could see the whole problem spread in front of him. The boy trying to be a man. The mom worried for her son.

"Ah, maybe I could help," Aidan said to Dr. Pingree. "I'm not a professional tutor, but I did go to St. Bart's, so I understand the culture." He lowered his voice. "When I was a student, I failed my algebra pretest. I had to work with a tutor myself—and work hard—but I managed to pull my scores up. To this day, math is one of my strengths."

"You certainly would have a wonderful perspective to offer a newer, struggling student," Dr. Pingree said. "You know how difficult it can be to catch up academically to St. Bartholomew's standards." He nodded. "Yes, I would support your choice as a mentor/tutor and give my recommendation to Brandon's parent."

He hoped she took his offer in the spirit of generosity with which he meant it.

But he managed a smile. "Please talk to Brandon's mother, give her my name, before I get any more involved in this process," Aidan said to the headmaster.

"Certainly, as long as Brandon is comfortable," the headmaster said. He peered at Brandon. "Would you like to talk more with Dr. Lowe?"

Aidan looked at the kid. He just seemed worried. Aidan remembered feeling shell-shocked at Brandon's age, when he'd realized he'd failed his pre-test. It had been the first time he'd ever failed anything in school. Maybe Brandon felt the same way.

"Come on," Aidan said to the boy, motioning to a table close enough that they weren't out of the headmaster's earshot, but far enough away that the kids at the other tables couldn't hear them. He was treading carefully with this situation.

Nodding, Brandon followed him. Sat down. Stared at a hangnail on his thumb.

"What's going on?" Aidan asked the boy. "Did you study for the pre-test? I don't know how it is now, but I remember that they recommended I study for it over the summer."

"Yes," Brandon said. He shrugged. "In my old school it was easier. I didn't expect it to be this hard."

"Yeah. I remember the same feeling."

Brandon glanced up. Aidan could see the pain in his eyes. "My aunt was an anesthesiologist at Wellness Hospital. She went to a regular public school, and she became a doctor."

"Well, yes." Aidan paused. "Of course that's possible. What's your aunt's name?"

"Dr. Elizabeth LaValley."

Aidan struggled to keep a straight face. He'd done surgery with Dr. LaValley once or twice. Seemed like a million years ago, and he'd been in such a different place then.

"You know her?" Brandon asked.

"Yes. I'm sorry I didn't realize your connection to her at first." He should have recognized Brandon's last name. He'd just been so… caught up in his own situation. He needed to rectify that. Aidan cleared his throat. "Dr. LaValley is a good anesthesiologist. We worked on some hip replacement surgeries as part of a team."

He'd been the bored hotshot surgeon blaring Led Zeppelin music while she'd sat in her anesthesiologist's chair wincing because she preferred Mozart.

But he kept his expression level. None of that was the kid's problem.

"My aunt tutored me this summer," Brandon said. "We used Skype every Monday and Thursday. She's in San Francisco now."

Ashley had mentioned that. But oh, here was potentially another reason for Dr. LaValley to dislike him. He would be stepping in to help where Dr. LaValley had failed. Some people wouldn't take that so well.

"Why do you suppose you didn't pass the pre-test?" Aidan asked him.

Brandon shrugged. "I don't know," he mumbled.

Aidan remained silent. Brandon fidgeted. Finally he sighed. "I'm a commuting student, not a boarding student. The boarding students get special help from the resident teachers that I don't get."

Aidan nodded. Perhaps it was a valid reason, but it definitely wasn't an avenue he was exploring. Brandon's living situation was really none of his business.

"What else?" Aidan prompted gently. "Do you think there are any other reasons you didn't pass?"

"Well...my aunt said I haven't learned to

be focused enough. My old school—the one I was in before this—I got all A's there and I didn't even need to try. I could just memorize stuff. But here, everything is faster. I guess I didn't believe her this summer, but now I do. I think I'll do better next time. Or I would if I was here at night with the other kids in quiet study session." He looked longingly back at the group of boys eating breakfast together.

"Okay," Aidan said. The last thing he wanted to do was to contradict either the aunt or the mother or the headmaster or his grandmother. "Why don't we go back to see Dr. Pingree?"

"So are you going to tutor me?" Brandon asked.

"Do you want to be tutored?"

"Um. Yeah." Brandon glanced at him. "Do you want to tutor me?"

Out of the corner of his eye, he saw Ashley in the corridor, being led to meet Dr. Pingree. She looked pretty, with her hair done up so that her long neck was exposed. He had to be content gazing at that attractive sliver of skin, because every other part of her was covered—in a conservatively cut tailored blazer and wide-leg trousers. She was making an effort to fit in, he observed, not wearing her trendy hairstylist clothes, and that just made her all that more remarkable in his eyes.

He stilled, remembering what Gram had said about Ashley going to alcohol rehab. Aidan didn't hold that against her. He thought highly of her for it. Still, he couldn't deny that it raised a warning flag. Would she think he was "interfering" in her home life? Would he have to worry that her alcoholism might influence her to do something she shouldn't?

He should have thought of that before he'd reacted so impulsively, wanting to help Brandon without thinking it through.

He tried not to wince as Ashley noticed his presence. He watched as her eyes widened. She seemed wary. Her lips pressed together.

It saddened him to see her react that way toward him. He'd liked her yesterday. He liked her calm manner, her inherent gentleness, even though she'd had a steel spine, too. In her own sweet way, she was no pushover.

Brandon was staring at him. He hadn't seen his mom yet. And he was waiting for an answer from Aidan.

"Let me talk with your mother," Aidan said to the boy.

"Okay. Um. Here she comes, the lady with Dr. Pingree. That's her."

Ashley was stalking toward them, ahead of

the headmaster. Brandon glanced at Aidan and smiled hopefully as she stood before them.

"This is your mother?" Aidan asked, by way of verification, even though he well knew it was.

"Yeah, this is my mom."

Ashley crossed her arms. Two bright spots of color blazed in her cheeks. The corners of her mouth tugged down.

She looked at Brandon, and Aidan saw hurt in her eyes. "We need to talk about our discussion earlier this morning, but not now. We'll do it when you get home this afternoon," she said to her son.

"But, Mom, I—"

"I *said* we'll talk later."

Brandon didn't argue. Looking pained, he shrugged and gazed at the headmaster, who led him away.

He and Ashley were alone. "What are you doing here, Aidan?" she asked.

"Ashley, I honestly did not plan this." But then he paused, because in a sense, hadn't he?

He gave her a guilty look and a shrug because he didn't know what else to do, but she stared at him, not buying the insouciant look on his face any more than she had with her son.

From his peripheral vision, Aidan was well

aware that not only was her son watching them but so was the table of boys he'd been sitting with.

"Let's talk out in the hall," he said, smiling broadly for the audience across the room.

"Yes. Good idea." She nodded and then turned on her heel.

He didn't follow her, though. He was damned if he'd let himself be given the questioning schoolmarm treatment. He could have easily outpaced her—his legs being longer—but he kept his strides even with hers.

Once in the hallway, she didn't stop. She marched straight into the closest office.

He followed her, raising a brow as he caught up to her. "Should we be doing this?" he asked.

"Yes. I'm not risking being overheard."

Ouch. She was tougher than she'd seemed.

She shut the door behind him and crossed her arms.

The room wasn't all that big. It was a very tight, very enclosed space.

"What are you doing with my child?" she asked.

He sobered. "I swear I didn't set out this morning intending to meet your son."

"Are you following me?"

"My grandmother follows you."

She gave him a look of horror. "Vivian Sharpe follows me? What are you *saying*?"

What *was* he saying? He'd just insinuated that his grandmother was a stalker.

"No, sorry, I just…" He shook his head and leaned against the edge of the desk. He was losing it. His pulse was elevated. His breathing shallow.

Aidan closed his eyes. Practiced slow, deep breathing to regain his equilibrium.

What had made him think he could do this—help another person? He'd just come back from a war zone. His nerves were shot as it was. He'd been neglecting dealing with that part of himself.

And his grandmother had been worried about Ashley being an alcoholic? What a laugh.

"Aidan?"

He opened his eyes and focused on her. She was the only one who'd been able to calm him lately. It really was great not to be called Dr. Lowe. Not to have to be so professional all the time.

"You'll be okay," he said lightly to Ashley. "Don't worry about my grandmother. She loves your son and sits in the background, doing what she can for him. You'll never really be in trouble with her watching over you like she does."

"Oh, my God!" she exclaimed. "It sounds like she's a spider!"

He couldn't help it; he laughed out loud.

But Ashley was horrified. By him, by his grandmother. And maybe she was right to be horrified—maybe he should be more so himself. His whole life, he'd been surrounded by people who ran the show for him. Spiders, creating a web around him. This wasn't what he wanted. In fact, right now he just wanted his freedom. Wanted to be outdoors, with a wide blue sky overhead and an endless possibility of paths before him.

"You're right," he said. "I made a mistake in offering to tutor your son. I only did it because my grandmother sits on the board of directors here, and she mentioned him. But I won't be getting swept up in helping anyone again. And I won't be having anything to do with the Captains, with baseball, with charities, with hip replacement surgeries. And I won't be going overseas and doing good with war-torn children. I'm done, Ashley. Although, honestly, anytime you want to give me a haircut, I am so there. Just call me, and that I'll be there for."

"Oh, my God…" She put her hands to her

cheeks. She seemed to be in as much shock as he was.

He was surely going crazy. The pressure had all caught up to him and he was coming apart in the most inappropriate way.

"VIVIAN SHARPE," ASHLEY WHISPERED, dying at the realization. "Vivian Sharpe is keeping tabs on my son." That's what Brandon had been referring to earlier. How could she have missed it? "And she sits on the board at St. Bartholomew's School?" She'd probably even gotten Brandon his scholarship.

While she stood in stunned silence, taking it all in, Aidan gave her a tired look. It was that same tired, dazed look he'd had in the salon yesterday. And she understood. He'd been through a clinic bombing. His girlfriend—or maybe fiancée—had died in his arms. That was what he was dealing with.

She rubbed her brow. It was so hot in this tiny, tight space. And Aidan, with that dazed look in his brown eyes, he was gazing at her like…like he was mesmerized by her. Like no man looked at her anymore, not since she'd become Brandon's mom.

Brandon. He'd failed his math pre-test and he needed a tutor. He needed her help. And she needed to focus—not on her worries and suspicions about Vivian Sharpe and certainly not on her physical attraction to this complicated man, Vivian's grandson.

She backed up. "Aidan...Dr. Lowe...please. Please, you need to tell Dr. Pingree that the school should find another tutor, someone appropriately qualified to work with middle school children on their mathematics studies. I'm not comfortable with your grandmother being involved in my son's schooling. It's hard enough that he's so involved with the Captains. I didn't realize that she was on the board of directors here, too. Will you do that, please? That way I can tell Brandon that we'll find someone else."

"Aidan," he said.

"What?" she asked. He kept confusing her. He was looking at her straight in her eyes.

"Aidan. Call me Aidan."

"Fine. Aidan. But did you even hear what I said?"

"Don't worry—I'm not going to interfere with your kid again. I promise."

"Okay." She nodded. "Then...why did you talk with him this morning?" she couldn't help asking.

He shook his head. "I don't know. Curiosity? I'm sorry. It was a mistake." He shook his head again. "I need to clear my things out of Boston and get on with my life."

She digested what he said. He was still new to being home. Still reentering his old life again, but that old life was gone.

Just like hers.

"Good luck to you," she murmured. She wished that she could say she thought he would be okay, too, but she wasn't sure of that.

He glanced away, very briefly.

"Aidan, I really am sorry about what happened to your girlfriend," she said softly.

He said nothing.

"Well, we should go…"

His gaze dropped to her mouth. She squirmed. It was so hot in this tiny school office that smelled of books and wood and leather from the big tan-colored chair behind the desk she was leaning against.

"Ashley…"

"Hmm?"

"Elizabeth would be a good person to help him," Aidan said.

"Elizabeth?" she asked, confused again. Aidan was still staring at her lips with that dazed look in his eyes.

"Yes, Dr. LaValley. She's tough. She can help Brandon settle down and study."

Oh, Aidan was speaking of Lisbeth. And

Brandon. Of course, her son was the whole point of their conversation.

She licked her lips. But that made it worse, because Aidan sighed as she did so.

She fanned her face with her hand. It was so hot inside, and she was just off balance, and she shouldn't be looking at his body, so close to hers...

"Um, what did Brandon say when you talked with him just now?" she asked. She knew she shouldn't ask—she'd just told him off, after all. But...he'd mentioned Lisbeth, her sister, as if he knew her, and that made it seem okay.

Aidan's warm brown eyes rose to hers. A slight flicker of concern crossed his face. Then she wasn't sure what he was thinking. But he was shaking his head again, this time vigorously.

"No. No, I can't get involved," he said in a loud voice.

She blinked, surprised.

"There's too many kids with too many problems, and I can't save them all. I couldn't even save...well, it doesn't matter." Aidan tore his hand through his hair. "But just know that I'm the wrong one. I'm not the one that saves people."

"Of course." She nodded, trying to smile,

trying to soothe him. What he must have seen in that clinic in Afghanistan…

"Let's…well, I'll call Lisbeth." She decided. "I'll explain the situation to her. And Brandon will certainly understand that you can't help him."

"He wants to board here with the other boys," Aidan said.

"Well, he can't do that." She pushed it all away, set her chin and went to find the headmaster.

TEN MINUTES LATER, Ashley stared at Dr. Pingree. She didn't know what to say to the news, other than the brutal truth.

"I can't afford to pay for a tutor," she explained. "Isn't there another option?"

"I'm afraid I don't have an alternative to give you," he repeated. "Other than Brandon can come here at night and take the extra tutoring study sessions with the boarding students before lights out. That's the best I can offer."

Ashley didn't like Brandon being out that late on weeknights. That option was impossible.

"Isn't there another volunteer tutor available?" she pressed.

"Not that I'm aware of." Dr. Pingree sighed.

"As I said, most of our tutoring is done in these extra study sessions. Dr. Lowe is an excellent choice to tutor Brandon in math. He actually failed his pretesting in his first year, as Brandon did, but Aidan came a long way from those preliminary scores and went on to be one of our best math students. I'm certain he has a wonderful perspective to offer a newer, struggling student. As a mentor, he would know how difficult it can be to catch up academically to St. Bartholomew's standards."

"That's a wonderful recommendation," Ashley murmured. "Thank you."

She wasn't going to say so, but it was apparent that now that she'd chased him away, Aidan no longer wanted to help.

Her biggest problem with the entire situation was that she'd been blindsided. She hadn't appreciated being caught off balance. By Brandon's mischaracterization of the note sent home, by Vivian's behind-the-scenes monitoring of Ashley's family, by Aidan's involvement. Even so, she was doing her utmost to be a good mom here. To keep her attention focused on Brandon and what was best for him.

"Thank you, Dr. Pingree. You've given me a lot to think about."

Dr. Pingree just sat at his large desk looking at her, tapping his fingers together. "I'm sorry, Ms. LaValley. As you recall, Brandon's entry examinations last spring showed him to be behind in math. He was to have studied for the autumn pretests over the summer. I thought we made that clear."

Yes, he had worked with Lisbeth. She was highly skilled and capable—even Aidan had said so.

"Maybe Brandon was simply nervous," she said. "Could he take the math portion of the test again, please?"

"I'm sorry, but we can't change the rules for one student. I'm sure you understand."

"It's not a change," she said. "It's more of a bend…"

Dr. Pingree shook his head.

At that moment, Vivian Sharpe's distinctive voice could be heard in the outer office.

"Thank you, but could you excuse me for a moment?" Ashley asked.

Dr. Pingree stood. "You're quite welcome, Ms. LaValley. Feel free to call me and make an appointment to talk anytime you need to."

She nodded, impatient to see Vivian before she left. "Yes, Dr. Pingree. Thank you for your time."

She finished the niceties and then hurried outside. A secretarial worker was on the phone, her back to Ashley, but Vivian Sharpe wasn't there.

She wasn't outside in the hallway, either. How did an elderly woman with a cane move so quickly?

Ashley sighed. She was still absorbing the fact that Vivian Sharpe had turned out to be a hidden puppet-master mentor for her son's education. She wondered if Lisbeth knew. She was the one who had helped select the schools for Ashley to apply to for Brandon. And other than feeling threatened and worried, Ashley wasn't sure what she thought about it.

The worry was for herself. It was scary to think she could lose Brandon—her influence over him, his love for her—to someone wealthier and more powerful. Vivian Sharpe controlled all the things that Ashley's son cared about. His work with the Sunshine Club charity. His weekend job as a Captains Club ball boy. And now even his entrance into his new school.

She pressed her hands to her cheeks. She was grateful, at least, that Aidan had told her. At least now she *knew*.

If she had met Aidan at any other time— before she'd had a son, or after her son had grown—then maybe things could be different. She was drawn to him, attracted to this gruff, sweet, complicated man who was dealing with even worse issues than she was.

Crazy as it sounded, the fact that he seemed to have a touch of a stress disorder from his stint overseas, even the fact that he was clearly still grieving, made him feel safer to her, because he was more like her than she'd first realized. Another woman might run away from the problems, but Ashley was flawed herself. Her alcohol issues. Her excessive worry. Her problems with being a single mom...

Brandon, she thought. When she'd left him, he'd been talking with Aidan, no doubt assuming that Aidan would be his mentor. Now that it wasn't happening, he would naturally blame her for shutting him down.

Brandon also wouldn't like it when she discussed curtailing his weekend ball boy activities. At least twice a month during weekend home games, Brandon suited up and did what every kid in Boston wished they could do, too. And now she would have to force him to make some tough choices.

He's twelve. He's old enough to make these basic choices. To understand consequences.

She at least needed to talk with him now. Pave the way for a more difficult conversation this evening. She didn't like that when she'd left him, she'd snapped at him. That wasn't like her, and she didn't want it to bother him.

She went back to the desk where Dr. Pingree's secretary sat. Ashley prepared to ask her to please allow Brandon to leave his class for ten minutes, in order to talk to her.

The secretary behind the desk brightened and then hung up the phone when she saw her. "I'm glad you haven't left yet, Ms. LaValley." She held out a slip of paper to Ashley.

"What's this?"

"Before she left, Mrs. Sharpe asked me to give it to you."

Her heart pounding, Ashley unfolded the slip of thick, cream-colored stationery.

Inside, there was no printed name or heading. Just a bold, cursive scrawl written firmly in black ink.

Three lines: Aidan's name. A Boston street address. A phone number.

Her hand shook. *Mrs. Sharpe, the spider.* She probably thought she was being helpful.

Ashley shoved the contact information into her purse. She had no intention of using it—or Vivian's implied approval that Aidan should tutor Ashley's son—but it reinforced to her that Vivian didn't want to have any direct, face-to-face interaction with her.

Fine. She was too tired to take offense right now. Too concerned about Brandon's future.

The most important thing this message showed was that the all-powerful woman didn't have the power to keep her son from flunking out of the elite St. Bartholomew's School. She thought that only Aidan could do that.

Poor Brandon, she thought.

FIVE MINUTES LATER, Ashley met Brandon at the bench beside Headmaster Pingree's office.

He looked at her hopefully. "Will Dr. Lowe be tutoring me now?"

Pushing away the guilt she felt for disappointing him, she shook her head and chose her words carefully. "Brandon, I want to make sure you're okay. You got some big news today."

He hung his head. "I'm sorry, Mom. I don't want to see you worried."

"When you told me not to worry this morning, did you know that you'd failed the pretest?"

He shook his head. "I found out for sure after you did."

"But you suspected it?"

He stared at his hands. "I try not to think

bad things, Mom. I always try to think positive thoughts. You know that."

Yes, she did. That was important to him—she knew her son. And at least she could feel better that he hadn't outright lied to her. "Could you help me understand something, Brandon? What happened with your studies this summer? You seemed to be working so hard."

He shrugged and didn't meet her eyes. "There was so much to do. I guess I just didn't get it." He looked bewildered.

"School has always been pretty easy for you."

"It's different here," he mumbled.

"I know. And Aunt Lisbeth used to spend hours locked in the library when we were kids. Maybe she studies differently than you do."

"I have a life, Mom," he said indignantly.

This was where it got sticky. She nodded. "I know you want to keep up with your friends and your social media. I know you want to suit up and be a ball boy this weekend, Brandon. But life is about choices. You need to decide which is most important to you."

"I can do both. My social life *and* school."

"Perhaps. But you aren't doing them well right now. And I'm afraid that if you fall behind in math, it'll just get worse. And all the connections you have can't help you if you don't pass the tests. It's on you, Brandon.

"If you're going to stay here, you need to take responsibility for the work, not anyone else. That was made quite clear with me today. That's why I've been in meetings all morning about it."

She sighed. "Look, I would tutor you myself if I could. But I'm afraid I was never strong at math. I took as little of it as I could get away with when I was in school. And now you're at a higher level than I ever saw."

He worried his lip. "What if I can't pass it?"

She looked at him sadly. "We can't think that way. Positive, remember?"

"I know, but...what if I can't pass the next test? It's in October. If I can't pass that one, then I'll have to leave at the end of the semester, right?"

She didn't say the obvious. "We will take one step at a time," she said firmly.

"You can tell me the truth, Mom," he said.

She sighed. "If you don't pass, it won't be the end of the world. You'll just have to go back to your old school." And he wouldn't get as good a foundation for a preparatory high school followed by college entrance exams. Medical school would seem that much more difficult to achieve.

God, he's only twelve! How can he have so much pressure on him?

Brandon glanced down. "Did Dr. Lowe not like me?" he asked in a small voice. "It seems like you're saying he's not going to tutor me. I have a feeling he could really help me."

She put her arm around her son, her heart breaking. It reminded her of the day, four years earlier, when she'd had to leave him to go into rehab. When they'd sat in the therapist's office and broken the difficult news to Brandon. He'd taken it in stride, but he'd been just a little boy then. The conversation had been harder for her than for him.

Now…

He was growing up. Things were different.

She swallowed, aware that she had to do this parenting on her own. No counselor to help her.

But she was doing it.

"Brandon," she said carefully, "Dr. Lowe has a lot on his plate right now. His decision has nothing to do with you."

Brandon hung his head sadly. "Yeah, it does. He said he wanted to help, and then after he met me, he obviously changed his mind."

Ashley's heart nearly broke for the millionth time that morning. Brandon thrived on making sure that people liked him. And he was so genial, so happy-go-lucky that most people did like him.

But that need could be a liability, too.

"Please, let's put it behind us, Brandon, and come up with new solutions."

He stubbornly set his chin. "I think Mrs. Sharpe wants me to work with him. She's his grandmother, you know."

Ashley inhaled. She liked her son's arrangement with Mrs. Sharpe less and less as time went on. "Did you speak with Mrs. Sharpe about any of this?"

"No," he admitted. "We don't see her much at the ballpark. She doesn't come down to the team rooms—she's too old. But I remember Dr. Lowe from the Captains bullpen when I was eight. He used to work with the team. He left right around the time I started, but I remembered him. I really think he could help us, Mom. He's smart."

She couldn't argue with any of this—except to tell her twelve-year-old that Aidan Lowe, like her, was a complicated person who carried baggage along with him.

She sighed and glanced at her watch. They weren't going to solve this problem now, and, unfortunately, she was going to be late for work if she didn't get moving. "Okay, Brandon. We'll talk more tonight."

"Please, Mom," he begged. "Let me talk to him if you won't. It's either that or you've got to let me board at St. Bart's with the rest of my class."

She ground her teeth. "You're not the only commuter kid in your class." She was sick of the boarding talk.

"You'll talk with Dr. Lowe?"

"I can try," she said reluctantly, thinking of that note that Vivian had left for her.

Brandon brightened. "Thanks, Mom." He looked as relieved as if she'd already made it happen.

"I'm not promising anything," she warned.

CHAPTER FOUR

THE NEXT DAY, before Ashley headed to work for her Saturday morning half shift, she placed a quick call to her sister. From the busy coffee bar in the lobby of her building, she stood facing the windows. The smell of brew and the feel of warm morning sunshine hit her skin, and she inhaled deeply.

"Ash?" Her sister's sleepy voice caressed her ears.

"Hope I didn't wake you," Ashley said softly. "I know it's early, but I'm counting on the fact that you're an early bird yourself."

"Yes, I'm up. I'm headed in to the hospital, but I'm keeping my voice down because Jon got in late last night."

"We watched his game." Ashley felt a twinge of guilt for letting Brandon stay up so late to see his uncle pitch. But after the day they'd had, she couldn't say no. Unfortunately, the game on the West Coast hadn't ended until almost midnight.

"Is everything all right?" Her practical, focused sister always got straight to the point.

"No, actually." Ashley lowered her voice even more. The coffee shop was crowded, and she didn't want anyone to overhear her business.

"I'm calling about Brandon," she said. She held her sister's opinion of academic matters in very high regard, since Lisbeth had been the one who'd encouraged Ashley to seek out preparatory schools for Brandon in the first place. She'd helped consult with the entrance forms, with the recommendation gathering, with the entrance examinations. "He failed his math pretest."

"I was afraid of that." Lisbeth's voice was low, too. "Will you be getting him a tutor now?"

"Yes, the school suggested someone." Ashley paused. "But before I get into that, did you know that Vivian Sharpe was on the board of directors at St. Bartholomew's School?"

"I noticed her name," Lisbeth said mildly. "She has her fingers in a lot of worthy projects in Boston."

Ashley inhaled, taking a moment to process the news. "So...you don't think I have anything to worry about from her?"

"No. She's never directly interfered. She's

more of a patron to Brandon. She's very much in the background. As she should be."

"Has she ever said anything to you about Brandon? About directing his schooling?"

"No. When I recommended St. Bartholomew's to you, I based my decision on the scholarship offer they discussed. Vivian Sharpe never came in to the equation. Though frankly, when we listed Brandon's extracurricular activities with the Captains and the Sunshine Club on the application, I assumed it would be noticed."

Ashley swallowed. "Well, she's recommended a tutor for Brandon. Her grandson, Dr. Aidan Lowe. Do you know him from Wellness Hospital?"

There was a snort on the other end. Then a crisp, "Yes."

"That doesn't sound like a vote of confidence," Ashley said, her heart sinking despite herself.

"I've worked with him," Lisbeth said. "He's rude."

"He's not all that rude," Ashley found herself protesting. "That's just his prickly outer layer." If anyone, her slightly antisocial sister should understand that. Lisbeth could be prickly herself.

"You've met him, I see," Lisbeth said drily.

"He's…had a rough time. Aidan was over-seas at Doctor's Aid, and his clinic was bombed. His partner, Dr. Fleur Sanborne, was killed."

"Oh." Lisbeth's voice was soft. "That was *them*. Last autumn, right? I heard about the bombing, but I didn't…." She trailed off.

Ashley understood very well why this was news to Lisbeth. Her sister was obses-sive about those things that interested her—like Pompeii exhibits and academia and now, thanks to her husband, the sport of baseball. Everything else was outside the scope of Lis-beth's concern. Her intense focus had made her a great student, but unfortunately, some-times people misunderstood her. Ashley didn't. Ashley loved her wonderfully smart, loyal baby sister.

"Given that, and what you know of him per-sonally," Ashley said, "do you think I should go ahead with asking him—" begging him "—to tutor Brandon?"

"Did the school recommend Dr. Lowe?" Lisbeth asked.

"Yes."

"And Brandon wants him?"

"He does."

"Then I don't see the problem in asking him to do it. If the teachers at his school trust

Dr. Lowe, then that's what's most important. I just don't *personally* like him. *Personally.* Professionally, he's respected."

There was Lisbeth's logical side coming out yet again. Ashley knew how to take care of her baby sister—she'd spent her childhood managing some tough situations, for herself and for Lisbeth. If she could handle that, then she supposed she could handle whatever Aidan threw at her, too. She hoped.

"Thanks, Lisbeth. I'll go see him after my shift and ask him if he'll do it. Wish me luck."

ASHLEY WAS ABLE to scoot out of work a few minutes early, and when she did, she headed directly to Aidan's high-rise on the water.

Her feet were killing her in the heels she'd worn. She'd tucked her old clogs inside her bag, and when she got to the street, she slipped those on.

Copley Square was bustling just before noon. She took public transportation—the T—to the stop closest to the address that Mrs. Sharpe had left for her.

She walked down the street by the waterfront, where expensive hotels and restaurants and tall office buildings cast shadows over the wide boulevard. Across the street was the long park, a swath of grass known as the Rose Kennedy Greenway, after the mother of the late president. At one end was a pretty rose garden that Ashley had visited once when Brandon was small. They used to have "family fun days" together back then, as she had called their tradition of spending weekend time together. They'd gone everywhere together, all over Boston. Ashley, her friend Sharma, Sharma's son and Brandon. Now that Brandon was growing up and starting his new, intense school, she was feeling nostalgic.

Sighing, she turned on the GPS map app on her smartphone and followed the directions to Aidan's building.

The lobby was busy with residents and visitors. She pulled her purse tighter to her shoulder and headed for the elevators in the back.

She unfolded the slip of paper that Vivian had left her. Aidan's apartment was on the top floor. The penthouse.

Unfortunately, a doorman controlled the elevator to the penthouse. "I'll have to call upstairs and announce you," he said. "What's your name?"

"It's a trap," a woman said behind Ashley. Ashley turned. "If he announces you, then Dr. Lowe will instruct him not to let you up."

The doorman cleared his throat. "Are you another journalist?" he asked Ashley.

"No, sir. I'm a hairstylist." She opened her bag and, in a fit of optimism, showed him the full metal can of superhold hair spray that she always traveled with. She also showed him her trimming scissors, a mini set of shampoo and conditioner, and a barber's comb—in case he didn't believe her.

The doorman smiled at her. "Bill," his nametag read. "People have been feeding me lines all morning," he said to her. "But you, I believe. I've seen Dr. Lowe's hair since he returned home."

She laughed. "I know. He reluctantly came to my shop yesterday, but I'm still working on him. I'm Ashley, by the way." She held out one of her business cards.

"Nice to meet you," Bill said. He glanced at her card. "Perceptions on Newbury Street. Sweet."

"Feel free to spread the word," she said. "I'm open to new clients."

"Absolutely." Bill moved aside and held his hand forward to her. "Step inside. I'll take you up."

"Seriously?" asked one of the journalists as the elevator doors closed on the lobby.

Once inside the elevator, Bill pressed the

button for the penthouse. "I love tweaking journalists," he confided to Ashley. "Vultures. The *Globe* ran a story on Dr. Lowe's homecoming last night, and now everyone else wants to talk to him."

Ashley hadn't seen any newspapers today. "I'm sorry to hear that. It's been hard for Dr. Lowe to adjust to being home."

"Yes," Bill agreed. "I've noticed that, as well. And I'm glad you're here. Maybe it will calm things down."

"Isn't…he alone?"

"No, there are two people up there already."

Her heart fluttered with alarm. "Oh?"

Bill nodded but didn't elaborate. Apparently, that was as much gossip as he was prepared to share.

She wasn't getting a good feeling.

The elevator doors opened. A middle-aged man and woman were in the hallway, knocking on Aidan's door.

Ashley paused, shrinking back.

The sound of something breaking came from within Aidan's penthouse.

The man knocked on the door again. "You have to let us in, Aidan!" he called.

"Good luck in there," Bill murmured to Ashley. He looked expectantly at her, as if she was the one to fix this dilemma.

"Thanks, Bill." She mustered a smile and stepped onto the landing.

Immediately the elevator doors closed.

The man and woman in the hallway by Aidan's door paused to stare at her. The man stopped knocking, and the woman looked Ashley over, up and down as she tentatively approached.

"Who are you?" the woman asked.

Ashley smiled wanly. It was too late to head back down. The elevator was gone, and it likely wouldn't be coming back anytime soon.

Ashley licked her lips and told the truth, since it seemed to be working for her so far this morning. Again, she opened her monster bag and displayed the tools of her trade. The fact that she was wearing comfortable clogs didn't hurt, either. "I'm a haircutter," she explained. "I work at a salon called Perceptions."

The man turned to the woman. "He's that afraid to go outside?"

"Well, he was in the newspaper this morning. He's obviously upset about that."

The woman turned back to Ashley. Her lower lip quivered. She wore a bit of mascara, but it was smudged and starting to run. "A reporter called us yesterday and we answered all her questions. I'm afraid he's angry with us now."

"I'm sorry," Ashley said. "Are you Fleur's parents?"

"Fleur was my daughter," the woman whispered.

Oh no. Ashley ached for them, and for Aidan. Though she still thought he was being rude leaving them out in the hall.

"I'm so sorry for your loss," she said. "I never met Fleur, but from what I've heard about her, she was very brave."

The man nodded eagerly. "We were proud of our daughter. She always wanted to be a doctor. Our little town was too small for her— she wanted to go and save the world instead."

"That is so admirable," Ashley said, struck by their obvious need to talk about their daughter, even with a stranger.

The woman wiped away a tear, smudging her mascara a little more. "This has been hard for us. We never imagined…"

"I have a son." Ashley touched the woman's arm. "I can't imagine what I'd do if I lost him."

The woman reached for Ashley's hand.

"May I hug you?" Ashley asked.

Nodding, the woman hugged Ashley without speaking. A soft, motherly hug. She sniffled, and Ashley squeezed tighter. She wished she had her mom to hug sometimes. "What's your name?" Ashley asked Fleur's mother.

"I'm Flo. This is my husband, Albert."

"Albert, it's nice to meet you, as well. My name is Ashley LaValley." She held out her hand to shake it, but Albert caught Ashley up in a hug of his own.

He was a slight, sad man with a gray, bristly beard. Ashley hadn't grown up with a father. She counted Fleur as lucky in that respect, too.

"So, what's happening with Dr. Lowe?" she asked carefully, looking from Flo to Albert. "Did he know you were coming today?"

They exchanged a look. Flo gave Albert a slight nod.

"We arranged a time to come for our daughter's things. He told us noon, and here we are, but when we came, he immediately asked us to leave."

"He told us that he's not ready," Flo interjected.

"Oh. Dear. And you don't want to leave?" Ashley asked, for clarification's sake.

"No. He has been putting us off for eleven months now. First, he didn't come home for the funeral. He stayed overseas. Now that his contract is up and he's home, he's been avoiding us."

"We want to have a memorial service," Flo

added, her lips quivering again. "The funeral was rushed and private, and we were in such shock. Now that it's been nearly a year, we want to have a service in our church, with tributes from those who knew her from her childhood as well as her professional years."

"That's a wonderful idea. Have you told Dr. Lowe?"

"We've tried to. We need his help to invite the colleagues that she was close to."

Ashley saw the problem. Aidan didn't want to do it.

"It sounds lovely to me," she said honestly. "Very healing to have a lovely tribute for your daughter's life."

"Exactly." Flo nodded. "You understand."

"I do. So, if I'm understanding right, you want Dr. Lowe's help with the service. And you also want to retrieve her things?"

"Yes."

"Well...if he is...ill today...perhaps the things could be sent to you later?"

They exchanged looks again.

"We need to get inside," Albert said. "I know it's his condo, not hers." His lips curled. "But there's something inside we want to look for that we think she might have hidden."

"Perhaps if you told him..."

"We did."

"And he still said no?"

"It's a family heirloom," Flo added. "My late mother's wedding ring. I really want it back."

A wedding ring? "Ah. Perhaps she had a jewelry box?"

"Yes, but after it happened, Mrs. Sharpe brought us Fleur's jewelry box and the ring wasn't there."

"You think she might have hidden it inside the apartment?"

"I do think so. She…hid things in her closet as a girl. Perhaps it's tucked inside a box of shoes."

"We have a right to get her things," Albert said.

Of course they did. What was the matter with Aidan?

Ashley tried to imagine for a moment. Perhaps Fleur had wanted to get married. Her mother had sent her a wedding ring that might help things along. And Aidan, maybe angry, had done nothing.

This was none of her business. It wasn't what she'd come for today. But she felt sorry for these parents. She could certainly see their point.

Before she could decide what to do, the door to the apartment opened.

And Aidan stood there, looking like he badly needed a haircut.

"YOU'RE STILL HERE," Aidan said to Albert.

He had a splitting headache. He'd tried to grab a glass of water and some aspirin in the kitchen, but he'd dropped the glass, and it had shattered all over the floor. He'd left it there, but then he'd heard silence in the hallway. He'd come out to be sure the Sanbornes were gone. "I thought you left?" he said.

"You told us to call on you Saturday at noon," Albert replied stubbornly. "Now it's Saturday at noon, and we've rented a van."

"You said you were going to *call* me Saturday. *Call* me, not *call on* me."

"What's the difference?"

"There's a huge difference!" For one thing, he was standing there in bare feet, old jeans and a too-tight T-shirt he'd grabbed from the back of his old closet in his grandmother's house that morning. For another thing, he wasn't feeling up for dealing with people.

Behind Albert, Aidan heard a throat clear. And then Ashley LaValley stepped out, taking a place beside Flo.

He stared at her, blinking. Not believing his eyes.

She looked like she'd come straight from

work. A cute take-me-out-to-dinner dress, but with scuffed old working clogs. Her hair was up, and she was wearing makeup that made her big eyes look even bigger and her plump lips even plumper.

He stared another long moment, unable to speak.

She gave him a small, hopeful finger wave, which actually amused him. He laughed aloud like a crazy person, which by now, she should be well aware that he was.

He shook his head. The woman never stopped surprising him. Just like that, Aidan's anger evaporated a bit.

He glanced from Flo and Albert—the two people he'd once hoped would be his in-laws—to Ashley. Unpredictable Ashley.

She strode forward and touched his arm. "Dr. Lowe, please, you need to let us inside."

"And why is that?" he asked her.

"What is going on with you?" Albert sputtered, rushing to Ashley's aid. "You're not only rude to us, but you're rude to your hair-cutter?"

His haircutter?

Ashley put her hands on her hips and shook her head at Aidan as if he were a naughty boy. "Dr. Lowe, you do need to let Flo and Albert inside."

"I didn't call you," Aidan reminded her. "Somehow you snuck your way up here."

She set her chin. "Of course I'm needed here." She smiled at Albert as if they were co-conspirators. He should have known.

"While you meet with your haircutter," Albert said, "Flo and I will take a look at Fleur's things. We're entitled to her belongings, you know. She had a will. I'm sorry, Aidan. We waited until you came home, but we don't want to wait any longer."

Fleur had had a will because Doctor's Aid had asked them both to write wills before they'd left for overseas. Fleur had thought it a joke at the time.

The memory punched Aidan in the gut. He'd still loved her then, and the fact that Albert had rubbed that damn will in his face, no matter how inadvertently, didn't sit well with him.

Now he just seethed. "You'll get her stuff—don't you worry."

Flo's tears started flowing again. "She had a ring that belonged to my mother. I gave it to her the Christmas before she left. All I want is to have it to remember her by."

It was a *wedding* ring. Fleur had been irritated by it at the time because she'd considered it a hint and a criticism of her lifestyle choice. Although Aidan couldn't tell Flo that. It was the truth, but it wouldn't be fair to leave them with a hurtful memory of their daughter.

He knew he was acting badly today not letting them in. Even Ashley was giving him a censorious look. It was obvious she'd talked with them. They'd probably poured out their whole sad story.

"Please, Aidan. I just want to look for my mother's ring," Flo begged.

He had that splitting headache, and he suddenly also felt dizzy, as if he was going to pass out. The thought of dealing with the contents of Fleur's closet—her personal things— was a prospect so uncomfortable to him that it brought up physical symptoms.

He grabbed at the edge of the door. "No," was the only word he could get out as he waited for the feeling to pass.

And then Albert started speaking loudly, something about a judge and a will and an executor again, and Aidan had had it. Sick of all of them. He stood back to slam the door shut, but Ashley stuck her foot in the jamb. She was wearing those heavy white hairdressing clogs, like the female doctors and nurses at his hospital wore.

"I'll find it," Ashley said quietly. "My sister put everything in hidey-holes. If Fleur hid things in this apartment, I will find them, Mrs. Sanborne."

"Thank you," Flo said, dabbing at her eyes.

Ashley opened her purse and handed her a clean tissue. "I'll also call downstairs," she added, "and get some packing boxes sent up. If you and your husband will come back in two hours, I'll have your daughter's things boxed up for you."

Aidan just stood there dumbfounded, unable to speak.

"And then I'll walk you through the apartment," Ashley was promising, "and you can see that her things are out. Are you parked nearby? I assume there's a garage downstairs?"

"Yes, we left the van there."

"That's good. I saw a coffee shop across the street when I arrived. It seemed very clean, and they have nice sandwiches in the window, too. Why don't you have something to eat? Here, I'll take your phone number down and call you when I'm done."

"Are you finished?" he said to Ashley sarcastically, but she was paying attention to Flo, who was thanking her profusely and hugging her.

Flo then shot him a look as if he were evil.

Aidan swallowed, saying nothing. He watched Ashley walk them both to the elevator. When she came back, he opened the door and let her inside.

She stopped in the middle of the dusty parquet floor, and they looked at each other. She put both hands on her cheeks. Her skin was pale, and she was trembling. "I can't believe I just did that," she whispered.

He could. "You're a kind person," he said quietly.

"Why, Aidan? Why the cruelty?"

He sucked in his breath, hurt. He hadn't considered that he was being cruel.

"I'm wondering why you came today," he said, instead of answering her question. "Is it about your son?"

She nodded. Glancing down at her scuffed clogs, she whispered, "I made a mistake." She glanced up at him again, her big eyes appealing to him. "I never should have discouraged you from helping him. I would be grateful and honored if you would please tutor my son." She tried to smile, but her lips quivered. "Please, I'm begging you to reconsider. Brandon really wants you to, as well."

He toed the edge of the closet door. They were still in the entry hallway. He'd intended to stay for less than twenty minutes, just to see about grabbing some of his clothes. But then the reporters had been in the lobby, and that had spooked him, and then when he'd unlocked the door and come inside, he found that he couldn't even go as far as the bedroom to get anything.

"You don't mind boxing up a dead woman's things?" he asked Ashley.

Her cheeks paled even more, but she shook her head.

"So that's it, then? You mediate the family argument, box up Fleur's belongings, and in return I agree to tutor your son? That's what you want?"

She swallowed. "Yes, I very much want you to help Brandon. And I also want to help you and Fleur's parents."

He gazed hard at her. "You'll do a lot for your son," he noted.

"He's everything to me," she whispered.

He thought about that. What must it be like to be *everything* to someone? He didn't think he'd ever really experienced that. The boy was lucky, in Aidan's opinion.

He pointed the way to the living area. Those low black leather couches he'd bought with his first real paycheck—dusty. The huge windows with no curtains—Fleur had loved them that way—also dusty. A year's worth of dust settled everywhere while they'd been off having an adventure and he'd been hoping to salvage his relationship.

Which hadn't worked. But that was a year ago. *Move on*, he told himself.

He followed behind Ashley as she tentatively walked ahead. He didn't mind following her—such a beautiful woman to watch. Her bag was slung over her shoulder, and her gaze darted about his and Fleur's old apartment, taking everything in.

Fleur would never have done such a thing in Ashley's shoes. Like his family, she would have hired someone to do the job. Easy and neat, without getting too involved.

He sat on the couch. The action kicked up dust, and he wrinkled his nose. The whole apartment smelled musty from being shut up. They should have gotten a tenant, or at least covered the furniture with sheets, but neither of them had even considered it. They'd been so damned busy…

Fleur had lived with him off and on for almost ten years. They'd finished their residency together, then had both worked at Wellness Hospital. Busy all the time, they were.

He pushed his hand through his hair. Really, all that was a lifetime ago now.

There was a knock on the door. He tensed, but Ashley strode forward and answered it, handling the caller. Bill—his doorman—from downstairs, had arrived with a pile of flattened cardboard boxes.

Bill seemed to have developed a first-name relationship with Ashley over the course of an elevator ride, and he lingered with her for a moment. Even in the depths of Aidan's headache and bad attitude, he noticed a twinge of jealousy.

He frowned. But Ashley closed the door, and then stood before him, setting down the pile of flattened boxes on the bare floor.

"Could you help me assemble these and tape the bottoms?" she asked him. "Bill gave me a roll of packing tape, so why don't we get started?"

"Bill," Aidan said. "Did you know him before today?"

"No." Her cheeks flushed as she bent over to assemble a box. "I had to convince him to let me upstairs, so I showed him my business card." She smiled at him. "He found it very believable that you needed a haircut."

He smiled back at her. He suddenly felt sad. "You shouldn't have to be here, doing this," he said. "If it were up to me, I'd have locked the door behind me and then found a real estate agent to handle the whole thing." He glanced at the boxes. "I'd have sent all the clothes and furnishings to charity. That's what I would have done."

He stood and paced. Outside the floor-to-ceiling windows, the sun glittered on the sea of the inner harbor. Far below, white sails flashed. He'd give anything to be leaving with those boats.

He glanced back at Ashley. Her cheeks were pink. Her eyes were downcast, and she wasn't looking at him.

"What?" he asked.

"Nothing."

"You think I'm cruel again?"

"No." She kept her eyes on the box she was taping. "I think that if you want the right to make those decisions, then maybe you should have married her."

He paused, his whole body frozen.

Ashley groaned and squeezed her eyes shut. "I didn't mean to say that. I'm sorry."

He gave a dry laugh. "No, I'm interested in what you really think. You think I'm the one who didn't want to get married?"

A look flashed across her face, showing him that she was surprised. Wondering if she'd made a mistake, or if he was just arguing with her to pick a fight.

"The point is, you made an assumption about me," he said to Ashley.

"Well...yes." She gathered up the boxes and went into the bedroom. He found himself following her.

"Of course I made that assumption," she said, plopping a half-assembled box on the floor and then kneeling beside it. She lifted a piece of tape with her fingernail. "I grew up in a house with a mother who was always upset because she wanted our father to marry her." Viciously, she jerked the tape. "Oh, he came over a few times to visit that I remember, anyway, but that was the extent of his commitment."

Aidan leaned against the doorjamb. He hadn't considered that she would have such a personal stake in the issue.

"That...must have been hard," he said.

She tore more tape and assembled the box. "I spent most of my childhood consoling my mother. The rest of the time, I took care of my sister."

And no one had taken care of Ashley, it seemed.

"So you see, Aidan, in a way, I can relate to your dilemma. You weren't married to Fleur, so you don't have the right to settle her estate or even choose which of her things to give away or not. My mother never had any legal rights like that with my father, either. My sister and I might have, if she'd pursued it, but she didn't."

She finished assembling the box, and set it aside. "Shall we start?" She swallowed. "Where...did she keep her things?"

He walked over to the large set of double doors that led to Fleur's closet, and he swung them open.

Inside, it smelled like her. Tears stung his eyes, and he had to blink, hard.

Nothing brought her back to life like seeing her dresses hanging there. Her cubbyholes with shoes. A mirror.

How many times had he watched her check herself in that mirror before she rushed out to work or to a meeting or to the airport?

But Ashley was there with him, too, so he sucked in a breath and got a hold of himself. On the left side of the closet was a rack of drawers. Four of them. He opened the middle drawer. Sweaters, T-shirts, her running stuff. Her gym stuff. She'd been a huge gym rat.

He stepped back. He knew he had to do this. Knew he had to get this stuff cleaned out so he could sell the condo and finance his move out of the city.

He glanced at Ashley. It was as if they were speaking telepathically. With a search of his face and a silent nod, Ashley reached into the drawer he opened and gently, reverently and with care moved a stack of sweaters from the drawer to the packing box.

Then she smoothed the sweaters on top.

"Thank you," he said. He had to choke back his emotion at seeing Ashley's respect for Fleur's memory. Once, he had loved this woman.

"We'll get you through this, Aidan," she said quietly.

And then she started on the bottom drawer. Sinking to her knees on the plush white carpet, she began filling that box with pajamas. Nightgowns.

He turned away, overcome. This was so hard. It had to be hard for Ashley, too. She must really love her son to go through such a difficult task with him.

ASHLEY BROUGHT HER third packed box out to the pile accumulating near the front door. She rubbed her arms and glanced around her. Normally a place like this would intimidate her. The view of the waterfront took her breath away; the height of the floors made her dizzy. Aidan lived in a world of wealth that was out of her league.

She turned and looked for him, but he wasn't in this main room.

Instead, there was a pile of belongings, heaped like an unlit bonfire. On the bottom, two huge paintings. Modern art—they looked like splashes of paint enclosed in plain black frames. Beside the paintings were stacks of smaller frames. Diplomas. Awards. Piles of mail. Also frilly pillows. A side table. A small desk and matching chair. Boxes filled with books and files. Some knickknacks. A clock. A laptop computer. Some electronics. A box of things from the kitchen…mugs, some glasses with initials on them. A set of expensive luggage. A mountain of winter coats. A leather jacket and some boots.

Aidan had been busy, too.

Her heart ached for him. She knew this had been hard for him. In essence, it sounded like he'd been rejected by Fleur, and yet he couldn't be honest and tell anyone about it. He had to pretend, alone. Of course he grieved her death—whether he was aware of that or not.

Now Ashley could see where the prospect of removing Fleur's belongings had made him so angry. But he wasn't callous; he was grieving.

Ashley sighed. The awkwardness and sorrow she'd felt touching a dead woman's things filled her, as well. She knew the awesomeness of her responsibility. It made her think of herself, to put herself in a role-reversal situation. What if it had happened to her? Or worse, to her son? It made her shudder. She felt for Fleur's family. She felt for Aidan, too.

She woke from her reverie as she came across a cache at the bottom of Fleur's underwear drawer. Ah, women and their underwear drawers.

She'd dutifully put those things into the cardboard box for Flo and Albert. There were some small boxes of old jewelry hidden there. Into the cardboard box they went. At the very back of the drawer, there was a journal. Ashley's heart nearly stopped. Of course, she should have expected it. She shouldn't have been surprised.

The journal was an ordinary one. Plain tan leather. No lock. No name on the cover.

Ashley had kept a journal while she'd been in rehab. It had helped her sort out her feelings. She'd thrown it away—burned it, actually, in a private, triumphant ceremony—because the worst thing that could happen would be for her curious young son to find something so deeply personal. She no longer did a lot of things because of living with her son, protecting her son, above all being a good mother.

That had made her think of throwing the

journal away. Or destroying it. Certainly, that is what *she* would have wanted, in the woman's shoes.

Maybe Ashley could tuck the diary into the bookcase. Let Aidan find it and decide what to do with it himself, later in a more private moment. Perhaps he'd see it when he felt less raw.

Ashley slid the diary between two volumes on the bottom shelf of Aidan's bookcase.

She continued on through the living room toward the kitchen. To the side, there was a nook, again with the floor-to-ceiling windows, where Aidan sat alone at a table, staring out the window.

She backed away, slipped into the kitchen, sidestepping some broken glass and a spill of water—that must have been the crashing noise she'd heard earlier. She looked for a broom but didn't see one at hand. Later, she would sweep up the glass for him. For now, he needed something else.

She opened a cabinet door until she found a box of English tea and some sugar packets. No kettle that she saw, but there was a microwave and a refrigerator that had a water filter.

There was one thing that Ashley knew how to do well—her go-to reaction to any difficult situation—and she made the decision then and there to take care of Aidan.

Quickly, she made two tall glasses of iced tea. By habit—because it was what Brandon liked—she stirred a packet of sugar into each glass. Brought the glasses to Aidan at the table in the other room.

He looked up, distracted, and she almost dropped the glasses. By goodness this man was beautiful, even in grief and pain. Maybe especially in grief and pain. His dark eyelashes contrasted against pale skin. His gaze was distant.

She longed to go and put her head on his shoulder. It was curious that she could admire him from afar because it was safe—he was grieving and therefore not interested in her.

She sat down beside him as he lifted the glass and took a sip. He wasn't looking at her; he was gazing out the window at the sailboats in the marina.

She crossed her legs and sipped at her own drink, watching him over the rim of her glass. He was so beautiful; he made her long for something. For what she couldn't have. But it was okay to long, because it was impossible. Lisbeth may have wanted Tony to come back and marry their mom, but Ashley had always known it was a fairy tale that wouldn't come true. She hadn't even bothered to feel bad, one way or another.

Imagining Aidan kissing her was safe. It was only a dream that would never happen. The poor man was still grieving, for goodness' sake.

She glanced around at the nice apartment. The pretty things. The outwardly gruff, though inwardly kind-at-heart Aidan. It struck her again that Fleur Sanborne had been one lucky woman.

Aidan suddenly glanced at her. "Thanks for this," he said hoarsely, indicating his drink. "And for packing those boxes. I appreciate it."

She nodded. "You're welcome."

"I'm not a monster," he said.

"I know that." She smiled at him. "I wouldn't let a monster tutor my son."

That made him chuckle. He shook his head and looked directly at her. It was a look of awareness, of her body, of how close and alone they sat, and it made her freeze.

"I can't commit to the whole semester," he said, "but I can promise to work with him every day, if that's what you want, for the next two weeks. After that, I can help find someone else to take over for me."

She tried to mask her disappointment. She'd hoped for more than two weeks. Glancing at her glass, she asked, "Do you plan to leave Boston then?"

"I do." His frank gaze made her want to pull her thin sweater tighter across her breasts.

"Okay," she murmured. "Thanks for telling me." And then she babbled. "Brandon will be very appreciative, he—"

"I'm not doing it for Brandon," he said sharply, "I'm doing it for you."

"For me?" She could feel her cheeks heating.

"You're a good person, Ashley. So I'm going to say this. You should prepare yourself for things not to work out the way that you'd like them to."

She blinked at him. "Excuse me?"

He swept his arm over his apartment. She glanced back and saw the pile of jumbled household goods scattered there, and it occurred to her that he was talking about himself more than about her. He'd lost his love. His life had fallen apart around him. He wasn't handling it particularly gracefully. "Tell your son that life sometimes blows up in your face no matter what you do to stop it."

"No!" She leaped out of her seat and stood, her hands shaking, her knuckles white on the back of the wooden chair.

But the look he gave her appeased her anger. She remembered that he had been through a heartbreaking tragedy. "Your wife died in your arms, Aidan. I know—"

His cheeks reddened. "She wasn't my wife," he spit.

"I'm sorry. I'm so sorry. That was a slip of the tongue, but—"

"She turned me down, Ashley. I wanted to marry her, but she said no. And that's not even the worst of it. Those last few months together, we'd fallen out of love. Both of us. Our Doctor's Aid assignment was a last-ditch effort at making something work again. It didn't happen. Instead, we broke up for good."

"You…?"

"A week before she died." He tore a hand through his hair. "I couldn't tell anyone. You saw her parents. They've been through hell— she was their only daughter. You think I could tell them the truth?"

"I…"

He shook his head. "Fleur was a complicated person. Forceful." He glanced at her. "I'm never gonna talk about her with you, but suffice it to say, there's more than what's apparent on the surface. That's what I was arguing about with her parents when you first got here. They want a memorial service. I understand. But the truth of the matter is,

I'm not comfortable being a part of it, given the circumstances."

He glanced at her again. "Your sister would probably call me arrogant for saying that. No, I think 'rude' was her word for me."

"Well…"

He shrugged. "I know how it looks. I know how I *seem*. And I know that maybe I was tough about things sometimes—regular, everyday things. But it's what I was taught in life, to be tough. I wasn't taught to be kind. But honestly, I'm doing my best. And I do feel for Flo and Albert. I really do."

"It's okay to ask for help with this," Ashley said softly.

He slumped in his chair. He passed his hands through his hair. She knew how hard it was to ask for help—she'd had to learn that lesson in rehab. But she'd learned it. And so would he.

"I'd thought I was over it," he muttered. "I thought I'd dealt with the breakup and her death during the last eleven months."

"You're human," she said gently. "Healing is a process."

He stood. "All right." He blew out a breath. "We'll start working together with Brandon on Monday evening at seven o'clock. Give me your address."

"My—"

"Address. Or is there another place you want me to tutor your son?"

She swallowed. He'd segued so quickly, her head was spinning. "Um, actually, I thought you'd be tutoring him at school…"

Aidan shook his head. "Brandon isn't a boarder, so it would be better for him to be in his own space."

Ashley twisted her hands. She suddenly wasn't sure she liked this. Having Aidan in her tiny apartment seemed too personal. Too risky to her.

Aidan in her house? Every night?

"I recommend going from seven to nine every night except Sunday," Aidan said. "Two weeks should be enough to get Brandon started. You can be present, but it would be better if you were in another room so as not to distract him. No matter how much you might want to jump in." He laughed suddenly. "Though not jumping in to help might be hard for you—I'm starting to see that."

"Are you saying I'm overbearing?" she protested.

"No. Just a mama bear taking care of her cub."

"Hey! That's not a bad thing."

He laughed again. "We'll see." He picked

up their empty glasses and headed to the kitchen. When he was confronted with the pile of household goods, plus the broken glass on the floor, he grimaced.

"Aidan, where's the broom? I don't mind cleaning up for you."

"No, it's my mess," he said. "I'll handle the rest from here. And I'll meet Albert and Flo when they come back."

"Are you sure?"

When he nodded, Ashley sighed and handed over the boxed ring she'd tucked into her back pocket. "This is for Flo," she said simply. "The family heirloom she was asking about."

Aidan's jaw tightened, but he met her gaze and then gave her a steely nod.

It had to hurt him. It had to hurt him a lot.

HOURS AFTER ASHLEY had left—after they'd all left—Aidan went outside to the marina and borrowed his neighbor's boat. He motored past the moored sailboats in the inner harbor, going slowly, and once in the outer harbor, lowered the controls, pushing the engine to its fastest, until he was alone in the Atlantic.

He cut the engine. Bobbing alone, the air smelling like sea and water, the city far in the distance, he pulled out the slim volume from the backpack on the seat beside him.

Fleur's diary. He'd found it in the bookcase tucked into the bottom shelf. He hadn't known what it was until he'd opened it and had seen her large, bold printing. No cursive for Fleur; she printed everything. Sharply, confidently.

He slammed the book shut. Hadn't wanted to read it, then or now. It wasn't his to read.

She'd embarked on an affair with another man toward the end. Aidan hadn't known until they were already overseas. He'd found out through a mistakenly addressed email. Or maybe not mistakenly addressed. It hadn't mattered how, just that he'd known.

Aidan wound up his pitching arm and hurled the diary as far as he could. Fleur's secrets would go to Davy Jones's locker.

He sat for a moment, still bobbing alone in the waves. He could taste the bitterness and the regret. Even though he knew it did no good to wallow, he let himself. Five minutes. That was all.

And then he fired up the engine. Smelled the faint tint of gasoline, the gurgle of seawater churning in the propellers beneath him.

At least nobody else knew. Nobody else would ever know he knew, but himself and Fleur, and she wasn't around to tell anyone.

CHAPTER FIVE

LISBETH WAS TALKING to Brandon via Skype on the computer in Ashley's kitchen. Lisbeth rubbed her very pregnant belly and gazed with adoring eyes at her husband and Ashley felt a brief moment of envy.

But then Ashley looked at her son. She was lucky to have him. She didn't have a husband like Lisbeth did, but that couldn't be helped.

"Did Uncle Jon leave for the ballpark yet? He's the starting pitcher tonight, right?" she heard Brandon ask his aunt. Ashley dried her hands on a dish towel. She always let Brandon watch Jon's games. Brandon idolized his professional ballplayer uncle.

"No, I'm still here." Jon appeared in the screen, lowering his head and giving them a quick wave. "Hey, Ash."

"Hey, Jon," she said.

"Whatcha cooking?"

"Frozen gluten-free pizza for Brandon." Her brother-in-law knew about Brandon's wheat allergy. When Jon had lived in Boston while

Ashley had been in rehab, he'd fed her son often and he knew the challenges.

"Are you going to the game tonight, Auntie?" Brandon asked Lisbeth. "I think they're going to the World Series this year," he said excitedly.

The timer near the stove dinged, so Ashley turned it off and then took out their pizza dinner. She calmly dished it onto plates while she listened.

"You need to finish up your call," she finally told Brandon. "Your tutor is coming over soon."

Aidan. She felt herself smiling. To her surprise, she'd found herself looking forward to his arrival, not just for Brandon but for herself. After the long afternoon in his apartment, she'd gone home and thought about all that had happened and been said between them. Her initial anxieties about his presence in her home had been calmed by the realization that despite his gruffness, Aidan listened to her. He took her advice, and he worked with her. He honestly seemed to respect her.

Yes, he was healing from a difficult experience. Maybe mentoring Brandon would help him, too.

Brandon certainly needed the help.

"Good thing the game doesn't start until eight," Brandon said to his aunt. "I want to see Uncle Jon win his sixth straight game."

Again, Ashley felt the slight sting of envy. Her baby sister's husband was talented, rich and a good partner to Lisbeth. She was happy for her.

"Who did you get to tutor Brandon?" Lisbeth asked over Brandon's open laptop screen.

"Dr. Lowe," Ashley said evenly. "We spoke about it, remember?"

Brandon momentarily dipped his head to scarf a slice of pizza. While his attention was away, Lisbeth mouthed to Ashley, "Call me."

Ashley hesitated only a moment. Nodding, she took out her phone and called up Lisbeth's number.

Lisbeth answered. "Honestly," she whispered to Ashley, "I never thought he would actually agree to do it! How did that happen?" Her face went off Brandon's laptop screen, and her husband appeared in her place, chatting casually with Brandon, keeping him occupied while the two sisters talked privately.

"Why didn't you think that Aidan would agree to tutor Brandon?" Ashley asked.

"So you're calling him Aidan now?" Lisbeth said on the other end.

"Yes. He asked me to."

There was a snort.

"What, Lisbeth? If there's some other problem I don't know about, then tell me quickly, because he's going to be here any moment."

The long scrape of the buzzer rang out. *Too late.* Ashley sighed. "I'm hanging up. He's here."

"I got the door!" Brandon said. He actually broke away from conversation with the uncle he idolized to go open the door for Aidan, down a short hallway from the cramped kitchen they sat in.

Ashley could see Aidan as the door opened. Darkly tanned skin, a serious expression. Clear brown eyes that stared directly at her, over her son's head.

And that new feeling skipped inside her. A short jolt of pleasure and happiness. The tiny spark of growing familiarity she had at seeing his face. The pleasure that they'd shared confidences, and that he still chose to help her.

Lisbeth groaned audibly over the monitor. "You like him," she mouthed, crossing her arms as if disapproving.

Ashley scowled at her sister, irritated, but when she turned back, Aidan was addressing her son. Aidan carried a white textbook in his hand, and Brandon helped the good doctor take off his windbreaker, wet with raindrops. Brandon hung it on a hanger in the tiny front coat closet.

Another groan came from the monitor, and Ashley turned back. "This is for Brandon," she said quietly to her sister. But her sister just stared at her in that quiet, focused, enigmatic, *judging* way she tended to have about her. As if *she* understood Ashley better than Ashley understood herself. And Ashley felt uneasy, reminded of the one time she'd imposed on Lisbeth. The one time she'd had to leave Brandon with her sister while Ashley went to inpatient rehab.

Maybe Lisbeth thought that gave her the right to criticize her mothering skills. If so, Ashley was ready for that to end.

"You know I'm a good mom," Ashley reiterated. "I always put Brandon's needs first."

Lisbeth sighed. "I know," she said. "I'm sorry." She glanced at her round belly. "Maybe it just reminds me of—"

"Of our mom?" Ashley asked.

Lisbeth looked taken aback. "Yes, of Mom."

She glanced up and saw Aidan looking at her, brow wrinkled quizzically.

Just wonderful. He was here, but the tension had returned to Ashley's shoulders. The magic and pleasure of his arrival had gone.

AIDAN PAUSED BEFORE the table in the small apartment where he'd obviously interrupted not only their dinner but some kind of heated sisterly conference. He couldn't shake the feeling that his presence was the problem.

He paused, textbook still under his arm. The goal tonight was to work with Brandon for just one hour to start. Have the kid do some quick problem sets with him. Assess where his difficulties were. Make a plan for his next tutor, because Aidan wouldn't be here long enough to finish the job. He was sorry, but that's the way it was.

Ashley put her phone away, then ran her hand through her hair and smiled at him. He coughed, not able to resist gazing at her. She wore yoga pants and a tight T-shirt, which showed off her great figure.

He swallowed. He needed to remind himself that he wouldn't be interacting much with Ashley tonight, since he would be with Brandon. He didn't need to worry about getting too close to her. He would just be with her son, the struggling student who said he wanted to be a pediatric oncologist. Just two weeks of tutoring and mentoring, just to get the kid started, and then Aidan would pass him off to somebody else.

"Would you like some pizza, Dr. Lowe?" Ashley gazed up at him. Her hazel eyes caught his.

"Ah, no. I'm fine."

"Dr. Lowe, meet my uncle," Brandon said. He pointed to a laptop sitting on the kitchen table. On the screen, a guy that Aidan recognized as one of his grandmother's former team pitchers was sitting in shirtsleeves, a San Francisco cap on his head.

Aidan sat in the chair that Brandon indicated. He nodded at the guy on the screen. "Hello."

"Hi, Dr. Lowe." A woman crowded in next to the guy. She looked about seven or eight months pregnant and was wearing scrubs.

"Hello, Dr. LaValley," he said.

"I didn't realize that you'd be coming to the house at night to tutor Brandon." Her tone was cold.

What could he say to that? Dr. LaValley obviously wasn't happy about it.

"Dr. Lowe went to St. Bart's," Brandon piped up. "He's going to help me catch up with algebra and stay in school."

Whoa. The boy was running political inference for him? Aidan glanced at Ashley, but she had crossed her arms and appeared to be silently communicating, sharing looks with her sister.

Both Ashley and her sister noticed him watching them, and they looked away.

There was silence all around. He glanced at Brandon, then at his watch. "So. Where do you study? Here? At the kitchen table?"

"Not usually." Brandon rubbed his nose. "I work in my room, but I'm eating right now." To prove his point, he took a bite of the pizza on his plate. "And my uncle has a game. I like to talk to him before he leaves for the ballpark."

The uncle gave Aidan a look that said, "Is that a problem?"

It was. This kid and his family had no idea of the deck stacked against him. Aidan had once been in Brandon's shoes, and no one had helped him. He'd had to figure out everything himself. At least Brandon had a mom and a family who cared, however clueless they were about the situation.

Aidan stood. "Look," he said to the couple on the screen, "good luck with your game tonight. I only have a short time with Brandon, and we need to get going."

Their mouths opened in surprise, and he was sorry for that, but someone had to give the wake-up call.

"Brandon," he said, "I need to talk to your mother. Alone."

"No," Brandon said. "I want to hear, too."

Aidan glanced at the computer, waiting for the aunt and uncle to sign off. When the screen went black, he turned to Brandon and Ashley.

Ashley just stood with her arms crossed, giving him a strange look.

Aidan exhaled. "Okay," he said to the boy, "you're twelve. Old enough to hear the truth. You're also old enough to make your own decision. I just left your school, and there's a room full of twelve-year-olds who are away from home, probably for the first time, and they're studying together. No one is talking, making internet calls or eating pizza with their mom."

Brandon clamped his mouth shut. He gave his mother a sullen look, which made Aidan remember that Brandon really wanted to be boarding with the other kids, but his mother preferred him at home with her. Wasn't that why she'd moved to Boston with him?

"Brandon is not going to board," Ashley said firmly. "But you're right. Study time should be designated study time. I agree with you on that."

"I'm glad you're on board," Aidan said,

"because I'm going to be frank. You both need to know what you're up against."

Ashley's phone rang. A ringtone like an old-fashioned telephone.

A line appeared in her forehead. "My sister." She swiped at the screen of her phone, connecting to the call. Her cheeks turned pink as she listened.

Faintly, he heard Dr. LaValley's raised voice. After a moment, Ashley said, "I'll call you back later."

"What's she saying?" he asked Ashley.

"She asked to speak with you."

"I don't mind."

He held out his hand, a silent request to take her phone and talk with her sister. He'd say what he had to say out loud. Brandon was watching with big eyes and, presumably, big ears.

She sighed and turned her phone over to him, then crossed her arms and cocked a brow. With a sidelong glance at her son, Aidan knew that she was on the same wavelength as him—it wasn't easy to communicate without letting her son in on what they were thinking, but somehow they were managing.

He took the phone. "Dr. LaValley?"

"Dr. Lowe. You are rude and arrogant, and you are out of line. But I'm not surprised, because you've always been rude and arrogant and out of line—"

Ashley gave him an apologetic look. He appreciated that. For her sake, he let her sister continue to say what she had to say. Her voice was strident, telling him all his flaws.

Okay, he got it. But she also had shown him something important.

"Everyone," he said, "we're going to have a family conference." And then he pushed the speaker button so that everybody in the room could hear. "Okay, we need to get Brandon's entire support system on board."

He cleared his throat and continued. "Your nephew is a lucky kid," he said, gazing at both Ashley and Brandon as he spoke into the phone to Elizabeth. "He's got you and your husband and his mom, all in his corner, all helping him out." Aidan hadn't had any of that. "He'll be okay. He's smart, and from what I see, he's a good communicator, like his mom."

He met Ashley's eyes, just as she was exhaling in surprise. Her hazel eyes fastened on his in gratitude. He guessed that in her family, maybe her younger sister got all the credit.

"We know he's smart!" Dr. LaValley snapped.

So was Dr. LaValley. But from his memory of her, she wasn't a great communicator.

He shrugged, not taking anything she'd said personally. "You all need to know that I have no pull with the school. Neither does my grandmother. If Brandon doesn't pass his classes, he will not be allowed to return next term. It's a serious threat." He stared at Brandon, who looked genuinely shocked. All the blood had drained from his face. "He needs to decide if this is important enough to him to take it seriously," Aidan continued. "To prioritize it over watching baseball games."

"But...but..." Brandon began to stutter out a protest at the same time Dr. LaValley was groaning on the other end of the phone.

"Quiet, please," Ashley said to both of them. "This is important, and you need to listen."

"Ashley," Elizabeth began. "Think about what we talked about."

Aidan had no idea what they'd talked about, but whatever it was, Ashley was driven enough to make a stand. "I'm Brandon's mother," she said into the phone. "I will handle it on this end."

She glanced at them all—him, Brandon and the phone, with her sister on the other end. "You know what," she continued. "I think Dr. Lowe has said everything that needs to be said. I'm going to sign off now, Lisbeth, and I hope that you and Jon have a great night."

Then she pushed the button, ending the call, then turned the phone off and stashed it in a drawer.

Wow, Aidan thought. He gave her a smile of encouragement.

She crossed her arms and stared hard at Aidan. "So let's continue. What is the situation with Brandon's tests? Tell us the absolute truth."

He spread his hands. "Well, you signed a release allowing me to see his scores. I assume you're okay with discussing them in front of Brandon."

She nodded. "Yes, please."

To Brandon he said, "It was a requirement of allowing the school to find you a tutor. Although honestly, in our case, I'm more of a mentor than a tutor. I'm not a trained teacher."

Ashley leveled a gaze at him. "We understand. Speak plainly to us, please. We're open to hearing what you recommend."

Aidan sucked in a breath. Brandon's lips were twisting. He moved closer to his mother, and she put her arm around his shoulder.

It blew Aidan's mind how close they were. He had been so alone. He'd always been alone, really. He'd never known the extent of it.

It just made him want to help them even more, however he could, for as long as he was here. Just a couple of weeks. He could get them pretty well started in that time.

But the final success was going to be up to Brandon. Aidan couldn't do his work for him, and he needed to learn that difficult fact now.

"Look," Aidan said to Brandon. "I know how hard St. Bart's is. Truthfully, I barely survived the place. I almost flunked out my first year, and I didn't have anyone to help me. I had all the expectations of the world on me…" *Aw, hell.* Brandon didn't need to know this. This wasn't about him; it was about the boy. He cleared his throat and changed tack. "Frankly, the math admissions aptitude pre-test shows that you're at the very bottom of your class. You did okay in your English and history tests, but—"

"His aunt helped him with those," Ashley murmured. "She loves literature and history."

Aidan nodded. "His science is passable for now, though he'll need to stick with it hard, but math." He shook his head. "What happened with math?" he asked bluntly. "He's starting behind most of the other students." To Brandon, he said, "Math is cumulative. You get behind just a little bit, and it's very difficult to catch up. Trust me—I know."

"Math is stupid," Brandon muttered. "I don't need it to be a doctor."

Aidan shook his head. "Math and science are key foundations for medicine. I'm sure your aunt told you that."

Brandon's lower lip stuck out.

"Your aunt Lisbeth helped you with math," Ashley said. "I remember she sent you a workbook. I *heard* you going over the problem sets with her over the phone."

Brandon scowled.

"She did, didn't she?" she pressed.

"There was an answer key in the back," Brandon admitted.

"Brandon!" Ashley looked appalled. "It's my fault. I didn't pay close enough attention." She stared helplessly at Aidan. "Honestly, math…well, it intimidates me. It's like a foreign language."

He smiled. "I remember when I felt the same way."

"Seriously?"

"I had to teach myself. And then one day, it clicked and it all made sense."

"Well…" Ashley shook her head as she turned toward Brandon. "I'm hoping that will happen for Brandon, too."

"He's capable," Aidan said. "The school gave

him an intelligence test as part of his entrance exam, and his raw scores are off the charts."

"Really?" Brandon asked, clearly pleased. "Cool!"

Aidan gave him a stern look. "But in your case, I think your natural talent has probably hindered you, discipline-wise. You never learned study skills, did you? You were able to skate by with a minimum of practice and focus, weren't you?"

Brandon looked warily at him. Aidan doubted that any adult had spoken so bluntly to him before.

Well, he had to hear it. He was old enough to be making his own choices and decisions. Aidan had had to learn this fact, too, many years ago. At some point, childhood ended.

"You have an important choice to make," Aidan said plainly. "If you want me to work with you, you have to be ready at seven o'clock. That means you have to be done with dinner with your mom. You should have your other homework finished, and that means you have to work during your study periods at school. You can't be goofing off with the other boys."

From Brandon's pink cheeks, Aidan knew he'd hit on the guilty truth. It had been easy to see that first day when Aidan had met him in the cafeteria.

But there was more Aidan needed to say, and it wouldn't be what Brandon, or maybe Ashley, wanted to hear. Or an easy choice for them to make.

"Another thing," Aidan said. "You can't be up late watching baseball games on the West Coast. Or any coast at all." He held up his hand to Brandon's protest. "We're just getting started here. Show me an area in your room where you can focus on your work."

Brandon glanced at his mother. Ashley gave him a nod. "Show him. This has to be your decision to make. I can't do the work for you."

Aidan gave her credit for that. A lot of people did do the work for their kids. They made the calls, did the legwork, wrote the checks. He'd seen it in his orthopedics practice. College-age student athletes who couldn't set up their own rehab sessions without their parents coordinating everything for them.

Brandon's thin shoulders sagged as he led Aidan into a room at the end of the corridor, off the kitchen. Across the hall was a second doorway, shut. Probably Ashley's bedroom. He wouldn't let himself think about that.

Brandon's room looked like an electronics store, with distractions galore.

Ashley had followed them. She stood to the side, her arms crossed, expression cloudy. But she was listening to Aidan. Not fighting what he had to say. That was a start.

"Do you want to thrive at St. Bartholomew's?" Aidan asked Brandon gravely.

"Well, yeah…"

"Then you've got to give some things up."

Brandon shook his head. "I'm not giving up the ball boy job." He set his chin.

Aidan's resolution flagged. He did have some sense of survival. Gram would kill him if he shut down her best fundraiser and kept him from her ballpark. "Weekends only," Aidan relented. "One home game per weekend, period, that's all you can handle for now."

"That's all I do anyway." Brandon looked like he was grinding his teeth. "And what if I get my math skills up in a week or two? Then I won't need you at all. Then I can go back to as I was."

"Nope. Sorry. Won't happen that fast." He glanced at Ashley. She was nodding slightly, backing him up.

"I *have* to go to the hospital on Sundays." Brandon looked like he was seething. "I visit the kids in the cancer wards. The Sunshine Club."

Aidan couldn't tell if Brandon was saying

this genuinely, or if he was arguing for the sake of arguing because he was upset. "The kids will understand if you need some time off for a few months to take care of yourself and get your studies in order."

Brandon glared at him.

"You need to take care of yourself, Brandon, the same as a sick child might. Your situation is serious. You would tell a sick patient to take all the time they need, and so should you."

"I'm not sick!"

"No, you're not. But you're in danger of not being asked back next semester. It'll happen sooner than you think, and when it does, there's no going back. Fix yourself and learn to study now, while you can."

The boy's eyes widened. Suddenly, he looked every bit the scared preteen that he was.

"Dr. Lowe," Ashley said in a warning voice. "Maybe you should get started with the lesson?"

She didn't understand. This *was* his lesson. He might not be a qualified tutor, but he knew he could be a damn good mentor. Aidan stalked over to Brandon's dresser and reached behind it, feeling for the plug. He found it and unplugged it from the electrical source. He disconnected the rest of the cords from the back. Then he lifted the television monitor and turned to Ashley. "Is there a closet where we can lock this up?"

She gaped at him.

"No!" Brandon said. "I need to watch the baseball game—"

But Aidan had turned and walked into the corridor. Ashley caught up with him and dashed ahead. She put her hand up, and he stopped obediently.

"You're overstepping," she said. "You're making a good point, but you don't need to be so pushy and nasty about it."

"Pushy and nasty?" Maybe he should be glad she hadn't said "rude."

"You will do it kindly," Ashley told him. "You will treat us as you would *like* to be treated, not necessarily as you *were* treated."

She gave him a knowing look, and he had to swallow at her wisdom. Nobody had ever put it to him quite like that before.

He put the television set down on the floor. Then he turned to Brandon, who had followed them out to the hallway.

"Please," Aidan said to the boy. "Your mom and I need to hold your electronics for you, just for a few weeks, while you're learning some new study skills."

Brandon glanced at his mother, then back

at Aidan. "So you're taking my television away—is that it?"

"Yes, Brandon," Ashley said softly.

Aidan watched her walk across the apartment and then disappear into a room behind the kitchen. There was noise as she did something he couldn't see.

Brandon scowled, his thin arms crossed. The two of them just stared at each other for a moment.

Ashley came out holding an empty laundry basket. "We'll keep his electronics in here," she said. "Just for a few weeks, until he learns to study without distraction."

Aidan saw how much easier it was, having her support. "Brandon, will you follow me to your room, please?"

Brandon scowled, but he followed.

In Brandon's bedroom, Aidan directed the boy to put his game controllers inside.

Brandon set his chin. "I don't see why—"

Ashley put the game controllers in the laundry basket. There was a radio on the cluttered desk, and she put that in, too.

"Hey!" Brandon said. "Sometimes I listen to the game in bed at night."

"Brandon," Ashley said calmly. "Please cooperate with us. I see what Dr. Lowe is doing.

He's ridding your study space of distractions. He's going to teach you how to study."

"He has no idea how kids study. I can't have quiet. I can't think with quiet. I need my earbuds." He pulled his earbuds from around his neck.

"Please, Brandon, put those in the basket," Aidan said.

"No. You two know nothing about kids today. You're both crazy."

Ashley gazed from Aidan to her son. She'd never seen Brandon like this, and it hurt. Usually, she gave him everything—he'd been such a sweet kid. And of course, after he'd been diagnosed with leukemia as a toddler, she'd fallen to pieces over it. She couldn't bear the thought of losing her sweet child. So she'd spoiled him maybe, but everybody had said he was a good boy. And she tried so hard to be a good mom. It was the only thing that mattered to her. The best thing she could do was to do what was best for him.

It hurt her to be this hard on him now. But she understood what Aidan was doing, helping him mature and grow up and learn to be the student he needed to be if he was to achieve his dreams.

"Brandon," she said quietly, trying not to

wring her hands. Trying to show him that she was serious. "Please cooperate with us."

"Mom—what is the point? I know how to study. I've been figuring out school on my own for my whole life."

She winced. It was a dig, a slight one, against her. She knew she was inadequate on the educational front. Unlike her doctor sister, Ashley hadn't even lasted a year in college.

She noticed Aidan watching her reaction to Brandon's words. She felt herself turning red with embarrassment. He was doing her a favor, helping her with Brandon. Tit for tat, that was all. She'd helped him with his deceased girlfriend's—deceased ex-girlfriend's—parents. She'd handled it well. Flo and Albert trusted her. Albert had even given her his business card when she'd left Aidan's apartment that day. She should *not* feel inadequate. They each had their strengths. She felt herself lifting her chin a little bit higher. She and Aidan would be a team on this.

"Ashley, would you please bring me the textbook I brought?" he asked her kindly. "It's out on the kitchen table."

She went and retrieved it, plus a notebook he'd brought, feeling a bit like his helper in a difficult procedure. *Please, Nurse, bring me my scalpel*. The thought made her giggle, despite herself.

When she returned, Aidan was sitting in Brandon's desk chair. He'd had to clear off a pile of dirty clothes to do so, and these she calmly picked up and brought to the hamper in the bathroom. At home—in their other home, the one they'd just left—the routines had been firmly established and clear, but here, in their new life, some had fallen by the wayside. She saw that she'd have to step up the rules again.

She came back, and Aidan was writing something on an empty page in the notebook. Her heart sank. It was a mathematical formula, but it looked like gobbledygook to her.

Brandon sat on the bed, sulking, his arms crossed and a frown on his face. She hated to see her normally happy boy in such a snit, but better to correct his bad habits now than to let him suffer devastating loss and failure at the end of the semester.

Aidan held out the math formula. "Brandon, pretend this problem is going to be on your next math test. Please solve it for me."

Brandon's expression warred between anger and curiosity. Even she wondered if Aidan had been given the test in advance. That couldn't be true—could it?

But the lure was too much to resist. Her son

glanced at the problem. His face fell. Obviously, it was Greek to him, too.

Aidan got up and picked up the laundry basket. In it, beside the game console and the radio and the headphones, he added a stack of sports magazines.

A beeping sound went off. She watched as her son reached into his pocket. He shut off his phone as stealthily as he could, but Aidan obviously wasn't that dumb.

With his eyes, Aidan asked for Ashley's permission to confiscate this most important tool of preteen communication. This would be her hardest test. Was she really on board with him? Because she knew there would be repercussions…

Ashley nodded, swallowing.

Aidan stood before Brandon with the half-filled laundry basket. "Turn over your phone, please."

"No." Brandon's eyes squinted. She knew that determined look. Her boy was drawing his line in the sand.

"You may keep your laptop, though your mom will be turning off the Wi-Fi while you're studying. But a phone… I'm sorry, Brandon. I know it won't be easy."

"Forget it!" Brandon cried. "I need my phone to stay in touch with my friends!"

"Exactly why it's not a good idea for you right now," Aidan said, his deep voice calm.

"You're old! You have no idea how it is for us! Nobody can live without a phone." He glanced desperately to her. "Mom, tell him! I need to stay in touch with my friends from home! From where we used to live!"

"Honey," she said, her voice catching despite her determination. "Your friends will understand."

"No, they won't! You don't get it, Mom! Neither of you get it!"

She well remembered how important friends were at his age. The opinion of one's peers made one's life or broke it. It was remarkable that Brandon had dared to step out as far as he had, dared to aim for something higher than the grungy streets of their old neighborhood. "I know it's hard to make a new life," she said.

But Brandon was crying. Full out crying. Tears rolling down his cheeks. She hadn't seen him like this in ages. From experience, she knew she had about ten seconds until he bolted.

Aidan cleared his throat, interrupting her before she could act. With a look at her, he spoke quietly to her son.

"I went to St. Bart's, too. I lost friends,

too." His deep voice had lowered, as though he were calming a distraught patient. "But then I gained friends. Friends that were going through the same things I was."

He gazed at her son, and Ashley's heart broke. "That's what life is, Brandon. Loss and gain. Loss and gain." He shook his head. It was more as if he was talking to himself, rather than to her son. "But it gets better every time. Each cycle brings you closer to who you are at heart. What you're meant to be." He glanced at Brandon again. "That's why I want you to be sure that staying at St. Bart's and fighting for a medical career is really what you want. Because to earn that privilege, you're going to have to leave some things behind. I'm sorry, but it's the truth."

A miracle had happened: Brandon had listened and he hadn't bolted. He was crying quietly by himself on the bed, his back against the wall. But he was listening. He was trying to absorb it. He hadn't shut down.

Ashley went over and sat down by her son, hugging him. She'd never realized he felt so responsible for keeping in contact with his old friends from the neighborhood. Like it was his responsibility to keep the whole gang together. That was how she'd felt with her baby sister, growing up. That she was making up for her alcoholic mom's failures, being a little mom herself. Brandon was being the dad, the ringleader to his old group.

"I'll take your phone tomorrow, honey, and when your friends text, I'll let them know that you had to lose your phone for school for a while, while you get settled," she said.

"That is so lame, Mom," he whispered.

"I know. But it will work out. And it's just for the short term, until you learn how to focus and then get all caught up with the rest of the class. You're a smart person, so I have no doubt you'll handle it beautifully."

He wiped his eyes with the back of his sweatshirt sleeve.

"Have you made a decision?" she asked him, ruffling his hair.

He gave a short nod, then got up and left. But he returned a moment later with a chair from the kitchen. Aidan nodded. He just switched chairs with Brandon. They both sat at Brandon's empty desk, one she'd bought at a flea market for him when they'd moved here. It was a huge wooden desk, old-school, as Brandon had called it. But it was roomy, big enough for two people to spread out their papers and have plenty of elbow room. There was also great lighting overhead. The two of them would be fine. She hoped.

Aidan gazed up at her. Whatever he was feeling, she couldn't read his face. Everything closed inside. All business. Perhaps it was his "surgery face."

"Please leave us for an hour, Ashley. We'll be fine."

She glanced at Brandon. He'd gotten his textbook out of his book bag and was opening it, eyes lowered.

"Okay," she said, trying to keep her voice from shaking. She cleared her throat. "But I'm leaving the door open."

Out in the kitchen, she started to clear up their supper dishes. She was shaking even harder. She ached for a drink. For wine in a plastic cup. The tart taste of the grapes. The ease in her mind and in her muscles when the alcohol worked its spell on her bloodstream...

Of course she was stressed out. This was hard, watching her boy struggle. Fail. Cry. Try again. It broke her heart, every time. But this time was harder, not like before. He had beat cancer. He had flourished in his old school, even without a dad. He had taken his uncle Jon under his wing, had even played matchmaker of a sort between Jon and Lisbeth, Ashley's prickly sister. But this...this was something he might not overcome. It didn't look hopeful, truthfully. Maybe Aidan really didn't know what he was doing. He was a doctor, not a teacher. Maybe she'd made a huge mistake.

A bottle of water fell over, and water streamed across the kitchen table. Her hands were just shaking so much. She wished, oh she wished, she had some wine. *Stay busy*, she thought, mopping up the mess. *Keep to your routines. You know the prescription.*

In rehab, she'd learned many tactics for keeping to her path. For not coming undone again. Brandon needed her now, more than ever. This was for Brandon. For herself.

The kitchen cleaned, she went over to the stove, by rote. Reached up to the shelf overhead and found her tea boxes. She always found comfort in her tea ritual.

THE BATHROOM DOOR clicked shut, and Aidan was left alone in Brandon's bedroom. Aidan leaned back in his seat, rubbing his eyes. He was exhausted. Brandon had done the best he could, but they'd had to go back to absolute basics. The rest of his class was working on Algebra I, and Aidan needed to get Brandon through pre-Algebra. In the two weeks before he left. Pretty much an impossible task.

Aidan sighed. He'd started with stuff the boy already knew, just to get his confidence going, but that didn't seem to have worked.

Now Brandon was in the bathroom. Aidan had the impression he was exhausted and had reached his limit. The kid mumbling under his breath, "You're not my father," had been a pretty big clue. Aidan hadn't known how to reply to that one, other than, "I never said I was."

The scent—the peaceful spa scent—he was fast associating with Ashley—wafted into his space, and he glanced up. She was standing in the doorway. "Aidan? I've made some tea, if you'd like a cup."

He lowered his head. Tea. In Afghanistan, after the bombing, after he'd changed clinics, he'd worked with a local man, a doctor trained in Miami, who had ended each day with a cup of tea. He'd gotten Aidan snagged in his routine.

"Yeah," Aidan said. "I'd love some." He followed her to the kitchen table.

But this wasn't Afghanistan. He was home, in a kitchen like one he'd grown up with. He was working with people who spoke English again, and who lived in peace.

His hand shook on the cup.

"How did it go?" Ashley asked.

He honestly wasn't sure.

"I guess we'll start with basics," Aidan said.

"That sounds good to me." She sat at the table across from him and picked up her own cup. "We'll start with basics."

CHAPTER SIX

ASHLEY SET OUT for Aidan's apartment, humming. He'd just spent five nights in a row with Brandon, working hard at the desk in his room. And in response, she was seeing a different son. More confident. Quieter. His expression more serious.

It had shown her a very sobering truth. After Jon and Lisbeth had left for San Francisco, Ashley had worried that Brandon no longer had a significant male influence in his life. And as he entered adolescence, it would be even more important for him to have that influence. That first night Aidan had come to the house to work with Brandon, she'd worried that he might not be the right person for the job. But now, five days later…

Brandon was showing real progress. Not the false bravado he'd had his first week of school, but a true confidence that he was building from within, slowly but surely.

Not once had he asked her about his phone. He had, however, taken a call on her phone, from his friend Cho one night during dinner. She hadn't discouraged it. And she'd been secretly pleased when she'd heard Brandon explain the answer to an American history question to Cho.

Then Aidan had arrived and he'd focused on Brandon, and she was grateful for that, too. He set a schedule and he was reliable.

She owed him a lot for that, and she wanted to show him her very real gratitude.

She went to his apartment building near the water, where he'd mentioned he would be this morning, "taking care of business," as he put it. It was a clear, warm, September Saturday, and crowds were mingling, taking selfies and eating sausages from the gourmet food trucks that lined the greenway. Somehow the Boston waterfront had turned from the slightly dumpy, almost seedy space she remembered from her youth into a fantastic, world-class city of parks and majestic buildings and open spaces. A gleaming, bustling city, the pride of the region.

She hummed as she waved at Bill, the attendant in Aidan's building. He smiled and waved back.

"Well, if it isn't the hairstylist."

"Ashley," she said.

"Hello, Ashley. Are you going up to see Dr. Lowe?"

"Yes, please." She smiled and stepped inside the penthouse elevator. "What kind of mood is he in today, Bill?" she asked.

"There's a real estate agent in his apartment with him. Is he selling?"

Oh no. She crossed her fingers, hoping that Aidan wouldn't move away too soon. He'd only promised her one more week with her son, and units in Boston tended to sell very quickly, with cash payments, if they were priced right. If Aidan were given the freedom to leave the city so quickly, then Ashley's plans would be ruined.

"I hope not," she answered. "I hope he isn't selling."

All things considered with Brandon—the magic Aidan was working with her son, the improvement he'd shown so far—she really needed Aidan to stay longer. In fact, she'd hoped to convince him to stay even longer than his original commitment. If he could just stay until Brandon's next big math test in mid-October, that would be ideal.

"Well, then for your sake, I hope he doesn't sell, either," Bill said. "But tell him that if he knows anyone else in the building who's looking for a good real estate agent, then let me know. I know all the good ones." Bill pressed the button to Aidan's condominium.

"So…you don't know the particular agent with him today?" Ashley asked politely, feeling off-kilter.

"No, I can't say that I've seen her before, and I thought I knew all the local agents." Bill gave her a look that let her know he saw all the comings and goings within his building, and that he kept track of everything.

"You must know a lot of people in the city," she murmured. It was weird, but she'd felt a kind of partnership with Aidan. It must have been the sharing they'd been doing with Brandon. As if they really were a small family. She was oddly hurt that he hadn't mentioned the real estate agent coming, not that he owed her anything beyond the tutoring.

She glanced at her toes; a fresh coat of coral nail polish peeked out beneath her warm-weather sandals. She'd planned on being optimistic today.

"I do have a lot of experience." Bill smiled at her. The elevator dinged and drew to a stop. "Ah. We're here. Have a good day, Ashley."

"Thanks—you, too, Bill," she said, trying to be cheerful.

On the landing beside Aidan's front door,

a woman waited for her to exit the elevator, hand on her hip, tapping her foot. She had an e-cigarette in her mouth, and was inhaling and exhaling furiously. A plume of water vapor wafted over her.

Ashley nodded to her, but the woman ignored her and got in the empty elevator beside Bill. "First floor," she snapped. Bill caught Ashley's eye and winked as the elevator doors closed.

O-kay.

Prepared for anything, Ashley knocked on Aidan's door, and he opened it quickly. Without looking at her, he growled, "What part of no don't you under—"

He finally noticed it was Ashley standing there and stopped speaking. A tired smile crossed his face, and he leaned against the doorjamb. He had bare feet beneath his cargo pants. His hair was damp from a shower, and she could still smell his soap.

"How," he asked, "did you slip up here again without them calling me first?"

"Bill thinks I'm your personal hairstylist and that you're already expecting me." She stepped past him into his apartment.

He laughed shortly and followed her across the great wide space with the floor-to-ceiling windows that took her breath away. "It appears that you've thoroughly charmed my doorman."

She would rather charm Aidan. Which brought her to the point of her visit.

"I brought you two thank-you presents for the work you've been doing with Brandon," she said.

His smile seemed to freeze, and she wasn't sure why. "Well," she said lightly. "First, I brought baseball tickets for next Saturday." She slid her purse off her shoulder and pulled out the envelope on top. "I know you can get them from your grandmother, but these are special. They're for the seats over the dugout, right above where Brandon works as ball boy."

"Those are good seats," he agreed.

She held the tickets out to him, and he made a move as if to take them, but stopped. She had no choice but to wait, holding out the tickets.

"Will you be there?" he asked her.

"Well...no. I have to work Saturday."

"That's too bad." He shook his head and still didn't take the tickets.

She lowered her hand, feeling rejected. "Well...it was an idea." She smiled at him, determined to smooth over the awkward moment. She was still figuring this man out. "Honestly,

Aidan, I appreciate how you've been working with Brandon. I'm seeing changes in him already. He's more serious, and he's actually focusing."

"That's good to hear. We'll know better if it's working in a week or so."

She bit her lip. He'd said something about finding another tutor soon...she hoped that wasn't still what he had in mind.

"Come on in." He turned and led her toward the living room.

The place was stripped bare. The pile of furniture and belongings that had been in the center of the floor the last time she was here was gone. Most of the other furniture was gone, too.

"I'd offer you something to drink," Aidan said, "but I'm out of groceries. I haven't been here much, but I did have an appointment with a real estate agent."

"Oh. Yes, I saw her when I was coming out of the elevator."

"I didn't hire her," he explained.

Ashley nodded. She was curious and wondered why, but she was determined not to snoop. Her goal had been simply to discuss extending Aidan's mentorship longer than the two weeks he'd committed to.

There was another awkward moment while she hesitated, wondering how to ask him.

"Well?" he teased. "What's my second present?"

"Oh." She blushed. "Well, I worked with my sister to get some names for the memorial service. For Flo to invite. I knew you needed help with the task, but that you weren't likely to ask. So… I hope it helps you."

His brow furrowed.

She opened her purse again and took out the handwritten list. He accepted it and scanned it without comment. He seemed to study each name intently.

Finally, he lifted his head. "Your sister gathered this? Why would she help me?"

Ashley took a breath. *Because she loves me, and I asked her to do it.* But she couldn't explain it that way to Aidan, because he obviously wouldn't understand.

Instead she said, "Because you really do need the help, and it's the kind thing to do. If it were for my child, I'd appreciate the gesture. As a parent."

"You only met her parents that one time," Aidan remarked.

"Yes. And I've met you eight times, five times at my house. It's still the right thing to do."

He smiled at her. "You're counting."

She sighed, exasperated. "May I ask why you're so suspicious? I'm thankful to you, and I'm doing you a favor back."

"Okay. Duly noted." He walked toward the door.

"Are you seeing me out?" she asked, incredulous again.

He turned to her. "Is there more, Ashley?" he asked calmly.

She blew out a breath and stood. Aidan could be the most maddening man imaginable. "Never mind."

He gave her a slight smile. "Am I being rude again?"

"Well...you could say 'thank you'. Lisbeth even offered to contact the people on the list, if you'd rather that she did it than Flo."

"Thanks." He stared at her. "But I really did think your sister hated me."

She gave him a look. "But she likes *me*," she told him plainly. "And I asked her to do it."

"Because of Brandon?"

She was starting to lose her patience. Must he always fight with the world, questioning every motivation?

She crossed her arms and glared.

He sat down again. "Sorry. You just caught me in a bad..."

She looked expectantly at him, waiting for him to finish.

He sighed. "You're right—I'll tell you. That real estate agent out there? She just used the entrée to my home not to help put my house on the market, but to proposition me."

"She…?"

"Yeah."

"How dare she?" Ashley said, angry for him. "Why do you think she did that?"

"I don't know. Maybe she supposes my trust fund is worth more than this condo?"

"Oh!" Ashley said. "Oh." Her eyes were probably popped wide-open. Aidan no doubt thought she was naive.

"I've dealt with things like that for most of my adult life," he said matter-of-factly.

"That's terrible." It made Ashley uncomfortable to think of him going through that.

And then, in a horrible thought, she wondered if he ever thought that of *her*? Did he think she was an opportunist, as well?

While she stood in his living room with her mouth opened in horror, he looked at her questioningly.

She *had* come to seen him with ulterior motives in mind. She *had* considered that if she'd flattered him with gratitude, if she'd encouraged him to become more involved with the memorial service, then hopefully he would stay in town longer than the short two weeks he'd promised. It was undeniable that she'd schemed for it.

But...she hadn't wanted to *use* him. Certainly not for his money. And she really did want him to stay.

Not for what he could do—his skills or his family connections.

But for him—for all of him.

She licked her lips and gazed at him at the same time she caught him gazing at her.

She glanced away. But looked back again.

"Do you want to get something to eat with me?" His voice was low.

It was an invitation. An entrée—as he'd put it—to something more...

Heartfelt?

Possibly even romantic?

Oh, yes! Ashley's heart cried.

Without thinking things through, she said it aloud. "Yes. I do."

Aidan gifted her with a smile, one that showed his dimples. She felt an ache come over her all of a sudden. A feeling that she hadn't felt in years. An urge to press her body close to a man's, to tilt her head upward for a kiss, to feel his hands move up her back, caress her skin...

She pressed her lips together. He stared at her mouth. She wondered if he could read minds.

Abruptly, he stood. "I'll get dressed and walk down to street level with you."

"You—"

"I'm out of food, Ashley," he said.

She nodded and ducked her head. He got up and put on a pair of socks, and then his sneakers. Patted his back pocket to make sure he had his wallet. Grabbed a phone and his house keys.

"Let's go." He held the door for her. Outside, he locked up behind him. They both waited for the elevator.

"Will you…be over tonight at seven?" she asked him.

He smiled and nodded. "Of course."

"We look forward to seeing you." A stupid thing to say, awkward, and she glanced away, embarrassed. She'd been nervous all of a sudden.

The elevator arrived, and he politely waited until she walked in ahead of him. "Good morning again," Ashley said to Bill.

"Good morning, Ashley." Bill nodded to Aidan. "Dr. Lowe."

The ride down to the lobby was quick. On the one hand, she was disappointed with herself that she'd chickened out of asking Aidan to stay longer. But...in light of what he'd told her, she just couldn't do it.

She *cared* about him. She really did. And that shocked her.

Her heart pumping, she watched him scan the lobby before stepping out. A shadow seemed to cross his face. Perhaps he expected more journalists. Or gawkers. She really didn't know much about what his life was like, beyond what she saw with him and Brandon.

He glanced back at her because she'd fallen behind. "Are you all right?" he asked.

She caught up to him. "Aidan," she asked, "where will you go next, once you leave Boston?"

The question seemed to startle him. He looked into her eyes, as if searching them.

Then he looked toward the sandwich shop across the lobby. "Come have lunch with me."

"Will you tell me then?"

He gave a slight smile. "It's not the usual thing, Ashley."

"You're not the usual person," she said honestly.

He liked that response. He laughed so that his eyes crinkled.

She itched to reach up and wipe a lock of hair from his brow.

"If I tell you what I'm planning," he said, "you'll laugh."

"I promise I won't!"

"Hmm." He turned and scanned the other end of the lobby. "Do you want to go to a sandwich place or pizza place?"

She put her hands on her hips. "Why do I always feel like you're distracting me from what you don't want to talk about? Honestly, Aidan, I'd like to hear about it."

"So you can talk me out of it?"

"No!" She rolled her eyes. "So I can understand you."

"Let's get a sandwich," he insisted.

"After you tell me your plans."

He smiled at her. "I'm hiking the Appalachian Trail."

"The…?"

"The Appalachian Trail. It's a hiking path two thousand miles long. It runs north to south, Maine to Georgia, along the East Coast. I'd like to hike it alone. It's something that's always been on my life list, and I've decided I want to do it now."

She struggled to understand. "So…where do you sleep at night?"

"There are shelters—camps—along the way. Every day you hike to a new shelter. Ten, fifteen miles of hiking through the most beautiful, remote scenery. Lots of time to think."

"To heal," she whispered.

He glanced at her shyly. "Maybe."

"Is it safe?" she asked.

He grinned. "Maybe not."

"And you'll be by yourself!" She gaped at him.

"That's the point, Ashley. It'll just be *me*, the wilderness, the stars at night. Maybe I'll get a dog," he mused.

"Aidan! I'll worry about you! You'll have to call me now and then to let me know you're okay."

He threw back his head and laughed. "You've known me a little over a week. I'm sure you'll get over it," he chided. "Come on inside. Let's eat."

This time she did follow him inside the sandwich shop. His favorite one, he said. A server took them to a booth near a window in the back overlooking a park. She couldn't even look at the menu; all she could do was watch him. His shy expressions, as he glanced from her to the menu and back again. The cute dimple that formed in the corner of his cheek. The unruly hair that she was just itching to sift in her fingers again.

After the waitress brought their grilled cheese sandwiches, she just had to ask him.

"How long have you wanted to hike the Appalachian Trail?"

"Since I was a kid," he admitted.

"But are you sure now is the right time?"

"It's the perfect time," he said between bites. "There's never been a better time."

She felt like weeping. Just when he'd met her and Brandon? Just when her son needed him?

He caught her expression and put his hand on hers. "I mean…it's the perfect time now— or next week when I'm finished with Brandon's sessions—because if I wait longer, then I'll have to break up my pace into a shorter section, and stop when the winter weather kicks in. If I leave sooner rather than later, I'll still have a couple of good months of autumn hiking."

"Oh." She gazed down at the bowl of tomato soup she'd ordered but wasn't eating.

The whole thing just made her feel…lonely. Lonelier than she'd been. She'd been missing something—the sweet feeling of a new partnership—that she hadn't even realized. Maybe something like the male role model she'd hoped for for her son.

Aidan's hand was still on top of hers. Warm

and comforting. He clasped her hand and turned it over, as if pondering her palm. With a light caress, he drew his thumb gently across the lines in her palm.

His touch on her skin felt...nice. It gave her tingles across her breasts, but he didn't appear to notice that. He seemed to be thinking.

Finally he gazed at her, a lock of dark hair over his brow, and the look in his eyes took her breath away.

"You're right," he said finally. "I've been teaching Brandon to be responsible, and yet here I am neglecting my responsibilities."

Was *she* a responsibility? She didn't want to be that to him.

"I'll stay until Brandon's test," he decided. "That's in three and a half more weeks. That will also give me the opportunity to go to the memorial service. Then I'll be free to hike the Appalachian Trail for at least a month." He smiled at her. "My staying for Brandon's test—that's what you're most concerned about, isn't it?"

She nodded. It had been, but...

He must have felt her mood, because he gazed at her hand in his. Stroking it absently. Making those shivers run through her...

"It's been almost a year," he said softly. "I'm

ready to sell my place and move on now. I don't want to be caught in the past."

He glanced up at her, and she swallowed. "I'm glad to hear that," she whispered. It helped, hearing what he was saying. Getting a deeper insight into who he was. She didn't often talk with men one-on-one, because she couldn't afford to indulge in romantic relationships. She had a son. Usually she didn't want to be tempted—she'd made a mistake in judgment once, with Brandon's father. Ever since then she supposed that she'd convinced herself that she wasn't any good at dating. That she had bad instincts when it came to men.

Like her mom.

"You should eat your sandwich," he said, smiling at her.

She kept her right hand in his. With her left hand, she took a big bite of the warm, gooey cheese. He laughed at her, and she felt warm all over.

Aidan ate his sandwich the same way. She watched his left hand go to his mouth, his tanned skin smooth. The secret smile he gave her lit up his soft brown eyes.

No, I'm not tempted, she told herself. A lie, of course.

Swallowing her bite of sandwich, she asked

him a question. "What kind of doctor are you, anyway?"

"Orthopedics," he said, then lowered his gaze and took another bite.

She felt like a dummy, but she had to ask to be sure. "That's broken bones, right?"

He nodded. "Right. Broken bones. Sprains."

"Wow. You're accomplished." And then she thought for a moment. "Thank you for your service," she said.

Aidan tilted his head as if he didn't understand.

She laughed self-consciously. "When I meet a veteran or an active-duty soldier, that's what I say. But you put yourself in harm's way, too."

"Oh, Ashley. I am no hero." He laughed at the thought.

To her, he was. She just smiled and drank her iced tea.

And then she noticed someone staring at them from two booths down. A woman, with long brown hair and a tight blue shirt. She looked a lot like the woman who'd been at his condo earlier.

"What is it?" he asked her, immediately noticing her expression.

"Don't turn around," she said in a low voice, looking away from the woman.

"Who's there?" They were doing a good job

at communicating without saying too much. He was a good reader of her body language, and that made her feel more comfortable.

"The woman from your apartment." She took another sip of iced tea. "The real estate agent."

He frowned. "My cousin Jamison sent her over." He paused. "Is she gone yet?" he asked, as Ashley took another covert glance.

"Nope. She's approaching. Twelve o' clock."

"In that case…" He leaned forward, took her hand in his, and pressed her knuckles to his lips.

She jumped. She couldn't help gasping.

And then he smiled and winked at her. "Do we look like we're in love?" he whispered.

"I'm…not the best one to ask," she admitted, as the woman stalked past them and left. "Though we did chase her away, it seems."

"Why aren't you the best one to ask? You mean you don't date?"

She shook her head, her cheeks warm.

"Ah, because you have a twelve-year-old son?" He stirred his drink thoughtfully. "Then what do you do for fun?"

"Well, I go on outings with my son." Every weekend since Brandon was little, they'd had a habit of doing something special together, usually an outing or an activity. They called it "family fun day." Since their new life in Boston had started, however, their fun days had been few and far between. "Or at least, I did," she clarified. "The intensity of St. Bart's seems to be getting in the way of that old life."

"Hmm," Aidan said. "Do you still have those two tickets to the Captains game this weekend?"

"Yes. Brandon will be serving as a ball boy."

"May I have *one* of those tickets you offered?" He smiled at her.

"Of course." She reached for her purse but then paused. "What about the other ticket? Aren't you going to bring a friend with you?"

"Yeah. You."

"Me? But I have to work!"

He shrugged. "So, meet me when you get out of work. You were going to pick up Brandon at the game, I assume?"

She was. But suddenly this seemed more complicated. She felt shy all of a sudden. Something had changed between them this afternoon, and it surprised her.

And then he put his head close to hers. And threaded his hands through hers. He had large, strong hands. He was a surgeon after all. He set people's bones. He healed them.

She swallowed. She was actually going to spend family fun day with Aidan.

She hoped Brandon was okay with that.

LATER THAT NIGHT, Ashley stood at the stove making gluten-free pasta for the meatballs she'd cooked and frozen last weekend. She glanced at the clock. Twenty minutes until Aidan was due to arrive.

"I can't believe I have to study on a Saturday night," Brandon grumbled from where he sat at the table.

"Once you're caught up with your math, it won't be so bad." She tried to keep a hopeful tone.

"I don't like him, Mom."

"You…don't?" She swallowed. "I'm sorry, I thought you did."

"He took my phone away. That's crazy. Can't you give it back?"

She drained the hot water from the cooked pasta, and then with a large fork, served a generous portion to Brandon.

"What will you do when you get your phone back?" she asked mildly.

"Nothing."

She couldn't help smiling.

"My friends from school can't even text me. It's ridiculous," he complained.

"Your friends from your old school?"

"No, my new friends." He picked up his fork and began to dig in. "I miss a lot of what's going on, you know. It's totally stupid."

"Is everybody so social?" Ashley asked.

He looked at her pleadingly. "Please, Mom."

In the old days, pre-Aidan, she probably would have relented. Maybe she wasn't relenting now because she trusted Aidan. She wanted to trust him. She wanted to believe that he knew better than her how to handle St. Bart's, as Brandon was calling his new school.

"Plus, without my phone I can't even text Uncle Jon to wish him a good game!"

"We'll call him before we leave for the park tomorrow," Ashley promised.

"At least Aidan's letting me be ball boy," Brandon grumbled.

"*I'm* letting you be ball boy."

"Good." He rolled his eyes. "He's not my father."

No, he wasn't. And it gave her a chill to hear Brandon speak the word aloud. First there had been that conversation with Lisbeth back in August. Then Ashley had heard him angrily tell Aidan one night that same thing he'd just said, that Aidan wasn't his father.

Her hands shook. She didn't want to think about this now.

"Brandon, why don't we go out tomorrow, you and me? We could grab dinner and a movie together."

"No, Mom. I have stuff at school."

"You do? Like what?"

"We're doing a play in English class. The girls' school down the street are taking the girl parts."

She put down her fork. "You didn't tell me that."

"Maybe if I had my phone, I could keep you posted."

Oh, great. She was weakening already. Maybe she should just give Brandon his darn phone back.

"What play?" she asked her son.

"Romeo and Juliet."

Ashley almost choked. "Isn't that old for you?"

"I'm thirteen in December."

"Um." *Oh, God.*

Suddenly *she* felt old. Unprepared for that. "Dare I ask what part you have?"

He gave her one of his old grins. "Romeo, of course."

Of course? Ashley tried not to choke again. "Um, who is Juliet?"

He smiled slyly. "Some girl named Julia. Get it? Julia is playing Juliet."

She thought she might faint.

But then Aidan's familiar knock sounded on the door. Brandon rose to let him in. Aidan came in with a nod, smelling of fresh air. He put down the knapsack he carried. A copy of her son's textbook would be inside, she knew.

He gave her a private smile. Oh, she wished she could talk to him alone…

"What is it?" he asked, concerned by her expression.

"Brandon is playing Romeo. As in *Romeo and Juliet*."

"Cool." He grinned at Brandon. "Good job."

"Exactly," Brandon agreed.

"What's that about?" Ashley snapped.

"I played Mercutio," Aidan explained to Brandon. "I got to die in this really excellent sword fight scene we choreographed."

"That's who my friend Cho is playing," Brandon said excitedly.

"It's a St. Bart's tradition for the first-year students," Aidan said matter-of-factly to Ashley.

"But they're so young! Just babies!"

Brandon groaned while Aidan just laughed.

"You two are ganging up on me," she said.

"No," they said at the same time.

"When can I have my phone back?" Brandon said to Aidan.

"When you pass your first math test," Aidan said without missing a beat.

"And then I can have my phone?"

"I won't be here to keep it from you," Aidan said.

"Good," Brandon retorted.

Aidan nodded calmly. "You done with dinner?" He pointed to the clock. "Because we need to start studying."

She watched the two of them walk away, the beginnings of tears in her eyes.

Life was changing, and it was bittersweet.

CHAPTER SEVEN

AIDAN CAUGHT HIMSELF SMILING, which was a very strange feeling these days. Ironic that now that he was leaving Boston, he was beginning to appreciate some of the things about it that he'd either never noticed before, or that he'd looked down upon.

The city's ballpark, for example. Gram was owner and CEO of the New England Captains baseball team. Had been since Aidan was young, when she'd inherited it from his grandfather, a man that Aidan barely remembered in person. During his lifetime, Aidan's grandfather had been a fixture in the media. In those photos, he wore a business suit, a hat and a perpetual frown. A self-made man, he'd been in the trucking business. And he'd encouraged all his children to study medicine, presumably as affected by his son's death as Aidan's grandmother was. Aidan's aunts and uncles were all doctors, and married to doctors, just as Aidan's parents were.

Aidan was taking a break from all that. A

six-month-long break, he hoped, and maybe more, depending on what he decided on the trail, eventually, once he got there.

But for now, he drank in the excitement that was Lansdowne Street before a big home game. Vendors were selling the distinctive blue Captains caps with the white letter *C*. The smell of sausage and pepper grinders filled the air. Also big, doughy pretzels, with lots of salt. Throngs of people—families, couples, groups of friends, young and old—crowded the street, now reserved for foot-traffic only. Most people got into the spirit and wore Captains-themed clothing. His grandmother made a fortune on that stuff.

Aidan also knew that she was leaving most of her huge fortune to charity. Years ago, he'd been part of a big family meeting where she'd informed them all that it was never her intention for them to be so wealthy that they were tempted not to work, not to continue to "improve humanity," as she put it. She took fierce pride that *her* progeny—she, a second-generation immigrant to America—continued with the "improvement of mankind." And thus, some of Aidan's cousins worked in research—high-tech drug development—others were highly respected medical specialists. His uncle was chief of staff at Wellness Hospital.

An aunt was one of the top breast cancer doctors in the city.

He doubted *they* ever took an afternoon off to watch a Captains home game.

Chuckling to himself, aware that he probably looked like a maniac, he walked alone, swept along with the happy crowd into the front of the monstrous stadium located in the heart of the city.

When it was his turn at the entrance gate, he held out his ticket to be scanned, then was inside the massive lower floors. There were storefronts for programs, caps, popcorn, peanuts, hot dogs. The groaning organ music played loudly, making him smile with the childhood memories of coming to a game and sitting with his grandmother.

He stopped off to purchase a program with a half-size pencil nub—the better to keep score with—and then on a whim, bought a hat, too. Two hats. One for him and one for Ashley. He'd noticed that while Brandon seemed to live in his beat-up Captains hat, Ashley didn't wear one. She would need a hat for the game, though, to show her team pride. It was practically a rule at Captains games.

Enjoying himself, Aidan headed up the escalator to the section of the park where his seat was located. First base line, directly over the

Captains dugout. He was glad he'd bought the cap, because his seat was in full sun. But it was the shock of stepping out from the cool, shady overhang and facing the baseball diamond that made him blink. The field was so green, so wide. Batting practice was going on, and quite a few kids were seated with their baseball gloves aloft. Sometimes a foul ball was tipped into the stands, to the kids' delight.

Aidan took his seat and opened his program. Crazy, but he felt like keeping score as he'd loved to do when he was a kid. With his pencil nub, he began copying the players' names in the starting "batters order" displayed on the big screen across the field. He didn't recognize any of them. Damn, when had he stopped following his favorite sport? He really should do more of the things that *he* enjoyed doing…

"Bee-yah hee-yah!" A concessionaire, a thin guy in his twenties carrying a tray of freshly poured brews, stood at the top of his aisle.

Aidan flagged him down. The guy deftly descended the cement stairs, and Aidan handed him cash in exchange for a beer in a plastic cup bearing the Captains logo. He could almost taste the cold brew in anticipation. When a hot dog vendor came by, he'd grab one of them, too.

He sat through batting practice and then a display of local kids showing their marching band skills. Just when he was wondering when Brandon LaValley would make his appearance on field, Aidan saw him.

The announcer called out his name, and the entire stadium stood and cheered. Aidan's jaw dropped. He had no idea how well known and beloved the kid was by fans. Brandon raised his gloved hand and waved to the crowd.

And then, on the big screen where the scores were shown, a video played.

"Please direct your attention to the scoreboard while Brandon LaValley, childhood cancer survivor and spokesperson for the Sunshine Club, tells us about the contributions that you can make. Friends of the Sunshine Club will be appearing in the aisles to take your donations. Please give generously."

And then men and women, who had been previously carrying trays of pretzels and popcorn, walked the aisles with canisters. Attendees dropped loose change inside, occasionally bills. Aidan checked his wallet, took out a ten and stuffed it inside.

All the while, the video of Brandon, talking about what the Sunshine Club had meant to him, played overhead.

Aidan couldn't believe it. He was in shock.

The scruffy kid, the lazy student who seemed to want nothing more than to get his phone back, was a citywide celebrity? A true fundraising phenomenon?

His grandmother's machinations made sense to Aidan now. She wanted this kid on board with her organization, and to stay there.

Slack-jawed, Aidan sat with his half-eaten hot dog.

His grandmother had gotten Brandon the ball-boy job. Gotten him into St. Bart's so he could pursue his dream. Kept him working just enough that he wasn't overexposed—one weekend home game a week was enough, apparently. Aidan ran a quick calculation of what he was bringing in, in exposure and donations and goodwill, to Gram's pet charity.

The Sunshine Club was her baby. Gram liked to mention—and Brandon had in his talk, as well—that there was still a long way to go and a lot of work to be done.

Aidan had been railroaded into helping Brandon for his grandmother. He'd known it, of course, but he hadn't realized the scope and impact of it until now.

Ashley had been caught up in it, as well.

Aidan sat there in the sun. A couple sat beside him—between him and the aisle. The empty seat for Ashley was on the other side.

The woman in the couple smiled at him. "Are you a friend of Ashley LaValley's?"

She was probably asking because these were likely the "ball boy" seats, designated for family of the volunteers.

Aidan cleared his throat. "Yes. She's coming later."

"Our daughter is a team ball girl."

Aidan glanced out at the field. The players were being introduced. "The Star-Spangled Banner" would be played soon. Brandon was lined up, cheering as the New England players entered the field, one by one. A young woman stood by Brandon; she looked college-age.

He wondered if she was a Sunshine Club alumna, too. He didn't ask her parents, though. He didn't want to be impolite.

He settled his cap lower on his head, sank into his seat—as uncomfortable as it was—and picked up the stubby pencil. His way of coping with the world had always been to buckle in and work, and that's what he was doing now. Shutting out everyone and everything but the game, the score sheet and the nice day.

Alone, among thirty-eight thousand people.

That's all he'd wanted when he'd come home. Peace. Maybe that's all he'd ever wanted.

ASHLEY FINISHED HER last client. She was getting better at her job, was starting to fit in better. One client had booked ahead with her for a five-week appointment, and that made her feel great. It was different working here, but it was giving her confidence that she was good enough. She knew it was crazy to feel insecure, but sometimes she couldn't help it.

"What are you doing tonight?" Kylie asked conversationally as Ashley cashed out her money for the day.

"I'm going to the Captains game," Ashley admitted as she pocketed her envelope.

Kylie brightened. "That's fun. I love Captains games."

Ashley just smiled. She'd rather skip it, given a choice. Captains games made her uneasy, in a lot of small ways.

The beer drinking. Her son on the field, getting so much attention and television exposure.

Early on, she'd been in constant panic that Brandon's father's family would see him, hear him, notice the resemblance. It was hard not to.

The older Brandon got, the more he looked like his father.

Ashley shivered. She'd never actually met his father's family, or even knew anything about them, and the opposite was true, as well—they didn't know about her or Brandon. She assumed they were local people. She'd barely known Brandon's father—but he had to have some family nearby. Didn't he?

It was her worst nightmare. She'd always been terrified that if they found out about her, they would think she was unfit and take Brandon away from her. She knew Brandon eventually needed to know about his father, and be given the chance to find his family, if he wanted to. But not now. Not while he was so young. She'd wanted to wait until he was older. He'd had so many health problems in his young life, she'd just wanted to be sure she could always protect him. She'd heard so many horror stories. She would never knowingly set up a scenario where she would be powerless to help him.

Except…Brandon had asked his aunt this summer if she knew who his father was. Was he a doctor, too? Lisbeth hadn't known—but she had told Ashley what her son had asked.

"He's deceased," Ashley had told Brandon

honestly. She'd been as honest with him as she could be.

But it was almost a certainty that someday he would push her to reveal more. She was lucky she'd gotten out of that conversation—that revelation—for as long as she had. She knew it. But what could she do?

Sighing, she headed downstairs and walked the half mile to the baseball stadium. She'd worn jeans with a pretty blouse and a light jacket—the day was sunny and warm, but in the shadows it could be a bit cool. As she got closer to the stadium, she could hear the roar of the crowd, and her heart plummeted.

But she'd promised Aidan. He was sitting alone in her seats. At the thought of his handsome face and the little center of happiness she felt when she was around him, she found she had a reason to keep walking.

She wouldn't mind sitting close to him. Rubbing shoulders a bit. The warmth of his body beside her.

The man at the entrance scanned her ticket and sent her on her way. She hurried past the beer stalls, the line of people watching the game from the food area.

From the top of the stairs, she glanced toward the two seats she was usually given whenever Brandon worked a game.

Aidan sat there, wearing a blue Captains cap. She smiled and felt an inner warmth at the sight of him.

He raised a beer cup to his lips and took a long swallow.

Just like that, she froze. Backed up.

And stepped on somebody's foot.

"Hey," said the man behind her. "Watch it!"

She couldn't turn around and go back up the steps—there was a line of people behind her trying to get down.

She dug her nails into her palms and kept moving forward. The field, so green, was ahead of her.

She got to the end. A security agent nodded to her. "Ticket, please?"

She showed him her ticket, and he pointed her to the empty seat beside Aidan.

When Aidan saw her, he stood, smiling. She walked past him, brushing his chest. Felt the back of the hard metal chair at the back of her thighs and sat, shaking.

He took out a blue Captains cap and settled it on her head. "For you."

She sucked in her breath. She was grateful he'd thought of her, but she was feeling overwhelmed at the moment and couldn't speak.

Aidan peered at her. "Are you okay, Ashley?"

She shook her head.

"What's wrong?" He put the back of his hand to her forehead. It felt cool and…nice. She leaned her head forward, into it.

A chuckle sounded from his throat. "You don't have a fever."

"No," she muttered. *Oh, what the hey.* She needed to tell him. "I'm an alcoholic," she whispered, leaning closer to his ear. She didn't want it broadcasted. "It's kind of hard for me to come here sometimes."

That was only part of the reason it was hard to come here, but it was all he needed to know for now.

He looked at her with grave eyes. "I'm sorry. I'll get rid of this."

His half-full cup of beer was in a holder between their seats. He put the lid on it, then slid the cup under his seat.

"You don't have to do that," she said.

"I would pour it out if I could, Ashley."

"Really, I don't want to stop you from enjoying yourself."

"I'm enjoying myself now that you're here."

She smiled at him. He really was growing on her.

He put his arm around her chair, around her. Then he put his head close to hers. She had the sense that he would make sure that she was safe. That no one else would hear them.

"Do you go to meetings?" he asked in a low voice.

Maybe because he was a medical professional, she didn't feel bad answering him. "I have a counselor I talk to. I've been with him since...I spent thirty days in an inpatient rehab." She took a breath. "I haven't slipped since then."

Besides Brandon's academic aspirations, and his physical and emotional well-being, it was the thing in her life she was most proud of.

Aidan nodded. "I'm sorry. I mean that. I shouldn't have ordered a beer."

"You can, you know. It's not usually a problem for me."

He cocked his head. His eyes were so brown. "Why is it a problem today?" He glanced at the stadium. "Brandon is doing really great. I didn't realize what a superstar the kid was."

She must have grimaced, because he looked at her strangely.

And then she found herself pouring out her heart to him. "I already told you I grew up with an alcoholic mother, so I knew the signs. Wine—I used to drink wine. And when it got too bad—I mean, I was functioning, but it scared me that one day Brandon might find me, like I'd found my mom. I knew I had to stop. I knew I needed help. I spent the thirty days in rehab when Brandon was eight. I left him with my sister. When she stayed with him—well, he came across Jon Farell—he's a baseball player, he used to be with the Captains—"

"Yeah. He was on the computer with Brandon the other night. Your sister's husband."

"Yes, and because of Jon, Brandon ended up making a television commercial for the Sunshine Club. They'd wanted Jon to do it, but Brandon was with him and Brandon did it better, so…" Ashley sighed. "The point is, I came home from rehab excited to start fresh with my son, and instead found that my son was a Captains ball boy and a regional celebrity. He loves it, of course. And his celebrity has only been building since then." She couldn't help feeling miserable about it.

Aidan's voice was close to her ear. Low and deep. "Tell me why that's a problem."

She thought of it from Aidan's point of view, leaving out the truth that she hadn't told him. That she could never tell him. She realized how it looked—most moms in her situation would feel happy for their sons' success. "You think I'm a major control freak, don't you?"

He laughed gently. "Aren't you?" he teased.

She sighed. "If I am, it's to protect him."

"You can't protect him much longer. He's growing up, Ashley."

She sank deeper into her misery. She tried not to think about that point when Brandon would grow up and leave home. Brandon at eighteen? She shivered.

She followed Aidan's gaze toward the field. The Captains were up at bat. Brandon was doing his thing, one eye on his job, one eye on the crowd. She smiled to herself. Always such a ham, her boy.

A cloud passed over Aidan's face. He shook his head. "I just hope that St. Bart's doesn't dampen his natural enthusiasm."

Great, something new to worry about. "Do you think it will?" she asked.

"No. He has you looking out for him."

Something occurred to her. "Did your parents look out for you?"

He gave her a sad smile. "I was expected to suck it up and go be a doctor, whatever it took. It's what my parents did. My aunts and uncles. All my cousins."

"Oh." She digested that. Out on the field, Brandon was doing a funny dance to the organ music that was playing over the speakers.

The crowd tittered. A lot of people clapped for him.

"He's a funny kid, but he's being himself."

"Yes, he's an original," she said with wonder.

"I think we're all originals. Some kids just have it beaten out of them at a young age."

"Did that happen to you?"

"Maybe." Aidan stretched his shoulders a bit. Leaned closer. He said, "You smell really nice, like that shampoo you used on me that first day."

She leaned closer to him. This was the most enjoyable ball game she'd been to in a long time. Aidan's score program had fallen to the floor.

"You should come in to the salon." She dared to reach up and touch his hair. "I could trim it for you this time, too."

He smiled at her. "I just might."

She nodded, her heart hammering. It felt very comfortable with him, nestled in the crook of his arm, cocooned in a seemingly private world, even though the seats around them were filled with yelling baseball fans.

The man on the other side of her stood at his feet and started booing.

She jerked up her head. "What's going on?" she asked Aidan.

"The game is tied. New York is up to bat.

It's actually been a good inning so far." He had to lean close to make her hear him; it was so loud around them.

And then he leaned even closer to her, nuzzling her ear.

It was a really good inning…

While they watched, heads together, Brandon danced out to get a bat that had been left behind by the last New England batter. He was such a goof.

"I wish I could protect him from everything, especially at St. Bart's," she mused. "But I can't."

"No one can," Aidan answered. "That's both the beauty and the tragedy of the place, in my opinion. He's going to have to find his own way."

She let that digest. It was so frustrating being unable to do anything else to help. It reminded her of when Brandon was sick. She could fight by interviewing doctors, by running fundraisers, by sitting up all night with her child. But she couldn't make it all better. Not really.

"I can only do what I can do," she muttered aloud to herself.

"I wish my parents had been like you," Aidan remarked.

"Really?" She turned to gape at him. That was a revelation.

"You put your son first, before everything else. Literally. I don't think I've ever really seen that before."

"That's…" *Sad.*

"Yeah. And here I am talking to you instead of watching the game." He laughed with wonderment and with good humor.

She dared to lean her cheek on his shoulder. It felt nice. He'd said she smelled good—well, she liked how he smelled, too. Like a man. A really sexy, solid, kind man who—God help her—she was starting to enjoy spending time with.

She sighed and gazed up at him. "Thanks for inviting me," she said lightly, and leaned up to give him a peck on the cheek. Nothing heavy, just something to smile at.

At the last second, he turned his head so that instead of kissing the slightly stubbled skin of his cheek, she kissed him on his lips.

Holy hell. She couldn't gasp and she couldn't jump away; she just seemed to freeze in place, shocked at herself.

He kissed her—a sweet kiss on her closed lips.

So nice.

When he pulled away, she put her hand to

her mouth. "I'm…sorry," she said. "I meant to kiss your cheek."

"I'm not sorry."

"No?"

He gave her a sweet, roguish smile. "Nope."

"Oh." She stared straight ahead at the green baseball diamond. Her heart was hammering, and she could hardly believe what had just happened.

She hadn't kissed or been kissed by a man in…

How old was Brandon? Plus nine months? *Oh, God.*

Aidan's arm tightened on her shoulder. "Don't be embarrassed. I won't tell anyone that you kissed your son's tutor."

"*I* kissed?"

"Sure." He grinned at her in a way that let her know he was teasing. "You made the first move."

"And you intercepted me," she protested.

He looked at her and laughed, his eyes crinkling. "It's okay, Ashley," he said gently. "It's more than okay."

She wondered if maybe he hadn't kissed anyone since Fleur had died, either.

Almost a year ago.

"Well, I need to focus on Brandon right

now, and you're…leaving Boston," she reminded him.

"Yup," he agreed. Still teasing her, his eyes twinkling, he added, "Though I know you've been planning something else behind my back that you haven't been telling me about."

"What?" she whispered, indignant. She didn't want anyone overhearing them. The crowd had quieted down, it seemed. A batter was up—he'd been up a long time, and Aidan was keeping one eye on him, too. "I have not been plotting."

Aidan leaned close again. "Flo called to tell me she's set a date for the memorial service. And she told me something funny, which was that she's been calling you, coordinating the details. She said she likes you."

"Well…yes, we did have that long talk outside your condo that day and I left her my business card. You already knew I was helping her because I told you, but I'd hoped to surprise you with the extent of it."

He chuckled. "You're lucky that I like you so much, or I wouldn't have taken it well, guaranteed."

"So… Flo booked the church?"

"She did."

"Um, when?" Ashley asked, hoping it didn't conflict with Brandon's math test.

"Two weekends from now."

That would work! She felt pleased that he was staying for it.

He saw her good mood. "I haven't completely agreed yet," he teased.

"Aidan, of course you're going."

"Then you're going with me," he insisted.

"Won't that cause a problem?"

"Not for me. Or for Flo and Albert. Honestly, they would like you there." He glanced sideways at her. "Maybe I need somebody like you by my side, just for that one day."

"Like me?"

"You're supportive. I'm not used to that."

She wasn't sure how she felt about what he was saying.

She sat back in her chair, watching the action on the field. The crowd was still relatively quiet. There was tension in the air.

"We'll see," she said.

Aidan said nothing. She expected him to give her a joking response, but his silence made her turn toward him.

He was leaning forward, his hands on his knees, staring intently at the field. "Aw, hell," he muttered.

He gazed at her, and she saw the concern in his face.

"What is it?" She looked back at the field

but saw nothing other than the New York players standing at their field positions. The New England batter was outside the batter's box. A group of officials huddled near the dugout, in front of them, but she couldn't see much from her angle.

The man next to her was standing, so she stood, too.

Peering around the group of officials, she could see that they were leading her son into the dugout. She could only see the back of his head, but that was enough. What caught her attention was the way he held his arm in the air. He was hurt!

Ashley screamed aloud. Without thinking she reached for the railing. She had to get to Brandon. She could just jump over and then onto the dugout roof—

"No." Aidan's strong hands were on her waist. "They'll arrest you if you do that. Come with me. I can get you to him."

Blindly, tears in her eyes and panic threatening to set in, she nodded. Aidan took her hand and led her quickly out of their seats, up the cement stairs of the stadium, through the open concourse and then down a set of back stairs, guarded by an official.

Without missing a beat, Aidan pulled an ID out of his wallet. "I'm with the team. Dr.

Lowe. I have Brandon LaValley's mother with me. He's injured and she needs to be with him."

"I'll radio ahead." The guard waved them on. A few more twists and turns down corridors and they were inside New England's dugout. She'd been here once, a long time ago during Brandon's first season as a ball boy, but that hadn't been in the middle of the game with the dugout full of players. Players intent on winning and getting themselves into the playoffs. She didn't watch baseball, but that's what Brandon had told her was happening right now. All she cared about was finding her son. She held on to Aidan's hand for all she was worth.

"Where's Brandon LaValley?" Aidan barked at one of the managers.

"In the back, through the tunnel, first training room," the manager said. He acted as if he knew Aidan, as if it was perfectly natural that Aidan was here, unasked and unannounced in their heavily guarded team areas.

"Hey, Dr. Lowe! Take care of our kid!" one of the players called to Aidan.

"Come on," Aidan muttered to Ashley. Her purse was clutched to her chest and she still held on to Aidan with a death grip.She was trying not to scream, trying not to cry. She knew she was overreacting, but she couldn't seem to stop herself. Anything to do with hospitals just reminded her too much of when Brandon was young and sick…

They ran through more rooms until they got to an outside door. On the street, an ambulance was running, and an attendant was at the open door, tending her son, who was sitting on a gurney, inside.

"Brandon!" she cried.

"Mom!" He looked up and waved at her. Then he blanched.

"It looks like he hurt his wrist," Aidan muttered. He pushed his way to the front, speaking quietly to three men at the back of the ambulance. They wore Captains jackets and obviously were from the team.

She ran over, needing to know what was going on.

"We're taking him in for an X-ray," she heard the attendant say to Aidan.

"Well, I'm his orthopedic doctor. Let me take the ride with you." Aidan looked up and caught Ashley's pleading look. "His mother is here, and she needs to come, too."

"Sorry, Aidan, I've got to go," one of the officials said. "Team policy."

"If he's riding as physician, I can only let

you go if you're family," the ambulance attendant said to Aidan.

"He is," Ashley interjected. She gazed at Aidan. "I need you at the hospital with us."

"But…"

Ashley looked at the attendant. "I said he's family. Let's go."

"He'd have to be the boy's father, ma'am," the attendant clarified.

"Yes," she shouted. "Now let's go!"

There was a split second where she got a look from both Aidan and from her son, telling her that she was out of line. She was way, way out of line. Not only that but she was crazy. It was a dark look from both of them. First at her, then at each other.

But what they didn't understand was that stupid rules didn't matter. Brandon was all that mattered. She didn't know who these team people were. Her sister was no longer at Wellness Hospital. The only person she knew for sure that she trusted right now with her son's health was standing next to her. He'd spent the past week plus in their home, helping them both with one of the bigger problems that they'd had to face. Aidan had also cared enough to bring her back here, to her son when he needed her. Aidan would know what to do once they got to the hospital.

She didn't want to think it, but Brandon's arm looked broken. *His writing hand*, she thought desperately. How would he manage his schoolwork? How would it affect the rest of his health? Would it make his cancer come back? So many questions whirled.

But there was no doubt in her heart. Maybe she'd fibbed, but she needed Aidan there, with both of them. What if they needed to start treatment right in the ambulance? She couldn't risk him trying to find them at the hospital. He needed to be consulted immediately on any decisions she needed to make.

"Hurry up!" she snapped at the attendant. "Let's go!"

CHAPTER EIGHT

AIDAN HAD CALMED Ashley down enough that she was seated in the emergency waiting room, nursing a cup of coffee and filling out forms for the hospital. He was still incredulous that she'd implied he was the boy's father. Furious, too, and with good reason, in his opinion.

But now wasn't the time to go into any of that. Or to think about the fact that he'd kissed her. No, now was the time to concentrate on the patient. And Aidan was very good at concentrating.

He sat opposite Brandon in the examination room, keeping the boy's eyes focused on his.

"I was so stupid," Brandon was saying. "I don't know how it happened, Dr. Lowe, but I was walking backward and I tripped over a bat."

Aidan nodded. Brandon likely was waving at a cute girl in the audience. Focus wasn't Brandon's strong point.

But now wasn't the time to go into that, either.

The door to the examination room opened, and Dr. Rodriguez walked in. A former colleague of his.

Dr. Rodriguez did a double take when he saw Aidan. "Dr. Lowe! I didn't know you were back in the country." Without even greeting Brandon, he shook Aidan's hand.

"Thanks. I, ah, just got back two weeks ago."

"You'll be joining us on staff again, I suppose." Dr. Rodriguez took a stool beside the computer. As he spoke, he drew up Brandon's file.

Aidan cleared his throat. "This is Brandon," he said by way of introduction. "He's a student at St. Bart's. I've been tutoring him lately."

Dr. Rodriguez glanced at the chart the emergency workers had keyed in. "It says here that you're his—"

"No," Aidan said flatly. He wasn't the boy's dad, and he didn't want that repeated, especially not in front of Brandon.

Brandon was too distracted by the fracture in his right wrist to worry about what the doctors were talking about. It was a closed fracture. The bone wasn't protruding through the skin, thankfully, but there was obvious displacement. Despite the ice pack the ambulance attendants had applied, the limb was swollen to twice its natural size.

"Brandon," Dr. Rodriguez said, showing him the X-ray on the computer screen. "It looks like you have a clean break. That's good news. None of the bones in the wrist were crushed. We're going to prep you for surgery, set the break and when you wake up, you'll have a cool new cast on your wrist."

"I can't have a cast!" Brandon protested. "And I don't want surgery! It's not that bad!"

Dr. Rodriguez exchanged a look with a nurse, who'd just knocked and entered the small examination room.

"The surgery is so you won't feel any pain when the bone is set," Aidan said quietly to Brandon. "If you can handle some pain and are brave enough, the bone can be set here in the office."

At this point, Brandon perked up. "I'm brave."

Aidan nodded. "I know." Good, he'd hoped the kid would agree to an office procedure. Aidan didn't think that Ashley would hold up so well if her son was in surgery for a few more hours. Besides, when Aidan had first begun training, children's simple breaks were routinely set in outpatient settings. Now surgery and general anesthesia were more often used. In Brandon's case, though, in Aidan's professional opinion, a set in the office was the better choice.

"There will be a big needle involved," Aidan warned. "And some pain. But the good news will be you can go home in a couple of hours. The cast will be on for just a few weeks, while the bone heals."

"How long?" Brandon snapped. He looked angry now, rather than scared or hurt. His eyes were red-rimmed and he was no longer crying.

Aidan exchanged a look with Brandon's doctor.

"Four weeks," Dr. Rodriguez said.

Aidan relaxed. Better to say that to Brandon than four to six weeks and hope there were no complications.

"Four weeks! That's a month. I can't do that." He looked at Aidan, pleading. "I'm supposed to be Romeo in the play with St. Brigid's. They won't let me do it if I'm wearing a cast."

"I'm sure they'll make an exception."

"They won't! My friend Allen wanted to try out for Romeo, and they said he couldn't because he has his foot in a cast. They said it's an active role. He had to be the narrator instead!" Brandon pouted.

Dr. Rodriguez was looking mildly annoyed. Annoyed with Brandon's protests, annoyed with Aidan's presence.

"I'll scrub in and do the bone set, if you want," Aidan said to him.

Dr. Rodriguez shook his head. "Can't. You know protocol."

Yes, he knew all the rules with insurance, with lawyers.

"In fact, you probably shouldn't even be in here," the doctor said.

"Brandon's mother asked me to be here. She's signed all the appropriate forms." Aidan turned his attention to Brandon. "This is the best we can offer you," Aidan said to the boy. "I'll help you through it. We'll work with your teachers at school."

A tear leaked out of Brandon's eye. He was angry and frustrated and disappointed. Aidan could see it. In some respects, he was still very much a child.

Aidan leaned forward and caught his eye. "Hey. We have a lot to be thankful for. I just did a year in Afghanistan, working with kids your age and younger. I just wish I was setting simple bone breaks for them. Instead, I fitted prosthetic limbs for kids who'd lost their own when their towns and even schools were bombed."

Brandon's mouth fell open.

"Your wrist is going to heal a lot faster than you think. You'll be out of the cast by Halloween. By Thanksgiving, you'll be wondering if it had even ever been broken at all. The only thing it will do is give you a little bit more of a roadblock to overcome. You'll come out of this more resilient than ever."

Brandon's lips set. Aidan figured that the pain medication had kicked in, that the wrist wasn't hurting him. The thought of what he was losing at school in the short term had been what was hurting him. Aidan hoped his instincts were right. He wasn't the boy's father. He wouldn't even be in his life by Halloween.

"You ready?" Aidan asked him. While he'd been speaking, he'd become aware of the movement in the room behind him. The nurse had come in. Aidan remembered that her name was Nurse Hinton—and he also remembered that she didn't like him. He didn't blame her for that. Aidan always *had* been pretty aloof, bordering on rudeness. He knew some people had attributed it to his being Vivian Sharpe's grandson.

It didn't matter now. He hadn't been feeding Brandon a line of bull about being grateful and recognizing the good things he had. What Aidan had seen and done in Afghanistan, plus his interaction with Ashley, was going a long way toward changing his attitude.

Aidan turned slightly. Yes, Nurse Hinton had brought in the equipment Rodriguez would need to set the break.

"Everything's here now," Aidan told Brandon. "You sure you want to do it like this?"

"Yes. I'm tough. I beat childhood leukemia, you know."

"That's the spirit." Aidan nodded to the doctor. The doctor nodded to the nurse. She took Brandon's right hand and began applying the traps to his fingers that would attach to the traction apparatus.

Brandon looked at what they were doing, and the bravery seemed to drain from his face. From his point of view, Aidan was sure the contraption looked like a medieval torture device.

"Look at me," Aidan said. "Don't look at them. They're going to put a needle in your wrist. You'll feel it, but don't look at it."

"I'm not afraid of needles," Brandon insisted.

"Excellent. I don't want to put any added pressure on you, but your mom is out there waiting for us."

"I'd never let her see me cry."

Aidan distinctly remembered him crying

when his phone was taken away, but he wouldn't embarrass the boy by mentioning that now. "Yeah, we know how brave you are," he said, speaking quickly, keeping the kid's focus on him instead of on the foot-long monster of a needle that was about to go into his wrist. As it did, Brandon flinched and gritted his teeth, but to his credit, the boy only made a slight groan.

"You're doing awesome," Aidan said. He gave a quick glance to Rodriguez. His former colleague was less experienced than Aidan, but Aidan knew him to be a good doctor.

The local anesthesia he'd injected was powerful, and worked quickly.

"Does your wrist feel numb now?" Aidan asked.

Brandon nodded. "Yeah. It…feels weird."

Dr. Rodriguez maneuvered the boy's arm, doing everything right to set the bone cleanly and properly. To a layperson, though, it would look upsetting—the arm being pulled and twisted in positions and directions that a healthy arm shouldn't go.

But Brandon wasn't looking. He'd followed Aidan's instructions. He'd trusted him.

Aidan took satisfaction in that.

The bone was set. Dr. Rodriguez wheeled his stool over to the computer screen, where patients' charts were shown. Nurse Hinton took over and removed the traps from Brandon's fingers. Then she quickly gathered up a bucket and the materials to make a plaster cast.

"Wait," Aidan said. "He'd like a waterproof cast." In his opinion, the boy would be much better off in a lighter fiberglass cast with a waterproof liner.

"Well…" Rodriguez muttered, still staring at the screen.

"He's an active kid. It may help him with his ball boy duties for the Captains," Aidan said. "Brandon LaValley is the volunteer spokesperson for the Sunshine Club."

"Oh!" Nurse Hinton smiled at Brandon. "We've seen you on television. My daughter loves your promotional spots."

Brandon smiled genuinely back at her.

"We've got a celebrity here," Dr. Rodriguez murmured. He showed Brandon the sample clip with the color choices for the fiberglass casts. "You can have any color you want."

Right on top was a royal-blue color that matched not only the Captains team color, but the blue St. Bartholomew's blazers, as well. But Brandon pointed to the black. "That one. It's badass."

Badass? Was that because he'd survived the bone setting?

But Aidan remained silent. He sat back as the doctor and nurse made small talk with Brandon as they finished putting on his cast and giving him his routine instructions for home care.

"I'll need to talk to his mother about a follow-up appointment next week," Dr. Rodriguez said.

"Fine. I'll bring you out to see her."

The three of them—Dr. Rodriguez, Aidan and Brandon—headed back to the reception area where Ashley, hopefully, waited.

Aidan felt the tension increasing in his neck. When they'd left her, she'd been emotional, worried about her son. Excessively so, in Aidan's opinion. He'd gone with Brandon because that was the only thing that seemed to appease her. Now he hoped he'd done the right thing.

As they walked down the corridors, Brandon walked ahead of them.

"Now that you're home, are you coming back on staff?" Dr. Rodriguez asked him, his manner friendly.

"No," Aidan said. "I don't think so."

"That's too bad. Well, keep in touch. Let me know where you end up."

"I will," Aidan said. But the truth was, he was shaken up. His former colleague hadn't asked a word about Fleur. Nothing. It was as if she'd been forgotten.

Or maybe she didn't matter to people at Wellness, because people at Wellness hadn't mattered all that much to Fleur. She'd always been looking further ahead. Boston had never meant to be the pinnacle of her career. She'd wanted more.

He'd wanted less.

The truth was he liked working with Brandon. It gave him some meaning. Even if he wasn't—and never would be—the kid's father.

Once in the waiting area, Brandon met his mother first, and let her cover him with hugs. He hugged her back, speaking bravely, telling her that everything was fine.

He'd kept all the bad moments from her. Maybe it was for the best. Aidan wasn't sure.

Dr. Rodriguez filled Ashley in about the details of the procedure, the particulars of his care and the importance of a follow-up appointment. And then, within five minutes, the three were alone again.

"I need to go to the bathroom before we leave," Brandon said.

"Okay, honey. We'll be right here waiting."

They both watched him walk off, still in his team uniform.

When he was out of earshot, Ashley asked him, "Is he really okay? Tell me the truth."

"He's on painkillers right now. When he gets home, he'll probably want to sleep for a few hours."

Ashley nodded. "Good. I'll see to that."

"What I'm really wondering about is how you're doing," Aidan said quietly.

"I'm better." Frowning, she sat again. "I know I was pretty upset. Out of control even." She sighed, looking at her hands. "Brandon being hurt is one of my triggers. I...learned that through my work with my counselor. So I called him just now. We talked. I did some centering meditations." She glanced up at Aidan. "I want to apologize to you. You helped Brandon and me more than you'll ever know, and I reacted badly to it."

From the corner of his eye, Aidan saw Brandon returning with his black "badass" cast.

He forced a smile at Ashley. They still had stuff to talk about, but not here, not now. "I'm glad you're okay." And now that he thought about it, she'd been brave, too. Her kid had been through childhood leukemia. That had to affect a parent in really difficult ways. "He's strong, Ashley. He didn't make a sound when the bone was set."

Brandon joined them. "Can we go?" he said petulantly.

Aidan wondered if he'd had trouble using the bathroom. Soon enough, Brandon would realize all the things—everyday tasks that most people took for granted—that would be difficult if not impossible to do with a cast on his dominant hand.

"Actually, Brandon," Aidan said casually, taking off his new Captains cap and holding it out. "I bought this today, and I was thinking I'd like to go up to the Sunshine Club and give it to one of the kids in the cancer ward. We left during the third inning, so the game is probably still on." The television in the children's room always played the Captains games. It was his grandmother's policy. "Maybe one of the young fans would like to have it."

"They can have mine, too," Ashley said softly. She held out the cap that Aidan had given her. "If you don't mind, though, I'll wait here while you go up with Brandon."

Brandon rubbed his cast. "Okay," he mumbled. He looked at Aidan, surprised. Maybe even suspicious.

"Lead the way," Aidan said. "I've never been up there before."

"Seriously?" Brandon asked.

"I haven't. I'm ashamed to say…well, I was always too busy." Not only that, but to his mind, that part of the hospital had been his grandmother's province.

"I know everyone in the Sunshine Club," Brandon said. "Come on. The access is by the main elevator."

Aidan couldn't help turning as he walked off, and Ashley gave him a secret smile and a little wave. Every time he looked at her, he felt a warm glow. Damn, she was sweet. And caring. And…appreciative. That was it—she didn't take him for granted.

Yes, there were red flags. He still needed to talk to her about that whole insinuating he was Brandon's father thing just to get him in the ambulance. And she was fragile still, emotionally, no doubt about that. His grandmother had said it first—just the fact that she was a former addict was worrisome. Was a former addict ever really trustworthy?

She'd told him the extent of her problem, and it seemed relatively manageable. But did he really know? He should be wary. Especially for someone with the money and power his family had. This should be a warning to him.

But yet…he glanced back at her one more time. She was still gazing at them.

She didn't *seem* like a person to desert or cheat on a man. Yes, he was sure of that, to his bones, and yet, he was telling himself that without even really knowing her.

Tread carefully.

UPSTAIRS IN THE Sunshine Club, Aidan was shocked to find that a crowd was gathered around the large television in what was obviously the children's family community room.

Painted bright yellow, with colorful drawings and photos pinned up of child cancer patients who'd come through the Sunshine Club program, the room was a warm, inviting space.

Brandon moved about easily, seeming to be at home here. He took Aidan and introduced him to his doctor. Dr. Zedelkowsky gave Brandon a long, genuine hug. "What have we here?" he asked Brandon.

"Broken wrist," Brandon said, a hint of pride in his voice. "Nothing serious. I got the bone set today, and then I have four weeks in the cast."

Aidan was heartened to hear the boy take ownership of the situation. It eased some of his reservations and worry.

"This is Dr. Lowe," Brandon said to his oncologist. "He's been tutoring me in math. I'm going to St. Bart's," he said, his chest puffed up with pride.

Aidan smiled at the doctor, shaking his hand. "Nice to meet you. I've seen your name of course, but…"

"Wellness Hospital is a big place," Dr. Z said. "I rarely get out of the ward."

"I'm in orthopedics."

"Ah! A specialty that has come in handy to young Brandon, I see."

Aidan laughed. "Unfortunately."

"I'm an alumnus of St. Bart's myself," the doctor mentioned.

"Really?" Aidan asked, interested. Judging by the good doctor's snowy-white hair, he'd graduated years earlier than Aidan. "Ah, have you ever done any mentoring?" Maybe here was the answer to his problem.

"No." Dr. Z shifted his computer tablet to his other arm. "They always ask, but that's, ah, not my forte. I commend you, good sir." He winked at Aidan from behind his wire-rimmed glasses.

Oh, well. It had been a thought.

"Come on," Brandon said to Aidan. "Let's check out the game."

Aidan was well aware that Brandon hadn't watched any television or even seen his phone in almost two weeks now. "I have him on a no-media diet while we get him settled in his new school," Aidan remarked to Dr. Z.

"Then that explains this…" Dr. Z reached into the pocket inside his lab coat and pulled out his personal phone. He swiped the screen and showed it to Brandon.

"It's his social media page," Dr. Z explained to Aidan. "I saw the accident on TV and wanted to leave him a message."

Brandon grabbed the phone and swiped eagerly. "It's true. People are sending me get-well wishes! The announcer on television told everybody that I broke my wrist!"

"See," Aidan said drily, "the internet world doesn't end when you're not on it."

"Yeah. My mom posted a note on my front page. It said that I'm off-line so I can study. Here it is." He swiped some more. He appeared to be reading silently. Then he frowned. "I'm off-line, studying hard, because I really want to be a doctor and work in the Sunshine Club someday."

Brandon paused, frowning. Then he handed the phone back to Dr. Z.

"Is that true?" Aidan murmured to Brandon after Dr. Z had left them to make his rounds.

Brandon nodded. But he wasn't looking at Aidan. He seemed to be thinking deeply, keeping his own counsel.

"You have lots of time to change your mind, buddy," Aidan said. "You're only twelve. You could be anything you want. Just remember not to let anyone push you into a direction you don't really want to go."

"Yup," Brandon mumbled. "Okay."

Aidan wasn't sure what to do next. His point was made, but...he still wasn't sure that everything was okay. Maybe he shouldn't have said anything.

He wished Ashley was here.

"Come on," Brandon said to him. "Let's see if anyone wants those Captains caps."

"I'm on it," Aidan said.

Brandon caused a little bit of a stir when he entered the community room. He was still in his uniform, and he was holding out that solid black cast.

"Why is it black?" Aidan heard a little girl ask.

"It's cuz I'm a pirate," Brandon told the little girl, and at that simple, childlike statement, Aidan smiled.

The girl giggled. "Like *Pirates of the Caribbean*?"

"You like that movie?" Brandon asked.

"I like Captain Jack Sparrow."

"Me, too. Would you like a Captains cap?" He held it out to the girl. She was sitting in her dad's lap, and she must have been through chemo treatments, because when she took off the pink cap she wore, her head was completely bald.

Proudly she put on the Captains ball cap. "Thank you, Brandon!"

Aidan swallowed a lump in his throat. It was hard being up here, in what was still a children's cancer ward, no matter how brightly decorated or whimsically named.

He gave Brandon credit. The boy was more kindhearted—and focused—than Aidan had given him credit for.

He knew what he was doing. Maybe Aidan shouldn't worry. Maybe he should just trust him.

CHAPTER NINE

ASHLEY SET HER keys down on the table in the hallway and then opened the door wider so Brandon and Aidan could follow.

Her son's eyes were drooping. Aidan hadn't been kidding—the painkillers they'd prescribed for him had obviously kicked in, and Brandon looked like he could sleep until tomorrow morning.

She led him into the bathroom and helped by putting toothpaste on his brush. Yes, he was twelve—almost thirteen—but at the moment he was a small child again.

"I'll wash your hair for you when you need it," she told him. "Some things are going to be hard for you to do for a while."

"I was just wondering that, Mom. How am I going to write?"

That thought had concerned her, as well. "We'll go in to see the headmaster on Monday together."

"Do you think he'll let Dr. Lowe help me take my math test?"

"I'm sure they'll work with us on this special circumstance. I think the most important thing is to get a lot of rest tonight. Monday you can start studying again."

He nodded sleepily. "It could be a lot worse, you know."

"That's true." She smiled. She loved seeing this upbeat, positive side he had. She'd been worried he was losing it, truth be told.

"I think I need to go to the Sunshine Club more often, Mom. It helps me. Maybe on Sundays again, since that's my day off with Dr. Lowe."

"You know, I think that's a good idea."

"Okay." With a teasing tone, Brandon said, "You can go now, Mom. I'll put myself to bed."

She hid a smile. "If you need me to put your jammies on…"

"Mom!" he said in outrage, then rolled his eyes at her.

Ah, yes, this was more like it. Her almost-teen was back.

"G'nite, Bran," she said, and then closed the bathroom door behind her.

But when she got out to the kitchen, Aidan was still there. She wasn't sure why, but she'd thought maybe he would have excused himself and left. She had a feeling he'd been angry with her earlier, at her emotional reaction to Brandon's injury.

He stood at the stovetop, fiddling with her teakettle. "Hope you don't mind, but I made myself at home."

"No, I don't mind."

"Would you like some black tea with honey?" he asked.

"Sure. There's honey in the cabinet, but I'm not sure how old it is."

"It'll be fine."

She sat at the table, twisting her hands together while he gathered the supplies. His voice was so quiet and calm. His expression was thoughtful, though. It gave him an attractive quality. He hadn't yet cut his hair, and with the lingering effects of that desert tan, he still looked wildly sexual to her.

She swallowed. He'd kissed her today. She wished he would bring it up again, but there was this new, angry barrier between them. It made her sorry.

The teakettle whistled. Aidan took it off, poured the hot water over the tea bags in a pair of her best mugs and then stirred in the honey.

So strange to have someone else take over her kitchen. She never allowed that. But she allowed him.

He put the mugs down and then sat across

from her. With his head lowered, he gazed up at her, his wide, clear eyes steady.

She rubbed her bare arms. Crossed her legs under the table.

"I should have asked, Ashley," he said in that low voice of his. "I should have asked you before I ever started tutoring or mentoring Brandon."

She wasn't sure what he was talking about. But she suspected.

"Where is Brandon's father?" he asked.

Her fingers trembling, she placed them on the sides of the mug for heat. She knew she owed Aidan an explanation. But if she told him, she was pretty sure that he would start questioning some of her decisions. He might even take over. Or leave.

"Ashley, you can't say that I'm his father," Aidan said calmly. At least he wasn't being rude. She was grateful for that.

"You can't do that," he repeated. "It's not good for Brandon, and it puts me in an awkward position with him."

She hadn't considered the effect on him —she'd been mainly worried about Brandon—but he was right.

"I'm sorry," she said. "You're right, about everything you've said. I was afraid today, and the words just slipped out without my thinking about the ramifications."

Aidan sat back in his chair. "You know, I don't want to be the bad guy, but Brandon says things to me like, 'You're not my father.' Do you think it bothers him that his father isn't around?"

She inhaled. "He knows that his father is deceased."

"Deceased?" Aidan's eyebrows shot up. His mouth worked, as if he didn't know what to say.

Ashley slowly rose. Feeling numb inside, she went to the back cupboard in the pantry. High on the top shelf, she reached for the oatmeal box. Instead of oatmeal, it held a metal tin with a very strong lock.

She brought it to the table and then sat down again. Aidan was watching her. His brows were knit in curiosity.

"I've been keeping this for Brandon, for someday." She swallowed and looked down. "The counselor I work with said he'll help me show it to Brandon when he's older. Brandon will have a lot of questions to ask, and a lot of feelings to work through, so...so that's what we have decided to do. This...this is part of what I talked to my counselor about while you were in the surgical room with Brandon."

"You did?"

"I didn't mention it at the hospital because Brandon came back in the middle of the conversation that you and I were having."

His gaze flicked to the tin.

She knew she would have to show him. This wasn't like his history with Fleur —there were things Ashley wouldn't ever have to know about their relationship, because that one hadn't produced a son. This seemed different. Brandon was here. She'd taken a risk today, and she'd gone out with Aidan. Her first date in thirteen years. Her first kiss.

She pressed her hand to her mouth. She wanted to keep building on what she and Aidan had started. Tonight was a turning point. She had a terrible feeling it would end here if she handled things badly. Or, possibly, it could go on.

That part would be up to Aidan. But to not show him—that would end it for certain.

"Was he abusive to you?" Aidan asked angrily. "Because if he was—"

"No," she interrupted. And then more calmly, "No." She squeezed her eyes shut, but she knew Aidan was staring at her, in pain.

"*I* was abusive to me," she said.

"I don't understand."

"I've never discussed this with anyone. Not

a soul. Not even my sister." Her throat felt hoarse and painful. Like her words were getting stuck in it.

"Ashley…"

She felt like a patient…a perpetual, chronic patient, and that was making her angry. "There are reasons I stopped drinking," she said, her voice betraying her anger. "When I was young, before Brandon was born, I was a college student. Elizabeth wasn't the only one in our family to try and escape our background."

"What were you studying?"

"Business." Her voice broke. She felt so sorry now—to think about those old youthful ambitions that had no chance of ever being realized. "I was working so hard. I'd passed my beauty school tests during high school, but my dream was to open my own shop. I wanted people working for me, not the other way around." She pressed her hand to her mouth. Her dream had been so vivid. "I wanted a neighborhood shop, community based. I didn't want to have to depend on other people…" Her voice trailed away. In that respect, she'd gotten entirely what she'd wanted. She hadn't been dependent on other people, because the people she'd most needed had deserted her.

Aidan was silent, listening.

"Well, I told you that Elizabeth and I grew up in a house with an alcoholic mother. My father wasn't around, because he was married to somebody else and had been the whole time, and he didn't want anything to do with us." She blew out her breath. She still hadn't answered Aidan's question.

She dared to take her attention away from her tea, which she was stirring round and round with her teaspoon, and looked at him. Not quite in the eyes, but…she was ashamed of this part.

"I drank back then, too. I had friends… classmates that I went out to college parties with. Boston is…well, you know that there are a lot of young people here."

Aidan nodded. His face didn't look unkind.

"I got pregnant. I was…very frightened." She looked at her thumb again. "By this point, Elizabeth was in college. She was only sixteen and very intent on becoming a doctor. My… mother had moved. I was living in a falling-down apartment in Brighton with four other girls who were in my classes. We were all splitting rent."

She sighed. "I wasn't exactly dating the young man. I…barely knew him. A student at another college. I don't even know what he was studying." She shook her head.

"Did you tell him?" Aidan asked.

"Yes. Of course." She still couldn't keep the bitterness out of her voice.

"What did he say?"

"He told me to take care of it."

Aidan winced.

"My friends," Ashley continued, "room-mates, really…told me to go back to him and ask for money to pay for it. They said they would go with me."

"What did you do?"

"It was hard. It was really hard… I left Boston and moved back to my old neighborhood, my old town. I had my haircutting license, so I was able to get a job with Sal—he was the older brother of a friend from high school. He let me bring Brandon with me and sit him in his stroller while I cut people's hair. You should have seen Brandon—he was such a little cutie. Everyone loved him. He was personable and loving and…" Her eyes filled with tears.

Aidan reached across the table and took her hand. "When was the last time you spoke to Brandon's father?"

She shook her head. "I told you."

"You never…?"

Tears blurring her vision, she fumbled with the lock on the tin. She hadn't opened it since the day she'd put the article inside. Until tonight, she hadn't even realized why she'd saved it to begin with—probably because no matter how deep her denial was, a part of her knew, had always known, that Brandon would have to be told. He wouldn't be a child, easily dissuaded, forever. He would deserve to know, when the time was right.

But, oh, it was such a fear of hers. She'd been so reluctant to think about it...to talk about it. Even now.

The lock sprang free, and the lid popped open. Inside was the article, clipped from the Boston newspaper. Folded in quarters, locked away for almost twelve years.

With shaking hands, she passed it to Aidan.

He opened it. Spread it on her kitchen table with his broad, solid, doctor's hands. An accident report and a death notice, both on one page. And square in the middle, a photograph of the young man who'd tragically died on a summer construction accident, falling from the tall building where he'd been installing windows.

Aidan looked up at her, his eyes wide.

"By God. He looks just like Brandon."

She sat down at the table, hard. Looked over Aidan's shoulder at the photo she hadn't seen in twelve years.

It was her worst nightmare come true. He looked even more like Brandon than she'd re-alized.

Her hand went to her mouth, and she nearly choked.

"Now you know why I'm always so anx-ious," she said to Aidan. "It used to be that every time we went out…or when he was on television at the ballpark, or on one of your grandmother's public service announce-ments…" She gazed at him. "I even worried that you, coming into my new salon, could be someone from his father's family, there to take Brandon away from me because I'm not a good mother."

"Ridiculous! You're a great mother!"

"After everything I've said and done, you can still think that?"

He stood them. Scraped back his chair roughly and pulled her into his arms.

He felt good. Solid. Trustworthy. A safe place.

She leaned her cheek against his chest and felt free to sob her eyes out.

AIDAN FELT A surge of fierce protectiveness as he clasped Ashley in his arms. He smoothed her pretty auburn hair back from her shoul-ders and felt the warmth of her tears against his chest. "Please don't cry," he told her. "You are a good person. I don't think any less of you. I think *more* of you."

He did. It was true. He rubbed her back, rubbed the cool skin of her bare arms even as he closed his eyes and thought.

She couldn't know it, but she was such a contrast to Fleur.

Fleur, who'd never cared about another person as much as she'd cared about herself. Who'd always put her own needs and ambitions ahead of her personal relationships, no matter who it hurt.

It made him feel bleak, even still, to think of it. At times he'd wondered if there had been something wrong with him—if he hadn't been enough for her.

But sitting here, listening to the wrenching truth coming from Ashley tonight, it had struck him that he simply *liked* Ashley better. He liked who *he* was better when he was with Ashley—and Brandon—than when he'd been without them.

"Ashley?" He smoothed back her hair and peered at her face. "Thank you for telling me the truth."

She took a tissue from a pocket. Wouldn't look at him as she blew her nose. "Do you want to go now?" she asked.

"Actually, I want to stay," he said quietly. He really did. "Would you like to order something in? Watch a movie with me on television?"

Slowly she wiped her eyes, glancing toward Brandon's bedroom.

"He's sleeping," Aidan said. "He'll sleep until morning, I'm sure. We'll turn your TV on, quietly, and we'll just sit here together. We don't have to say anything."

"Do you think I'm screwed up?" she whispered.

"No," he said firmly. If anything, he was the one who was screwed up.

"Together we work," he said. "Together we'll figure it out."

She smiled tentatively, then gave a soft chuckle. She was laughing again, and that's what he wanted.

With the volume low, he found a movie for them to watch, an old Western in black and white. Where good guys and bad guys were clear, and the good guys always won in the end.

Ashley curled up in his arms. They didn't talk much, but they didn't have to. He didn't kiss her again, either, though he wanted to, because she didn't seem to be in the right place for it yet.

Instead he listened to her heartbeat against his chest. Stroked her smooth hair. Tried to lose himself in the movie, because he didn't know what else to do to help.

CHAPTER TEN

ON SUNDAY, AIDAN still didn't know what to do. It was pouring rain outside, and he sat on his couch, watching the sheets of water cascade down his windows. The harbor was fogged in. He couldn't see any boats.

Even without Fleur's belongings inside, the place was still a depressing reminder of the old life he was trying to forget.

The phone rang and he jumped. *Ashley*, was his first hopeful thought.

"My name is Gin Sanders," said the husky, smoke-filled voice of the woman on the other end. "Ashley LaValley gave me your phone number."

"Okay," he said, not sure what to think.

"Is this Aidan Lowe?"

Not Dr. Aidan Lowe, but Aidan Lowe. He smiled. "Yes. Who is this?"

"I'm a real estate agent."

He put his hand to his head. Was Ashley trying to get rid of him now?

The real estate agent—Gin—cleared her

throat. "I've sold quite a few units in your building, Mr. Lowe, and I can get a great price for you. I know your market."

"Okay. Sure." He *was* ready to sell the place. "Come take a look."

"Are you available now?" Gin asked.

"Yes, I am."

"I'll be there shortly."

He hung up. He thought about calling Ashley, but just then his buzzer sounded. Curious, he went to the door.

Bill with his newspaper. Bill used to always bring him his Sunday newspaper in the old days before Afghanistan.

Aidan took it from him. "Thanks," he said warily.

"Did you get the call from the real estate agent I referred to you?"

"That was you who called her?" Aidan asked.

Bill nodded. "Your hair stylist called me. Ashley." Bill's face grew red.

"Ashley called *you*?"

"She did. She said you were looking for a good real estate agent." Bill's face was still red.

Aidan held on to the edge of the door, not sure he wanted to hear this. "You like her, don't you?" he asked Bill.

"Do you think she would go out with me if I asked her?"

"No," he said. "She has a kid. She doesn't date because of that."

Bill nodded. "Thanks for telling me that. You saved me some embarrassment."

He turned and headed back for the elevator, and Aidan could only stare after him.

He wouldn't give up so easily. Thoughtful, he turned to close the door.

But the elevator door opened. Bill again. And a woman with very short blond hair and lots of heavy makeup.

"Aidan?" she asked him. "Mr. Lowe?"

Bill's eyes widened. He'd only ever called him Dr. Lowe, and Fleur Dr. Sanborne. Fleur would've ripped into this lady for the insult, but all Aidan could seem to do was to smile.

"Yeah, I'm Aidan. That was fast," he told Gin.

"I was actually on the floor below you when I called."

"Good thinking. Please." He opened his door wider. "Come in. Sorry, I haven't had time to clean yet."

Gin walked in, her head swiveling, taking in everything. The huge room without furniture. The dirty windows he hadn't had time to clean. The kitchen, with empty packaging left on the countertops.

Gin wrinkled her nose. "No one has lived here for a while, have they?"

Hey—he was living here. Had been for more than two weeks. "I was overseas for a year."

"Are you the sole owner?"

"Yes."

"A trust is listed as owning it."

She'd done her homework. He nodded. "I'm the sole trustee." Trusts were just something they did in his family.

Gin walked over to a counter, clicked on her pen and made some notes. "Do you mind if I take photos?"

"Um…you need to do that now?"

She sighed. "How about you show me the other rooms? This is a two bedroom, right?"

Aidan brought her in and showed her the second bedroom first, which still had his old office stuff and a folded-up cot, which he'd been sleeping in. Then they went to the master bedroom. He'd had Bill come up and haul out the bed, so there was nothing in the room but a clean rectangle on the dusty hardwood flooring.

Gin frowned and opened Fleur's closet. Nothing was left but empty hangers.

Then she walked to the bathroom. Aidan had emptied that out himself. All the drawers with makeup, the shelves with shampoo. He'd felt proud of himself.

Gin stood there frowning.

"What?" he asked her.

"This bathroom is at least twenty years out of date."

He shrugged. "That's how old the building is."

Gin sighed. "Come out to the kitchen with me."

He shrugged again and followed her. She put her papers down, then pulled up a chair at the breakfast bar. He followed suit.

"Look at this counter. It's chipped and worn-out. People want granite these days." Gin frowned. "Your appliances are old. There's no stainless steel. And the flooring… it's in rough shape. Not to mention the paint situation."

"Okay." He'd been a busy doctor.

Gin clicked open her pen and showed him some numbers. "This is what your unit is worth now, as is. But I'm telling you, it's not necessarily a quick sale. People who buy here want turnkey—they're busy professionals, and they want to move in to a renovated unit with all the latest amenities."

"Maybe a fixer-upper type will want it."

"Sure. You'll get some lowball offers from property flippers. I emphasize *lowball*." She scribbled another set of numbers and turned her yellow legal pad toward him. "For this much in renovation cost—and that's just your kitchen, bathroom and flooring, plus a paint job, you'll get this much return." She pointed with her pen.

It was a substantial difference. "Are you sure?" he asked, skeptical.

She pulled out a computer tablet from her purse and proceeded to show him some comps from the building.

"Wow," he said, understanding what she was getting at.

Gin tapped her finger on the screen. "I hired the team for the kitchen/bathroom renovation in this unit one floor below yours. The team is fast, they're mostly on budget and they report to me."

"Sounds like I can't lose," he muttered.

"Not likely. This is a primo unit. You're facing the harbor, and you're on the top floor. This unit will go fast."

He thought it would, too, once the renovations were done. "How long will the construction take?" he asked her.

"I'll talk to the team, see what they have

scheduled. But once they start, it's fast. Maybe a month. Maybe less."

He liked that. He liked it a lot. "Let's do it."

While he completed some paperwork with Gin and exchanged phone numbers, he couldn't help wondering what Ashley's motivation in all this had been.

They'd spent last night practically snuggling on her couch. And she needed him to help Brandon catch up with his math studies. So why was she doing this? Was it a hint to leave? Was she embarrassed about what she'd told him last night?

No sooner had he shut the door on Gin than he took out his smartphone and pressed Ashley's phone number with his thumb.

She didn't pick up right away. He frowned. Just before his call would go to voice mail, though, she picked up. "Yes, Dr. Lowe?"

Brandon must be with her. He hoped. "I got a visit from your real estate agent."

"Was she good?" she asked. "She didn't hit on you, I hope."

"I don't get it. Are you trying to get rid of me?"

"I…can't really talk right now," she said softly.

He heard what sounded like Brandon's

voice in the background. "Is everything okay?" Aidan asked cautiously.

"Not really. Brandon's frustrated because he's figured out that he can't type his essay paper on a keyboard the way he used to, not with two hands, anyway."

"Ah. Well, it just so happens I have a solution."

"Really?" She was interested. "What do orthopedic surgeons recommend?"

"I have to show you in person. Can I come now?"

She laughed. "I see how you did that."

"I'll catch a ride from the car service and be there in fifteen."

ASHLEY FINISHED PUTTING away the breakfast dishes and then straightened her back. She'd hoped to get outside for a walk around the park. The rain had stopped, and it was turning into a nice day outside and she needed to think. Specifically, about what had happened last night. And what was going to happen with the man who was on his way over to her apartment.

She passed Brandon, staring slack-jawed at his laptop. But he had no Wi-Fi, so he had to be focused on his assignments.

With her son occupied, she ducked into

the one tiny bathroom. Taking a critical look at herself in the mirror, she plugged in her flatiron, dabbed on some quick mascara and pale lip gloss, and then managed to get a few swipes with the comb and flatiron combination.

"Mom!" Brandon called from the kitchen. "Somebody is at the door!"

She stuck her head out. "It's Dr. Lowe. Let him in."

Brandon's face perked up. He trotted off to open the door.

She stared at herself in the mirror. "What are you doing, Ashley?" she asked aloud. She had a feeling that his rejection was going to come hard and fast.

She had so many strikes against her. She was a mom, Brandon's mom. She'd made enough mistakes for one lifetime. She struggled with an alcohol problem. She kept her son's father secret.

But she had told everything to Aidan. He knew all her shameful secrets. And he was still here. He hadn't left, not yet, anyway. Even so, she'd all but handed him the opportunity on a golden platter—doing the legwork, phoning Bill and getting a good real estate agent contact for him. He was free to leave her.

All that was left was for it to happen.

Rubbing her arms, she shut off the bathroom light and went to the kitchen to find Aidan standing beside her son, opening a box of some sort, and Brandon eagerly helping him, his new black cast notwithstanding.

"Um, what's happening here?"

"Dr. Lowe brought me a voice-typing program."

"Speech-recognition software." Aidan held aloft a CD. Her son was already trying on a headset that apparently plugged into his school laptop.

Ashley swallowed. Aidan looked...well, her attraction for him hadn't abated. Since that first day in her salon, it had only grown.

His eyes sparked when he looked at her. He seemed to have taken more care in his dress than he usually did. For once, he'd actually run a comb through his hair. Put on a clean, pressed shirt. A pair of jeans that fit him really well.

He was looking her up and down, too. It made her want to shiver. And squirm.

"Mom, look at this program!"

She licked her lips and reluctantly glanced at her son. He'd uploaded the CD and was eagerly reading the instructions. "I've heard of this kind of software. I speak, and it types what I speak. I won't need to type with a cast anymore!"

"That's...great." It really was. She should be more enthused.

She glanced back at Aidan, and he was smiling at her shyly.

"What?" she mouthed to him.

"Tell you later," he mouthed back.

Indeed, he did the perfectly reasonable and decent thing—he sat down beside her son and helped him with his homework. All of it. Not just the math tutoring, which he wasn't scheduled for, because it was Sunday.

"Would you two mind if I took a quick walk in the park?" she asked.

"No problem," Aidan said, not looking up from the screen where he worked with Brandon.

She went outside. Enjoyed a long walk, stretching her legs as she circuited the park. "Now what?" she kept asking herself. What happened if Brandon had gotten attached to Aidan? She hadn't thought that far ahead. She'd only been trying to get him through his first semester at St. Bartholomew's. Aidan was doing all that and more. But for how long? And to what end?

By the time she made it back to their building, she still had no answers to her fears. She picked up some bottled water and fruit from the small convenience store on the first floor, and then headed back to the apartment.

They'd moved on to math homework, obviously. Brandon was laughing. Evidently, he directed Aidan which numbers and symbols to write, and Aidan obliged, completely stone-faced as he did so, which Brandon thought hilarious.

She set her grocery bag on the counter. "Would anyone like some, um, fruits or nuts?" she asked.

Brandon just continued laughing.

"Ha-ha, funny boy," she said, glad that he was happy. It had been a while since he'd been anything but tense and worried about failing.

"Dr. Lowe said he'd be my hands for me during my math test. You'll ask the headmaster about that, right?"

She swallowed. She just kept getting in deeper and deeper where Aidan was concerned. But she had to keep a calm, professional front for her son. "Yes, I'll walk over to see him Monday morning." She glanced again at Aidan. "Thank you," she said quietly. Because she really was thankful for his help with her son.

He nodded. "It's the least I can do." He stood. "Well, I've got to get going. Are you all set now?" he asked Brandon.

"Yeah. Thanks. My homework is done." He glanced at his mother. "I'm kind of tired, so I'm just going to read for a while. I've got to finish *Tom Sawyer* by next week."

"Okay."

Aidan glanced at her. "Will you walk me out?" he murmured.

She kept her gaze pinned to his chest, the broad muscles covered by cotton. Dully, she nodded. Last night, she'd rested her cheek there, but the mood had been ruined by her crying. She'd had a tissue clutched in her hand for most of the night. He must have been appalled with her.

Her heart feeling leaden, she headed down the stairs and out to the street with him.

"Take a walk down to the corner?" he asked her.

"All right." She was just about to ask him if he was ending things with her before they'd even really started, when she glanced up and caught his gentle smile.

She stopped short, in the middle of the sidewalk. She could drown in that smile.

"Ashley," he said quietly, hands in his pockets. "I hope you don't feel bad about what you told me last night. Because I don't."

"You…don't?" She rubbed her arms. The sun had gone down behind the buildings, and the afternoon was getting cooler. "Maybe I'm just... I don't know. *Ashamed* is probably the closest word."

"I hope that's not on my account."

She bit her lip. "It feels strange telling someone, after all of these years."

"Nobody ever asked you?"

"They did. I just refused to talk about it. After a while, people stopped asking."

"And... Brandon. Does he ask you?"

She sucked in her breath. Did she really want to continue this conversation?

"This summer," she said cautiously. "And we handled it. I told you he knows his father is deceased."

"He never asked you when he was little?"

She sighed. "I think he took it in stride back then. My sister once told me that she overheard him explaining to Jon that people in our family didn't have fathers."

"That's heartbreaking," Aidan said.

"I know. It did break my heart. It still does."

Aidan reached over. Casually he put his arm on her shoulder and pulled her closer, even as they walked.

"Why are you interested in me?" she asked, not daring to look at him.

"Because you care about people first, before anything else. I'm not used to that."

"You, from a family of doctors?"

"Yes, me, from a family of doctors."

It seemed so strange to her. She could only shake her head in wonder.

"You want to see firsthand?" he asked her.

"What do you mean?"

"My cousin is getting married next weekend. And I need a date."

That made her laugh. "Oh, right," she said, snorting. "I'll just put on my best frock and mingle with the high society. Vivian Sharpe will love to see me walking in on your arm—don't you think?"

He looked hurt. "They're people, too, Ashley. And they are my family, such as they are."

She stopped laughing. "Sorry. You're right."

"So you'll go with me?"

"First of all, you can't just add a plus-one to a wedding reception the week before the date. That's not how it works, Aidan."

He pulled a card, now crumpled, from his back pocket. "A note from my formidable grandmother. It was in my mailbox, which I checked before I came over here. She said that she put me in for a plus-one, and that if I was looking for a date, in her opinion, I should take that very sexy hairstylist who gave me the best shampoo of my life, my first day back in town."

She stopped short. "Are you kidding? Let me see that note."

Laughing, he handed it over, and it was all true, except for the "very sexy hairstylist" part. That he'd made up.

"I thought she disliked me." Ashley handed him back his letter.

"Apparently not," he said. "But the main thing I liked about this note is that it's what I want, too. I'm not doing it for her."

That…was probably the nicest thing any man had said to her in a long time. She leaned against him, walking in silence, enjoying the moments in the day with him.

"I'm not sure what to wear. Do I have anything nice enough?"

"A, um, cocktail dress is fine. That's what women call them, right?"

She smiled to herself. He was trying. Oh, he was trying.

"Okay," she admitted. "But under two conditions. First, I don't think it's wise to tell Brandon about the wedding just yet. And second…"

He glanced at her.

"Second, you let me cut your hair."

CHAPTER ELEVEN

AIDAN SETTLED HIMSELF into Ashley's chair in her salon on the afternoon of his cousin's wedding. He was dressed in a suit but had folded his jacket over the chair in the empty salon station next to theirs.

He inhaled deeply and then stretched his shoulders, reveling in how great he felt. Ashley and him, nearly alone. The morning rush was over, and now few coworkers were present—just the receptionist, hidden from view around the corner, and a lone stylist clear across the salon, working on a man that he looked like he might be romantically involved with.

Aidan crossed his arms over his white T-shirt and prepared for another very sexy shampoo.

He heard a clicking noise approaching and he glanced up, watching as Ashley walked across the tiled floor in her stiletto sandals. He sat taller, craning to see her better. She looked like a knockout, dressed to kill, and this was an entirely new side of her that he enjoyed seeing.

She wore a black dress with a hemline just above her knees, showing off great long legs. The sandals were black and strappy, and her toenails were pale pink, like cotton candy.

Something strange was happening to him. He was overcome by the feeling that all he wanted to do was settle her in his lap and kiss her silly.

"I hope I'm dressed appropriately." She set down a pot with some of concoction that she'd been mixing—it smelled fantastic, like the most sensual oils possible—and then reached for an apron. Before she put it on though, she spun around for him. "What do you think, Aidan? Will I pass muster?"

Her back was bare, crisscrossed by several elegant, sexy black straps. He itched to put his hand on her skin and caress her. Slide it under that side strap and—

"Aidan?" She tilted her head and smiled at him. Her auburn hair was up, a few strands brushing the back of her neck. She'd put some pale pink gloss on her lips, also the color of cotton candy. He couldn't help wondering if it tasted like cotton candy, too.

"Aidan." His name was breathless on her lips. With a groan, he pulled her to him. Set her on his lap. In her ear, he whispered, "You look more beautiful than anyone I've ever seen. All I want to do is kiss you."

She made a small sigh and put her palms flat on his chest. Through the thin shirt he could feel her warmth. On his lap, she shifted slightly, the black hem of her dress rising up her thighs as she did.

He'd never felt such attraction. Feeling the heat rise in his lap, he leaned forward and nibbled her glossy cotton-candy lips. She squirmed some more, sighing again, and then kissed him. He clasped his arms around her, and they were making out like teenagers on her salon chair.

He laughed inside, loving it, loving what she was doing to him, making him feel young and happy again, as if his life was again full of possibilities and charm.

She leaned back finally, and with that breathless voice, said, "I will never look at this salon chair the same way again."

He grinned at her. "Good," he teased. He itched to mess up her hair, to see what it would be like if they were in bed together, but he restrained himself.

He would like to ask her to skip the wedding and be alone with him instead, but somehow it seemed important that she get comfortable with his family.

Strange, that.

Low voices sounded behind him. He glanced back, and saw that the couple was headed out. One man—the stylist—saw Aidan looking at him and gave a friendly wave. Aidan nodded back.

Ashley jumped off the chair, blushing furiously. "Goodbye, Anthony," she called.

"See you Monday, Cinderella."

She laughed.

"Why does he call you Cinderella?"

"It's the lipstick color I used one time. Cinderella Red. Quite a silly name, if you ask me."

"I doubt it has to do with the lipstick. You look…well, you look beautiful, dressed like that today."

A line formed in her forehead, and she frowned at him. "This is new to me. I haven't done anything like this in, well…ever. I take care of Brandon—that's what I do. I've told you that." Her voice was gentle, but the feeling behind it wasn't. She cleared her throat. "I know it's hard for us to talk during the week, with Brandon there, so maybe we should clarify things now."

"Uh-huh," he said, determined not to let

her give him excuses. "Single moms are allowed to date, Ashley. There's nothing wrong with that."

"For most single moms, Aidan, but I have to be careful. If I mess up…if Brandon's father has a family and they find out I've messed up…I'm afraid they'll try to take him away from me somehow. I can't afford to make any mistakes. Maybe that's wrong, but I've always felt nervous. I know some of it comes from my background with my sister and my mom and our tough childhood, but…"

"Hey," he said softly. "You're not making mistakes. And Brandon's a well-adjusted kid. He loves being with you." And then he made a joke, just to take away that distressed look on her face. "You know me, Ashley. If you were doing something wrong, wouldn't I tell you?"

She gave him a smile, but it was a sad one. "I'd like to keep this secret. Us dating, I mean. For now." She swallowed, looking up at him so pleadingly that his heart went out to her. "Can we do that, please?"

"A hundred people will see us together at my cousin's wedding," he reminded her gently.

"I know. I mean secret from my family. From my sister. And…Brandon. Especially Brandon. For now," she said again, glancing at him.

He thought back.

The two of them had met in the salon this afternoon rather than at her apartment. She'd specifically asked Aidan to come here, but he hadn't realized that it was because of Brandon. He'd thought it was a sexy thing she wanted to do with him, coming into her workplace toward the end of her regular Saturday work hours and getting a haircut.

"So...you're not going to tell Brandon anything about us," Aidan clarified. "At all?"

She shook her head. "Why raise his expectations? Especially if it doesn't..." She blushed.

"If it doesn't work out between us, you mean."

She nodded.

He crossed his arms, suddenly tense. On an intellectual level, he understood. She was protecting her son. But his heart wasn't taking it well. Not well at all.

He glanced at her, and caught her looking at him, worried and sad. It was just a flash of emotion across her face, but it told him that she wanted it to work every bit as much as he did.

"So...if it works, we'll tell Brandon. Is that what you're saying? Because it's what I want. And I think your fears are unfounded."

She nodded. "I know I have to tell Brandon at some point. But…maybe if we take it slow, I'll feel more comfortable."

"Get him through his math test. Is that a good goal?"

"Yes." She nodded again, relieved. "You understand."

"Yeah, I do."

His heart softened a bit. He would just have to make sure that it did work.

He wiped his face with his hand. Thought for a second. "What did you tell him about tonight? If you're not with me, then where are you?"

"I didn't have to tell him a thing about tonight, actually." A smile spread over her face. "I thought I was quite clever about it."

"You are quite clever," he agreed, intrigued at what she'd come up with.

"Well…" She put an apron on herself, and then the blue plastic cape on him. Then she put on a pair of rubber gloves and began stirring that pot she'd carried out.

"Because of his cast, Brandon isn't allowed to participate in his required club sport. He'd chosen soccer for the fall, but since that's out now, they gave him a choice of other fall activities."

"And you guided his choice, I'm assuming."

"Oh, yes. And quite conveniently, country hiking takes place on Saturdays."

"And since the Captains are on the road today…"

"Exactly." She nodded, putting down her spoon. "Brandon is climbing Mount Monadnock with the St. Bartholomew's Outdoor Club as we speak. They'll be down the mountain by sundown, then they'll have dinner and drive back to Boston."

"Ah." Aidan actually felt a bit envious of Brandon. He'd always loved hiking. And what he wouldn't give to have Ashley with him, alone, overnight in a tent on a mountainside in New Hampshire. What a fantasy.

"Now lean back," she told him, swiveling his chair away from the sink and to face the mirror. "After a quick shampoo, I'm going to put this conditioning treatment in your hair. It's quite goopy, but it works great. You'll be under the dryer for fifteen minutes, though."

"Wait, what? I thought I was getting a scalp massage first?"

She laughed delightfully. "That comes after the conditioning treatment and before your cut and blow-dry."

He glanced at his watch. "Do we have time for all that?"

"Yes, we have time for that, but I do have one bit of unfortunate news before we start."

He braced himself. "What?"

"I turn into a pumpkin at eight o'clock."

"Excuse me?"

She sighed. "Brandon's bus gets back to St. Bart's at nine o'clock. That means I need to leave the reception at eight o'clock. I know that's right after dinner, and I'm really sorry, so I won't feel bad at all if you just drop me off and then return to party with your cousins."

He shook his head. She really didn't understand him. "Ashley, you're my date tonight. I stick with my dates. I'm not going to go back afterward without you."

"If you're sure…"

"Yes, I'm sure. If you hadn't agreed to go with me, then I wasn't going to go to the reception at all."

She smiled at him. "Then I'm glad I agreed, because it's good for you to spend time with your family."

He laughed softly.

"What?"

"I realized why my grandmother seems to have given her approval."

"Well…that's one less thing to worry about. Now let me fix your hair."

"I don't know about this," he said, eyeing the jar of glop she wanted to slather on his hair.

"A plastic cap will cover it."

"Forget it."

"Trust me, Aidan. I am very good at what I do. When I'm finished, you will not only look better but you'll feel like the best you possible."

He thought the same thing could have been achieved if she'd stayed in his lap for a while longer.

Then again, if he played along with the hair thing, maybe she would reward him later.

"Go for it, Cinderella."

ASHLEY TURNED OFF her blow-dryer and then stepped back to admire her handiwork.

Amazing. Aidan looked fantastic. Without that wild, long hair always in his eyes, he looked like a new man entirely.

She stepped back farther. Maybe he looked *too* good. Too far above her. As he buttoned up his shirt, tied his blue tie, and tossed on his suit jacket, he seemed…

Unbelievably handsome. All eyes would be drawn to him with his natural magnetism.

She chewed her thumbnail. What had she done?

"You're right," he said, smiling. "You are good at what you do."

She crossed her arms, rubbing them.

He was glancing at himself in the mirror. Touching his hair. "I like it."

"I hope so."

He glanced at her sharply at her doubtful tone. "It's great. Let's get going."

They went outside, and down to street level. Ashley walked slowly, constrained by her high heels and the short dress. She clutched her purse in one hand, a shawl in the other. It had been unseasonably warm today, but the evening would get cooler.

Aidan had borrowed his grandmother's town car and driver. He opened the door for her, gently helping her climb in.

The back seats were plush and warm, the air in their compartment quiet and still. She felt cocooned from the world.

The engine started up and the driver steered the car down the street.

Aidan reached for her hand. "Everyone will see that you've tamed me."

"That's never what I wanted to do!"

"I like being calmer. I'm done with war zones."

"Tonight won't be one?" she said nervously.

He chuckled and laced her fingers with his. It felt sensual and heartwarming to her, both at the same time. And then she was leaning over, kissing him. Running her fingers through that hair that she'd always loved, though now shorter and softer to the touch, less wild-looking.

Their driver turned the car down a garage ramp, and Aidan gave her a long, soul-sighing kiss.

"You'll be okay tonight, Ashley. I promise." His eyes glittered in the light from passing headlights in the dim garage.

"Yes, I trust you Aidan."

INSIDE THE VENUE, Ashley's mouth dropped open at more of those floor-to-ceiling views of the inner harbor. The wedding was on State Street, in an upper floor of a high-rise just behind Boston's famous blue-lit clock tower. It was nearing sunset. Chairs had been set up so that the bride and groom could say their vows facing the water. Later, Aidan explained, tables would be brought in and the guests would dine beneath moonlight that would shine through those spectacular windows.

He was a model escort. As she'd hoped, he kept her arm in his. They circulated the room, and he kept up a commentary in a low undertone, explaining to her who each relative was.

Cousins. Aunts and uncles. His parents

couldn't make it, he explained, because they lived and worked in Florida.

"So does my mother," she blurted, and then blushed. Most assuredly, her alcoholic mother and his doctor parents did not move in the same social circles. Just as she and Aidan didn't.

"Where in Florida is she?" he asked.

She swallowed. Maybe the key was to accept it herself. To believe that she had no reason to feel ashamed of her past. She was doing her best now. She always did her best.

Smiling at him, she answered, "A small town near Orlando, in the middle of the state."

"Ah." He nodded. "My parents are in Naples. On the Gulf Coast."

"Do you ever make it down to see them?" she asked, curious.

"Not often."

"Me, neither."

He smiled at her, just as a waiter stopped before them with a tray filled with flutes of champagne.

Her first instinct was still to freeze, to stare at the flutes of sparking, bubbling wine with the siren scent of sweet white French grapes, her old friends. If she let herself, she would feel her nose twitch, her mouth water, her knees weaken.

Yes. Oh, please, yes. Just a sip...

Her palms itched to clutch the cool glass in her fingers, to feel the sweet tartness glide down her throat, to let the reality-dulling euphoria take over her inhibitions.

But she stepped away. Smiled tightly at Aidan.

He already understood—she hadn't needed to step back or to smile.

"No, thank you," he told the waiter. "But if you could bring us two glasses of sparkling water, that would be much appreciated."

She let out the breath she'd been holding. "Thank you," she said after the waiter left them.

Aidan gazed at her. "I care about you, Ashley. If you want to, I think we could really build something here."

She put her hand to her mouth, amazed at what he was saying.

But then the minister took the microphone. "Everyone? We will be ready to proceed with the nuptials in ten minutes, if everyone will please take a seat."

"I'll be back in a moment," Ashley whispered to him. "Ladies' room."

"Of course." Aidan nodded. "I'll save you a seat."

She gave him her shawl to hold and then,

clutching her small purse, she dashed off to the ladies' room. Once inside, she wet a paper towel and stared at herself in the mirror. She looked dewy. Bright. Alive.

Did she dare?

She was just about to leave when Vivian Sharpe entered. She walked slowly, using a cane, and her hair was freshly done.

Maybe she'd been inside the private treatment room with Ilana when Ashley and Aidan had been in her workstation at the back of the salon.

Ashley pressed her hands to her cheeks at the realization of how easily they might have been seen. Perhaps Vivian even knew how close they were getting.

Vivian nodded to her. She didn't seem surprised by Ashley's presence. "Hello, dear," she said mildly. "Are you enjoying the wedding?"

Afraid she would stutter, Ashley just nodded.

"And how is Brandon?" Vivian asked. "I heard he's in a cast. I'm sorry to hear that."

"He's…" Ashley cleared her throat. "He's fine, thank you. I'll tell him that you asked about him."

"Very good." Vivian nodded and slowly walked on.

"Mrs. Sharpe?"

Aidan's grandmother turned, and Ashley realized that although there were many questions she was dying to ask her—about her interest in Brandon, her possible influence on his school admission, the scholarship, her plans for the future—there was really only one that she needed answered right now.

"Mrs. Sharpe, do you approve of my dating your grandson?"

Vivian Sharpe smiled faintly. She rested on her cane and seemed to consider Ashley—her dress, her demeanor, her question. With that same bland smile, she answered, "If I didn't, would it matter?"

"Yes," she answered honestly. "Because he loves you."

A flicker of surprise shone on Vivian's face. Followed by another look—wariness. "My grandson has been deeply hurt. I urge you to be kind to him."

Ashley nodded. "That goes without saying."

If Vivian was taken aback by her answer, she didn't say so.

Ashley returned to the wedding, still considering their meeting. She held back, watching Aidan. He was seated up front by the windows, talking to his cousin, the groom. Aidan had introduced them earlier. But it wasn't his cousin that amazed her; it was the easy way Aidan sat, relaxed, conversing.

A laugh. A nod. A dimple-faced smile. He was so handsome, her Dr. Lowe. When she and Lisbeth had been children, they used to play an old board game with the girls across the street. My Favorite Date. The game's choices for the girls' escorts had been either a sportsman, a scholarly nerd, a cowboy or a millionaire in a dapper jacket and tie. Ashley had always chosen the dapper millionaire with his dark looks and confident smile. Perhaps she loved the security and power that symbolized. She, a child who'd grown up with so little of either. Lisbeth, bless her, had gone for the scholarly-looking date every time. Deeply studious Lisbeth, who hid from their home's instability and poverty inside the logic and promise of her books.

Aidan met that promise for Ashley; he was what she needed. He'd been kind to her, though often challenging and meddlesome, too. All traits that, while maddening, sometimes had also done her good.

And physically, he *drew* her to him. Heaven, did he draw her.

She made her way across the floor and sat beside him, her whole body tingling. He glanced at her, his smile growing wider. His eyes twinkling.

She felt as if they were the only two people in the room as he touched the small of her back with his hand, leaned over and kissed her.

"Are you ready?" he whispered in her ear and she nodded, just as the wedding march began and everyone stood for the bride.

The ceremony was short and heartfelt. As the sky over Boston Harbor deepened into shades of red and gold, the bride and groom made their vows, exchanged rings and sealed their promise with a kiss.

"I now pronounce you man and wife."

The guests stood again and cheered. Even Aidan was smiling. Ashley had glanced at him during the short service, and he'd been watching intently. No sense of any troubled feelings, which she'd worried about, given his experience with Fleur and her lack of commitment. A bad experience hadn't scared him away.

He'd reached over and threaded his fingers through hers. Maybe they could try. Slowly, very slowly at first. Take it as a test.

After dinner, the music started. "One dance," Aidan murmured in her ear.

"But it's almost eight o'clock! I told you I'll turn into a pumpkin."

He laughed. "My grandmother's driver is an ex-NASCAR racer. I promise I'll get you home on time."

So she relented, and she was glad that she did. The lights were low, and the band played a slow, romantic oldie from before she'd been born. She felt like she was in another world, a new world to her, and she felt glamorous and cared for as Aidan danced with her in his arms.

But it appeared he had another agenda, because he danced her toward a particularly dark spot of the room, on the edge of the celebration. When the music ended, he leaned down and kissed her deeply, his hands running through her hair, over her shoulders and down her back. She ached for him. Her whole body throbbed.

If she hadn't had to go home…if she hadn't had responsibilities, then she would have gone home with him in a heartbeat.

"Come." He broke the kiss. "I promised you won't turn into a pumpkin on my watch, and I'll keep that promise."

He whisked her into the town car. And as he'd promised, the car sped through the streets of Boston.

Until they came to a construction project—a group of workers huddled by a manhole. Her street was blocked.

"Oh no!"

Aidan opened the door. "We'll run. Hurry up! We have five minutes."

Giggling in a way she hadn't since she'd been a young girl, she dashed after him in her bare feet, holding her strappy heels.

She ran on her tiptoes, on the edge of the grass beside the sidewalk. He held her hand. "Hurry up, Cinderella!"

She reached the door to her building, breathless. He glanced at his watch. "One more minute," he announced.

And then he kissed her, his tongue mingling sweetly with hers, until the minute had passed.

She let go reluctantly. "Good night!" she called to him from the doorway.

He disappeared into the shadows.

TWO NIGHTS LATER, during their regularly scheduled Monday session, Brandon had buckled down.

Aidan said nothing, but privately he was amazed. However, he kept a poker face as he copied the numbers and equations that Brandon recited into a notebook.

Brandon finished dictating and sat back. He picked at one of two stickers on his black cast—the New England Captains sticker. The other sticker was for the Outdoor Club at St. Bartholomew's School.

"Well?" Brandon asked. "How did I do, Dr. Lowe?"

His student's answer was 100 percent perfect. "You're ready," Aidan said.

Brandon sighed with relief. "My math teacher wants you to call him. I asked him about you being my writing hand for the test next Tuesday, and he said he has some questions for you."

"No problem." Aidan set down his pencil. "I'll go in and see him tomorrow."

Brandon nodded. With his left hand, he pulled over his English text book. No nonsense. No chatting. He had homework to get through, and he was doing it without procrastination or complaint.

The kid had come a long way. He knew how to study now. He'd focused and was growing up, in Aidan's opinion. His mother and his aunt had been right—Brandon was very bright when he applied himself.

Aidan watched him turn the pages of the book despite the bulky black cast. That obstacle hadn't stopped him. On the contrary, it had seemed to motivate him even more.

"I'm proud of you," Aidan said quietly.

Brandon paused. He didn't look up at Aidan, but Aidan saw him smile.

Ashley came in the door, breathing heavily from her walk outside and looking beautiful. Her glossy auburn ponytail was slightly disheveled. He imagined the wind on the Boston Common blowing through it.

Aidan glanced away from her. If he looked at her, her son would surely know everything Aidan felt, and he'd agreed—albeit reluctantly—not to tell the boy anything about them just yet.

"We're finished here," Aidan said to Ashley, pretending to look over Brandon's shoulder with interest at what he was reading.

"Okay. Can you see yourself out, then?" Evidently, Ashley was determined not to look at him, either.

"Douglas is going to walk to school with me tomorrow morning," Brandon informed his mother.

Aidan saw that Ashley looked rattled. "Who?" she asked Brandon.

"Douglas. My friend from Outdoor Club."

"Oh. Okay."

"He's not a boarding student, either. He's a commuter like me. He lives in Brookline."

"Well, great." She gave him a shaky smile. "I'm glad you're making friends."

Brandon closed his books. "I'm going to read in bed. Good night, Aidan."

"Good night."

"Don't stay up too late," Ashley called.

Brandon nodded, headed into the bathroom and shut the door.

Quick as lightning, Aidan used the opportunity to motion to Ashley. Breathlessly, the two of them ducked into the hallway outside the apartment.

This time, she touched him first, placing her hands on either side of his waist and pulling him to her. "God, I missed you," she whispered as she stood on her tiptoes and kissed him.

He cradled her head with his palm and kissed her back. "Can I spend some time alone with you? Please tell me Brandon has an Outdoor Club activity on Saturday?"

Ashley nodded. "He's climbing Wachusett Mountain."

That was located in central Massachusetts. "Excellent," Aidan said. "That's, what, a three-hour drive from here?"

"It's a little over an hour. Sorry, Aidan."

"Well, it's something."

She pressed herself against his chest and sighed. "You have the memorial service to go to on Saturday."

He stilled. He'd been trying not to think about that.

She peered at him. "You're still going, aren't you?"

Idly, he smoothed back her hair. "Please come with me, Ashley. Sit beside me. I meant it when I asked you."

She hesitated. "I want to support you, and I'll definitely be driving with you to the church, but I wonder if it might be too early—too hurtful—for Fleur's parents to see me sitting beside you."

He thought for a moment. Maybe she was right about that.

"You wouldn't mind waiting outside?"

"Not for this. I'm thinking of their point of view. They don't know that you and her daughter broke up, that there are hard feelings, and it wouldn't be helpful for them to learn about it now. Let them live with that delusion. It doesn't hurt us, Aidan."

This woman thoroughly amazed him. "Okay," he said quietly. She was right. It was the kind thing to do.

Ashley hugged him even tighter. He wanted to stay in this hallway forever.

He hoped he could get through the service on Saturday without getting angry and giving everything away.

CHAPTER TWELVE

ASHLEY KNEW THE memorial service was a test for Aidan. Was he really ready for a new relationship the way that he said he was?

She sat in the passenger seat of his rental car, while he steered into a parking space.

"Destination arrived," the navigational software blared from the dashboard.

Aidan clicked it off. "Yeah, we're here," he said to Ashley. They both sat in silence, staring at the traditional New England church where Flo and Albert Sanborne had arranged for her daughter's memorial service to be held.

"It's beautiful here. Very peaceful," Ashley said. Two huge maple trees stood sentry beside the tall white steeple. The maple tree's leaves were just turning from green to scarlet and gold, and the effect was stunning. "Is this the town where Fleur grew up?" she asked.

Aidan nodded. "She invited me home for Thanksgiving once, in the early years. Honestly, though, she didn't come home that often."

Ashley glanced around at the picturesque

town. North of Boston, it was a much nicer place than the gritty urban street where she'd spent her childhood. "Why didn't she like it here?"

"It wasn't a matter of liking it or not," Aidan said slowly. "At least, I never thought so. She just...preferred to live near her work."

A small group of children were playing in a park across the street. Two were swinging on the swing set and one was romping with a dog. "This looks like a great place to bring up children," Ashley said wistfully.

Aidan just nodded. His gaze looked far away. Was he saddened? Was he comparing her with Fleur, wondering what might have been?

A car pulled up, close to the church walkway. People were climbing the stairs. Ashley glanced to the clock on the dash—ten minutes until the service started.

Aidan let out his breath. "I should go inside."

She nodded.

He glanced at her, as if to ask something, but then shook his head as if thinking better of it. "If you want to take the car for a drive, go ahead. Just be sure to keep the navigational software on. I'd hate for you to get lost."

She smiled at him. She knew where she

was. "Actually, I'm going to take a walk. There's a beach two blocks from here. I'll sit in the sand and watch the waves for an hour."

He looked surprised. "Have you been here before?"

She nodded. Although Aidan had rented a car today, this town was only a few stops north of Boston on the commuter train. "I came here with friends a few times," she said softly.

"On family fun days?" He smiled at her.

She smiled back, even though that hadn't been the case. But, oh well, just as she'd never know the whole story of his life with Fleur, there were things from her past that would also remain private. "I like to look at the ocean. I'll keep busy while you're gone. And I'll be thinking about you." She leaned over to kiss him. He held on to her arm for a long moment.

Finally he broke the kiss, leaning his forehead against hers.

"I have my phone." She held it up. "Call me if you need me."

"I really don't need to do this for closure, you know. This service is for Albert and Flo. It isn't for my benefit."

Maybe. She hoped so. That remained to be seen.

"I'm over her, Ashley."

She smiled at him. "Then it's nice of you to go, for Flo and Albert."

He winced. "Yeah." But he opened the door and let himself out.

She got out, too. The air was cool and scented with an ocean breeze. "Why don't you drive over to the beach parking lot and pick me up when you're finished?" she suggested.

He gazed at her over the roof of the car, his expression perked up. "Okay. Yeah. That sounds great." He paused. "Maybe you can look on your phone and find a good seafood place where you and I can have dinner."

She smiled at him. "I'd like that."

As she watched him walk off, it occurred to her that maybe he really was over his ex. Maybe he was ready to start anew again. With her, this time.

An hour from now, she would know better. Time would tell.

AIDAN WALKED INTO the small church, originally built for a village congregation hundreds of years before he'd been born. He was filled with a mix of emotions...awkwardness, apprehension and discomfort at being with people from a life he no longer wanted to remember.

But it was pretty hard to forget all that, because the first thing he saw was a massive photograph of Fleur's smiling face, set on an easel at the front of the church.

He turned away from it, managing to smile at Fleur's mother, who'd rushed forward to greet him.

He let Flo—not exactly a mother-in-law to him, not even considered a friend by her daughter—hug him. The two women hadn't been estranged exactly; Fleur had just lived a different life from that of her parents. She'd been adamantly unconventional. And Aidan, who'd thought his entire family was unconventional, too, hadn't been fazed or surprised by any of it.

Knowing Ashley had changed that for him. He was enthralled by the way she adored her son. That she wanted to spend as much time as possible with him.

In the early days, Aidan had always just assumed that he didn't want to marry or have children, either, like Fleur. Then they'd both turned thirty, and then beyond, and he'd been shocked to realize that *his* mind was changing. He was starting to want something that she didn't want to give. The deal they'd struck early on no longer worked for him.

In the end, he'd realized that they had completely opposing goals and values.

He'd grown into his values. Looking around at the church, at the local people—Flo and Albert's friends and neighbors—Fleur had grown up with the values of family and friends and love of community. While she'd shed them, he'd been acquiring them. Ashley had acquired hers in adulthood, too, and she'd passed them to Brandon, her son. Maybe that was why he felt he was growing into a relationship with Ashley that just fit him better.

He moved aside to let a couple pass, and in doing so he brushed against a sprig of white roses on the aisle. The whole place was bursting in white. White roses, white lilies. It looked nice.

"You did a lovely job," he commented to Flo, who was clutching his arm now, as if having taken possession of him.

"Roses were Fleur's favorite when she was a girl."

He nodded. Fleur had loved roses. He felt sad for her, that she was gone so young.

"There's a real big crowd," Albert remarked. His jaw appeared to be trembling. "It's good to see her doctor friends make the trip to say goodbye to her."

"Your friend Ashley was very helpful with the names," Flo said. "I sent out quite a few invitations."

Ashley. She wasn't just a friend; she was much more than that. But Albert was shaking another man's hand. Hugging a woman who'd stopped to whisper her condolences.

"We were too broken up to have a proper funeral service for her the first time," Flo said to Aidan. "It's nice that we can have this one now. For everyone who knew Fleur as a child. She was so smart and promising. Her father was over the moon when she became an important doctor."

Aidan nodded again. He was starting to understand how important this was for them. Maybe he was starting to understand how his and Fleur's difficult relationship might actually have made it more difficult for him to accept her death. Maybe while he'd been trying to distance himself from her memory, her parents had been trying to hold on to any of the positives they could find.

In any event, his heart seemed to be breaking open, finding more compassion than he'd known before.

Just as the music started and Flo took his arm to bring him forward to take a seat with her, Aidan saw the church door open. His grandmother, Vivian, had arrived.

He smiled across the room at her. She understood the importance of family in a way none of his other relatives seemed to.

Beside him, Flo cried softly. Fleur had been her only child. "Parents should never have to bury their children," she whispered to Aidan.

He clasped his hands and bowed his head. Concentrated on the words the minister was saying. Breathed in the fresh scent of flowers.

He was genuinely sad that Fleur was gone from life. Not that she was gone from *his* life, but that she was gone from her family, from her own life. She would never have a chance for a redo or for a fresh start, the way he had.

By the end of the service, he felt as if he'd said goodbye to someone he'd known a long time ago, when he was a different version of himself.

Anger had seeped out of him. Good times had been remembered. Grudges forgiven.

When it was all finished, Flo asked him back to the house for a buffet supper.

"I can't, but thank you for inviting me," Aidan replied.

"I understand." She smiled at him. "Doctors are important. You're always so busy."

He smiled back. Maybe that's how things had been in the old days. Now... Now, he was spending his time in relaxed contemplation.

"Good luck, Flo. If you ever need me—"

"I'll call," Flo said. "I have your number."

"Of course." He gave her a hug, wondering what Ashley would think of all this when he told her. Surely, she would understand. "You take care now," he said.

He sought out his grandmother, gathering up her cane discreetly in a back pew and preparing to stand. He helped her up by the elbow and held out her cane for her. "Thank you for coming, Gram."

"Of course, dear. You knew I would." She gave him a long, gentle hug and then pulled back. "Well. That was lovely. A very nice service. I'll go speak to Fleur's mother, and then I'll be heading home."

"Is Rocco outside?" he asked.

"Yes. I told him I'd call when I was finished."

"Then I'll wait until you're ready to leave, and I'll escort you outside."

She patted his shoulder. "Thank you. I'll be just a minute."

He waited quietly in a corner for her, watching as she approached Flo and spoke a few kind words for her. Flo seemed genuinely touched that Gram had come. Aidan was, too.

And then he did as he'd promised. He escorted Gram to her waiting town car, the engine idling in front of the wide church stair-

way, and helped her into the backseat. After
Rocco had driven off, Aidan went back inside.
He had one last thing to do in the church be-
fore he headed over to Ashley.

Aidan went down the aisle and stood before the oversize portrait of Fleur. He thought
briefly of the good times they'd had. He bowed
his head and said a private prayer for her.

And then he said goodbye.

ASHLEY HAD WALKED barefoot from one end of
the beach to the other. Except for one couple
walking a German shepherd and another in
an impassioned conversation on a beach blan-
ket near the entrance, the stretch of beach was
deserted in early October.

What had most surprised her was that the
beach was much smaller than she'd remembered. The water colder. The sand a shade
darker, more brown than white.

She turned to head back to the parking lot
just as Aidan appeared, walking toward her
in his regular loping, confident gait.

She watched him for a moment, feeling
happy. So strong and handsome, he grinned
at her, even from this distance. His black hair
danced in the breeze, his jacket was tossed
over his shoulder.

She ran to greet him then, and he scooped her up in a kiss.

It was on the tip of her tongue to ask him how it had gone, but any details had to come from him, at his pace.

Was he okay? Was he truly over Fleur? Or did he still feel guilty?

"This beach is great," he said, gazing around. "I can't believe you found it, tucked into the village like this."

"It's for residents only, but if you don't park in the lot, nobody bothers you."

He put his arm around her. "Walk with me."

She nodded, feeling as if he had something important to tell her.

They walked for a few moments, listening to the seagulls overhead. He pulled her even closer, so they were walking hip to hip.

Finally, just when she couldn't stand the suspense any longer, he said, "Thank you for helping Flo. I think it meant a lot to her."

She exhaled. "I hope she's all right."

"I think she will be." He paused for a moment. "I'm glad you encouraged me to go."

Ashley smiled. "It was the right thing to do."

"Yeah. I'm surer now of what I want."

What did that mean?

"You know, Ash, since Brandon is going on

an overnight hiking trip with his outdoor club next weekend, I was wondering if you would go overnight camping with me, too?"

She stopped short, dragging him to a stop with her. Next weekend would be four days after Brandon's test. That meant he was staying—for her.

"You okay with going camping?" he asked.

"You mean, you and me in sleeping bags? With bugs and ticks and outdoor toilets?"

He burst out laughing. "Only you would say that," he teased.

Oh. *Oh!* He wanted to kick their relationship up to another level. She hadn't expected that from him today.

"You…were just at a memorial service," she said weakly.

"I was. And it struck me, Ash. Life can be so short. There's no way to know what tomorrow will bring. I want my life to mean something to me. I thought about all the things I most wanted, and then what I realized is that I most want you, to go camping with me this weekend. I've always loved it and I want to do it more in my new life. But you know, I can compromise. How about if I find us a shelter with a bed? And screen doors and indoor plumbing?"

"But it's overnight…the two of us alone?"

"Yeah. Of course." He tilted his head at her. "Does that make you nervous? Because I love you, Ashley. I really do think I love you. And only you."

How could she say no to him after that?

Especially since after the way he had put it, she really wanted to go camping with him, too.

CHAPTER THIRTEEN

IT'S JUST A TEST, Ashley told herself.

Maybe she and Aidan wouldn't even be compatible. Maybe he would be tired of her after spending a weekend—two days and two nights together.

In such a case, they could both laugh it off. *Oh, well. It wasn't meant to be, sorry.*

Because honestly, there were so many reasons why they shouldn't be together, or even get along.

Her son, for one thing. The bulk of Ashley's time needed to be spent with Brandon, at least until she got him through the rest of his high school years and out of the house, hopefully to college. That was her biggest priority. Brandon always came first with her.

But Brandon likes Aidan, too.

Doesn't he?

These were the thoughts and questions that Ashley tormented herself with as she worked with her customers on Monday.

She'd promised Aidan an answer by Friday. He said that he'd already arranged the trip, that he would go by himself if she said no, but that he'd rather not.

Brandon wouldn't find out—he would be on a weekend camping trip of his own.

Why not go with Aidan? She wanted to. She wanted to share a tent—a bed—with him. Her cheeks flushed to think of it, her body tingled, her heart beat faster. Aidan was constantly in her thoughts, in the back of her mind nearly every moment. He said he loved her. It just felt…so remarkable to her. And so natural.

On Monday night at seven o'clock, Aidan arrived at her apartment for his last tutoring session with Brandon before his test.

She hadn't made her decision yet. She wanted to go with Aidan. She was *tempted* to go with him. But they couldn't even put their heads together and whisper about it, because Brandon needed all of their attention.

"You're ready for tomorrow. You know that," Aidan told her son quietly.

"I hope so." Brandon picked at the sticker on his wrist's cast. He and Aidan were sitting at Ashley's kitchen table the night before her son's big test, and all Ashley could do was agonize. Maybe give him a big breakfast in the morning and say an extra prayer.

"What's going to happen is that I'll go in

to the test room with you," Aidan told him. "We'll sit before the proctor, and the proctor will give you your test. You should take a moment to look the whole thing over, get familiar with it."

"What if I see a problem I can't answer?" Brandon asked.

"Then move past that question and read the next one. The problems that you're feeling unsure about, save until the end. You'll have an hour for the test, so you want to make the most of it."

"Okay." Brandon nodded. "That makes sense."

"You'll know what to do. You've studied, and you're well practiced. You just need to remember to stay calm and focus. One step at a time, the way that we've been working."

"Can I talk to you about the hard problems, Dr. Lowe?"

"Now or tomorrow?"

"Tomorrow."

Aidan shook his head. He looked so serious, and Ashley was touched that the two men in her life had become so important to each other. Aidan would make a wonderful father—she could see it in the way he interacted with Brandon. And Brandon obviously looked up to Aidan. He depended on him now.

"Brandon," Aidan said. "The proctor will be watching me closely. I can't give the appearance that I'm helping you with anything other than writing. Just like we do during our tutoring sessions, you tell me what to write and I'll write it."

Brandon sighed. "This is so stressful."

Tell me about it, Ashley silently agreed. She was washing the sink, giving it a good—if relatively quiet—scrubbing while she listened to the two talk.

"I really need to pass, Dr. Lowe." The panic in Brandon's voice was palpable.

"I think you can pass. But you know what, Brandon, it's more important that *you* think you can pass."

Her son sighed. "What will happen if I don't?"

"Don't think that way," Aidan warned. "That's called defeatist thinking, and it will bring you down all kinds of bad paths. Visualize the best results happening tomorrow. You'll be much better off, trust me."

Brandon was listening as intently as she was. He just wasn't showing it.

She met Aidan's gaze across the table. Calm brown eyes. Solidly faithful. Always dependable. She felt strong just looking at him.

Aidan swallowed, his Adam's apple rising

and falling. Glancing at his watch, he stood. "It's time for me to go now." He looked seriously at Brandon. "Get a good night's sleep. I'll meet you at St. Bart's tomorrow."

Brandon stood, too. "I'll walk you out," he said to Aidan.

At the door, Aidan paused to glance at her for the briefest of moments. In that one glance, he told her so much.

He was waiting for her answer. He still wanted her to go with him. He *yearned* for her.

She put her hand to her chest, taking a deep breath to calm herself. She just…wanted to be with him so much, too.

Do it! A new, bold part of her was speaking up, urging her to consider her needs. Because she did have needs of her own, apart from her child, and until Aidan, she'd been pushing those away, convinced that they weren't important, that Brandon's needs were all that mattered.

But Brandon was doing better now. More than that, he was doing well. Since Aidan had come into their lives, her son was focused on his studies. Making headway with his future.

Even Aidan's advice, "Visualize the best

results happening tomorrow," seemed to be speaking to her, as well.

I think he will pass his test, she actually thought.

They felt so relieving, so comforting, these messages of hope.

She believed them. She believed in Aidan. They could work. She and Aidan could make a future together happen.

If Brandon passed his test, and all was well with him, she would take it as a sign. His passing could usher in a new time for her. She could be safe to explore a weekend alone with Aidan, focusing on *their* relationship.

Please, Brandon, she thought, as she watched her son exit their apartment with Aidan, headed for the street, *Please pass this test tomorrow. Because if you do, then I will go.*

THE NEXT MORNING, Aidan walked into the examination room in a hopeful but reflective mood.

It had occurred to him last night that these weeks with Ashley had actually changed him. Who had ever thought that after Afghanistan, he could talk about positive thinking and best outcomes?

Aidan blew out a breath and gave Brandon an encouraging nod. The boy settled into his seat, black cast raised, and looking scared but determined.

That's it—believe, he willed Brandon. "You can do it," he mouthed to the boy.

Every fiber in Aidan's body was rooting for Brandon LaValley to overcome his challenges and rise to the occasion he'd practiced and worked and sacrificed so much for.

The room proctor entered. He passed out the test papers and a blue booklet for Aidan to write in. Aidan and Brandon had already received their instructions. At the proctor's nod, Brandon's test began.

The boy started slowly, a bit unsure. Aidan itched to send him an encouraging smile, but he was aware of the proctor who watched over the two of them as Brandon took his exam separately from the other boys.

Aidan wouldn't do anything to hurt Brandon's chances. He had to force himself to remain still and calm. To copy the numbers and symbols that Brandon dictated to him.

As the minutes ticked by, Brandon seemed to pick up confidence. He dictated more quickly.

He was doing a good job. Aidan privately kept track of the boy's progress. When the test finished and Aidan silently tallied the boy's results, it was all he could do to keep the knowledge to himself.

"Time is up, please." The test proctor collected Brandon's paper.

Aidan stood and stretched. Brandon did likewise.

"Well?" he whispered to Aidan.

Aidan approached the proctor. "I'd like to talk to Brandon privately for a moment before he returns to class."

"Certainly, Dr. Lowe."

Aidan took Brandon into the quiet hallway. While Brandon looked up at him with wide eyes, as if holding his breath, Aidan drew the boy's cell phone from his own pocket.

"Your mom told me to give this back to you if I thought you did well today. And you did really great." He handed the boy his phone.

Brandon clasped it and held it to his chest, which swelled with the emotion of the moment. Aidan couldn't hide his own smile at Brandon's joy.

"You think I did well?" Brandon asked. Moisture glittered in his eyes. It struck Aidan that Brandon seemed more affected by his praise than by the return of the phone.

Aidan hadn't expected that reaction. Not at all.

He felt his own eyes growing moist. He and

Brandon had grown gradually closer over the past weeks, but in ways that men bonded, not like he and Ashley were slowly bonding. Teen boys were unique. Aidan hadn't been totally sure that he'd been getting through to Brandon until this moment.

"You rocked it, kid," he said, his own voice sounding hoarse. "But I knew you could. I think you can do anything in your life that you put your mind to. I'm glad I got to work with you, and not just because you're a Sunshine Club kid, or a Captains ball boy or a St. Bart's student. I'm glad to know you because of you. You're a really remarkable person. Just keep being your best self, and everything will work out for you."

As he spoke, Aidan knew he was laying it on a little thick, but life was so short. He had to be honest and tell the people who were important to him just what they meant while he still had the chance.

Brandon didn't seem to mind. The kid was so emotional over the joy of having achieved something real, something that meant a lot to him, something he'd fought so hard for.

Brandon ducked his head, leaned forward and hugged Aidan, the cast on his arm solidly sticking into Aidan's back.

Aidan swallowed back the lump in his

throat as he hugged Brandon fiercely. "You'll be okay," he said. "You know that, right?"

Brandon held on to him for a long time. Aidan had never been a big hugger, but in this case, he would hug the boy all day if that was what Brandon wanted.

Finally, Brandon let go. His eyes were wet and the tip of his nose was red. Aidan felt a lump in his throat, too.

"I couldn't have done it without you," Brandon mumbled. He scrubbed the back of his free hand over his nose.

Then he straightened, smiling shyly at Aidan. "I should, ah, get back to class."

"Yeah," Aidan agreed.

Brandon looked up at Aidan as if he wanted to say something else. Aidan waited, giving him the chance to gather his thoughts.

"Um, will you type your number into my phone?" Brandon mumbled.

Aidan blinked. Brandon had just given him the highest compliment an adult could get from an almost-teen.

"Sure," he said, smiling.

Brandon pressed his finger on the phone's screen a few times, and then awkwardly handed the phone over.

It occurred to Aidan that this act might put more pressure on his relationship with Ashley.

She hadn't agreed to spend the weekend with him yet. She said she was still thinking about it. He understood; it was a big decision for her. She might not have had another committed relationship before, other than with her son and her sister. Aidan knew he was asking for a lot from her. But he had faith that she loved him, too. That she was ready to figure out how to build a new life, and that she didn't have to be a single mom forever if she didn't want to be.

He finished typing in his phone number and then handed the phone back to the kid. Even if the worst happened—which he didn't want to imagine—Ashley couldn't be upset if Brandon wanted to call him now and then. That's what a mentoring relationship was.

Yeah, but you've fallen in love with your mentee's mother, a small voice said in his head.

"So, um, are you still going to tutor me?" Brandon asked.

Truthfully, he hadn't been thinking beyond the short term much until now. He'd been drifting since he'd been home—healing, Ashley had called it—not really sure what he wanted or what he was going to do, beyond a vague plan of escaping from what his life had been before.

But now everything was changing. He

wanted to stay closer to Ashley and Brandon—and besides, renovations were still ongoing at his condo. He had time to see what developed with Ashley. And he did like tutoring Brandon.

"Sure," Aidan said. "If you want me to. And if your mom says it's okay. I'm not, ah, committed to anything yet."

Brandon nodded. "I'll tell her I want you to still come after dinner and tutor me."

"Okay." It might be sticky if Ashley decided she wasn't ready to be with him. But Aidan didn't want to accept that happening. He decided to be optimistic, just as she'd taught Brandon to be. And him, too. "I'll let you handle that conversation, then."

"I'm going to be away this weekend," Brandon said. "The Outdoor Club is having a hiking trip."

"Your mom told me. Where are you going?" he asked.

"The White Mountains."

That was a range in New Hampshire. Aidan nodded. "A part of the Appalachian Trail goes through that part of the state. I plan to hike that myself at some point."

"Will you do a section-hike or a through-hike?"

"You know about the Appalachian Trail?" he asked, surprised.

"Yes. Our science teacher showed us pictures. He's our Outdoor Club adviser, too. He's done the through-hike twice. Once northbound, and once southbound."

"I'll have to talk to him sometime."

"I can introduce you." Brandon gave him a shy smile.

"That would be great."

A buzz of teen voices sounded behind them, amplified by the echoing of St. Bart's high-ceilinged corridors.

"I gotta go," Brandon said. Then he got a big grin on his face. "I'm gonna find my friends Douglas and Cho and tell them my good news. See ya, Aidan. Thanks again for everything. I appreciate it."

Outside, Aidan blinked in the bright sunlight. But he didn't go home just yet, where his kitchen had been completely torn out and now resembled a construction zone. Instead he headed over to Perceptions on Newbury Street.

He walked right in, waving at Ilana as he breezed past her. Her brow lifted, but she didn't say a word, probably thanks to his grandmother.

Ashley was at her station, cutting an elderly man's hair. Aidan felt a stab of jealousy that he wasn't the man in the chair with Ashley's hands against his head.

When she saw him standing there, she blanched. The hand she held her scissors in fell to her side.

He just smiled and gave her a thumbs-up. "Brandon did it."

Ashley clasped her hands together. Maybe her knees had weakened, because she leaned against her sink, using it for support.

"He passed," she said to the gentleman in her stylist's chair. "My son passed his exam!"

"Good for him," the gentleman said.

Ashley hopped over and threw her arms around Aidan, laughing. He gave a bear hug in return, breathing in the comforting scent of her hair.

"I gave him his phone back like you asked me to," he murmured into her ear. "And he said he wants to keep up the tutoring. He's going to talk to you about it when he gets home."

She turned her head and spoke beside his neck, tickling his skin. "Thank you," she whispered. "Thank you for helping us."

He kissed her, cognizant of the white-haired man watching his every move.

She leaned back in his arms and smiled up

at him. "You and I are going camping this weekend, Aidan."

"We're—"

"Yes. You and I. And you know I don't like to camp." She raised her brows and then smiled shyly at him.

Before he could react, she stepped back to her job, resuming her clipping and humming to herself.

Aidan stepped back, happiness spreading through him. He hadn't expected this today.

He had a lot to plan.

TWO EVENINGS LATER, Ashley stood at the clothes dryer, folding the socks and active-wear that Brandon wanted to take on his hiking weekend. Brandon was leaving on the bus directly from school tomorrow afternoon— Friday—and she needed to make sure he had all of his things together before he left for school in the morning.

She wouldn't be seeing him until he returned on Sunday. And then one of his commuter friends from school was coming for dinner and staying with them until his grandparents could pick him up later in the evening.

"This trip will be the most awesome thing we've ever done," Brandon said to her as he sat at the kitchen table. Ashley just smiled to herself. She didn't think that Brandon's feet had hit the ground since he'd received his official test scores yesterday at school.

"Douglas and Cho and I are sharing a three-person tent," he said.

"Douglas—he's the one who's eating dinner with us on Sunday?" she clarified.

"Yes, Mom. He's a commuter, like me. His grandparents are stopping by tonight because they want to meet you and give you their phone number. They're the ones picking him up on Sunday."

"Right." She made a mental note to pick up something for dinner before she left. "Okay."

"And did I tell you that we're assigned an inflatable raft, too, so we can ride the river on Sunday? This is going to be the most epic trip we've ever taken."

"Wait a minute. River rafting?" This was the first she'd heard of that.

"Yes, Mom. But don't worry because I know how to take care of my cast."

Ashley thought it strange that the school hesitated about casting him in a play because of his wrist, but river rafting apparently posed no problem.

"Dr. Lowe said it will be okay," Brandon said, noticing the skeptical look on her face.

"Well then, I guess I can't say no, can I?"

Ashley had asked Aidan about Brandon's cast care, too, during water activities. Aidan had advised her that Brandon's fiberglass cast would be fine, thanks to its water-repellent liner, but that Brandon should still take care to wrap the cast in plastic. She'd bought supplies at the pharmacy, and now she grabbed them from her kitchen cabinet and tossed them into Brandon's backpack. She hoped she was remembering everything. Their lives were so hectic these days.

Beside her, Brandon scrolled through his phone again. She allowed him to use it for the few minutes before dinner. After dinner, he had his study session. Tonight, though, Aidan wasn't coming. She had so much to do to prepare for Brandon's trip tomorrow that she and Aidan had mutually agreed to suspend his lessons until he returned.

Ping! Brandon received a text message. Furiously he began typing with his thumbs.

"Is that your friend Cho?" Ashley asked, sliding Brandon's freshly fluffed-and-folded gear into his backpack.

"Yes it is. My brother from another mother," he said happily.

She had to smile at that, too. It felt fantastic to see Brandon happy again. Privately, she'd been worrying about the wisdom of working so hard, at such a young age, to the exclusion of much else.

It would be worth it, though, Aidan had explained to her, since Brandon had caught up to where he should be, skill wise. From here on out it would get easier for them.

Their buzzer rang, and Brandon opened the door to the other commuter student in his trio of besties. "You must be Douglas," Ashley said to Brandon's friend. "Pleased to meet you." The boy was squat and blond, his hair cut in the same style as Brandon's. Douglas's grandparents came up to talk with Ashley, as well.

"His parents are out of town this week," James, the grandfather, mentioned. "We're driving Douglas to St. Bartholomew's every day and picking him up in the evening. I hope you don't mind that we wanted to stop by and meet you tonight, since our boys will be sharing a tent this weekend. And the dinner on Sunday, of course."

"Anytime," Ashley said. "It's nice to meet you, too. If I can help out further, don't hesitate to call. Here, let me give you my phone number." She grabbed a pen and a slip of paper, and they exchanged numbers and addresses.

"Thanks," James said. Ashley followed

them back downstairs to the street, along with Brandon, to wave them off.

"Would you like us to give Brandon a lift to school tomorrow?" James asked her. "We could load his gear in the back along with Douglas's."

"Well…" She glanced at Brandon and he was nodding eagerly. "I was going to walk with him, but okay. Sure."

She went upstairs, into the apartment and went to flop down on her bed. Her sense of optimism was starting to wear away. As she'd hectically prepared to send Brandon off, it was dawning on her that he would be away from her for the whole weekend—two nights out of her reach—having his own adventures with his new friends.

He loped past her down the hall, wearing his Captains hat backward. "Where's the duct tape?" he called on his way to the kitchen. His voice seemed so much deeper lately. "I need it for my cast."

"Didn't I put it in your backpack with the plastic?" she called to him.

"Nope."

"Then it's in the junk drawer."

"I can't find it."

She heard drawers opening and doors slamming. "It's there." She got up, intending to go help him, but her phone rang in her pocket and she checked who was calling. Aidan.

"Hey," he said.

Relief stole over her, and she sat on the bed. Picking up an old afghan from the end of the bed, she draped it around herself. She needed the comfort of it. She'd been feeling so tired, with the weight of her decision, with the double shifts she'd been carrying so that she could take the weekend off...

"H-hey, Aidan." Her voice sounded shaky, even to her.

"What's wrong?"

He keyed into her moods so quickly. "Nothing. Just tell me I'm doing the right thing."

"What do you mean?"

"Brandon passed his test, but I wonder if I'm failing mine."

He laughed. "I didn't know you had a test. But whatever it is, I'm pretty sure you're not failing."

"I am. It just dawned on me that I haven't been separated from Brandon for more than a night since he was eight years old."

He paused. "Do you want me to come over?"

"I wish. But, no, Brandon's packing tonight. Tomorrow he has the day off because of his Outdoor Club activity. His bus is leaving at ten."

"He'll be okay, Ash. He's just growing up."

Yes, but that didn't mean it sat well with her.

"He will always be your son," Aidan said. "You don't have to worry about him loving you. He just will."

She chewed that over. He was right. "Thank you," she whispered into her phone. "You always know what I need to hear."

"Do you like doughnuts?" he asked.

She giggled at the non sequitur. "I love them, but I haven't had one in forever."

"Why not?"

"They're hard to find gluten-free. And, you know me, I eat gluten-free, because I don't want Brandon to feel left out."

"Well, these are for you. Do you like jelly, sugar or chocolate covered best?"

"Oh, chocolate covered!" she said, stretching her toes.

"And coffee, mocha or white mocha?"

"What, no tea?"

"We're gonna be decadent tomorrow, and the rest of the weekend, too. And there's nothing you can do for Brandon, because he's going on his trip. Think of it as a holiday from worrying. I'll bring you breakfast tomorrow, all right?"

Oh, she liked the idea of a holiday from worrying. And logically Aidan was right. Brandon had his trip this weekend and she had her…fun.

"Okay, I'll take a white mocha," she said. She'd never had one of those, but she loved the sound of it. In fact, she was starting to feel a wonderful sense of adventure.

Thank you, Aidan.

By the time she got off the phone with him, talking just to talk, just to hear his deep voice and the laughter just for her, she felt better. He had a talent for that.

She got up to check on Brandon, but his lights were off and he had gone to bed. She went out to the kitchen and cleaned up the dishes from dinner, and then sat and made herself a cup of tea. Alone at the table.

She wanted both of them, she realized. She wanted her son to stay safe within her orbit. And she wanted Aidan to continue to be a special part of their lives. But for right now, she wanted private time with him. Adult time.

Naughty time.

If that made her a bad mom, then she would be bad.

It was just for the weekend, and Brandon was safe with his school and his friends.

She went to bed with a feeling that she would be okay with Aidan.

"Bye, Mom. See you Sunday."

Ashley watched Brandon load his gear into the back of Maria and James's truck. She stood on the sidewalk for as long as the truck was within view.

Then she went back into the apartment. She was still sitting on the couch contemplating her open suitcase when Aidan rang her buzzer.

She didn't know how to tell him this, but when she'd finally gotten around to focusing on *her* weekend instead of her son's, she'd realized that she hadn't done any planning until it was too late.

So much for her own needs. She had no hiking boots. No sleeping bag. No tent.

And what did women wear camping?

She got up to let Aidan in. As always, her heart sang to see him. He wore a green jacket that made his eyes stand out, and his dimples were on full display. And the smile he gave her made her feel as if she was the most important woman on earth to him.

He put down the bag of delicious-smelling doughnuts and the twin cups of white mocha he'd brought, and then went to her, lightly cupping her cheeks with one hand. "Are you ready to go camping?"

She nuzzled against him and sighed. "Help! I don't know what to pack. I took care of Brandon, but I forgot to take care of me. Will you help me? What should I pack? What do I need?"

He crossed his arms, grinning, his hip against the back of a chair. "Um, nothing," he said. "I don't know, a toothbrush? Even then, I'd lend you mine."

That made her laugh. "Won't we have a tent?" She'd just been watching Douglas and Brandon with their gear in his grandparents' backseat. "You and I are going to be outside, aren't we?"

"Actually, I cheated. I rented a luxury cabin."

"You did?"

"Oh, yeah. I'm not stupid." He grinned.

"Did you do that for me?" she asked.

"Yes, I did," he said sheepishly. "But it is on a lake, and I'm partial to lake houses. The place looks amazing."

"Perfect!" That did make her feel so much better. "In case you didn't realize, I'm not the nature girl you might have wanted."

He laughed. "I promise you we'll have electricity, heat and running water. Just the thing for a city girl."

"Better by the minute."

"We can stop for groceries on the way up. The only other thing I can think we'll need is towels and, uh, sheets."

Sheets. For a bed.

She rubbed her arms again. Getting Dr. Lowe into bed with her was something that was very appealing. She'd been dreaming about it for nights and nights now. She fell asleep with visions of him on her mind.

"Is it a big bed," she asked in a small voice, "or a little bed?"

He raised an eyebrow at her. "I think it's a good size."

She snickered. He winked at her.

"The only sheets I have are for a double bed," she said once she'd finished laughing.

He looked relieved. "That will work."

"Great. Then we're all set." She went to her linen closet and tossed out a set of sheets and some bath towels. He caught them deftly and loaded them into a bag.

"What else?" Aidan asked her.

"Condoms." She looked at him. "Do we have any?"

He paused, gazing directly at her. "We soon will," he said.

Ashley smiled.

CHAPTER FOURTEEN

ASHLEY'S BONES FELT languid by the time they reached the cabin. During the three-hour drive into New Hampshire, she had found herself falling for Aidan all over again.

The sound of his rich, deep voice as he spoke to her. The way he looked over at her from the driver's seat. She'd never felt so cared for and protected.

And instead of the bugs and sleeping bags she'd been worried about, the cozy mountainside setting that Aidan had chosen reminded her of a fairy tale. A traditional design, the log cabin sat alone on a clearing at the end of a winding country road. She helped Aidan bring in their bags of groceries and gear, and he gave her a short tour.

A screened-in porch overlooked the prettiest lake she had ever seen. Inside was a cozy main floor with a stone fireplace. Upstairs was a bedroom with a balcony that overlooked the lake. There was also a large bathroom with a huge antique claw-foot bathtub.

She stood there, admiring it. This was exactly where she wanted to be.

"I didn't know you were such a fan of bathtubs," Aidan said.

"Love them." There was a nice bottle of bubble bath on the shelf. *Sensuous rose.* She picked it up. "It's extremely rare that I get a chance to have a nice bathroom to myself."

The smile he gave her seemed wistful. "Then you shall have your fantasy."

But before she could crook her finger at him, he headed for the door.

"Hey, wait!" she said. "I didn't mean for you to leave!"

He turned at the doorway and gazed at her, his eyes smoky. "I'm going to start a fire downstairs. You come get me when you're ready."

Oh, my. She put her hand to her chest, suddenly feeling hot all over.

But it had been a long day cramped up in the car. She looked forward to stretching her legs in that gorgeous tub. Relaxing with the bubble bath. Thinking about Aidan downstairs, waiting for her…

Smiling now, she filled the tub. Poured in the fragrant bubble bath. The scent of roses and earthy musk permeated the steamy air. She easily shucked out of her jeans and cot-

ton turtleneck sweater, dipping into the bliss-
fully hot water.

Ah. She sank in up to her neck, her ponytail
falling over the lip of the white porcelain tub.

She closed her eyes and rubbed the sudsy
bubbles all over her body. Feet. Legs. Breasts.

She hoped Aidan came in and surprised
her. Her body seemed to be humming all over,
waiting for him. She'd been waiting for him
for weeks now, ever since she'd met him in
her hair salon and had thought him the wild-
est, sexiest man she'd ever seen.

Sighing, she stretched out and relaxed until
the water turned cooler.

No Aidan. She felt very curious as to his
whereabouts.

Nibbling her lip, she hopped out of the tub
and onto a plush cotton mat. She cocked her
ear but heard nothing. On a whim, she dried
quickly and dashed across the short hallway,
into the bedroom she would share with Aidan
tonight.

He'd already made the bed. Pillowcases,
sheets, blankets—all were arranged. Fascinated, she reached into her suitcase and found
a long silky robe she'd packed at the last minute.

The silk felt luxurious on her warm and
freshly oiled skin. She wrapped the robe

around her waist and chest, tied it with a barely functioning knot and clutched the long end of the belt in her fingers as she slipped downstairs on bare feet and bated breath.

Aidan—handsome, sexy, kind Aidan—was on his knees, stoking the fireplace with a length of wood. When he saw her on the stairway, swinging her robe's belt like Mae West, his mouth dropped open. He staggered to his feet, speechless. They came toward each other and met at the bottom of the stairs in front of a long velvet couch, as out of place in the rustic cabin as she'd been.

She and Aidan stood toe to toe. She gazed up at him, into his dark eyes. A hungry look was on his face.

Her breath came in shallow gasps. Her every nerve ending seemed electrified.

"I was waiting for you," she breathed.

"You don't have to wait anymore." He took the silk belt from her fingers and gave it a sharp tug.

Her robe fell open. Cooler air grazed her skin. His eyes devoured her as he drew her to him and they both lay on the couch.

His breathing came in a jagged gasp, too, but he kissed her anyway, as if the feel of her lips was medicine to him. He caressed his hands up and down her body. Her arms. Her back. Her bottom. His touch felt even better than the sensuous bath she'd just enjoyed. Moaning, she pressed into him, fumbling with his belt buckle. With the button to his pants. With his shirttails.

His clothes were off, and then his hard, hot body was next to hers. She *needed* him. There was a hunger in her that had been building for weeks. She'd been wary of it at first, not trusting her body's feelings for him, but now she was sure. Now she was ready for that closeness with him. She wanted Aidan, badly.

His hand dropped to the juncture between her legs, and he worked magic on her. She sighed, wriggling, crying out. The flames and the hunger in her needed to be fed. She needed him inside her, making love to her. She reached down and stroked him. So hard. But something within her—that warning voice of experience—made her screech to a halt.

She opened her eyes. "The condoms!"

"Right." His gaze holding hers, he reached down and drew a wrapper from his jeans' pocket. Then he leaned over and kissed her gently.

"I'm sorry. I shouldn't have forgotten."

"No," she whispered.

"I won't ever forget again."

She smiled into his eyes. He understood.

Briefly, it occurred to her that maybe some-day she would like to have another child. With Aidan. He would make such a wonderful fa-ther.

Feeling teary, she reached out and touched his slightly scratchy cheek. Without breaking their intense, soulful gaze, he put on the con-dom. While he kissed her, more deeply and slowly this time, he lowered himself over her and she met him, enveloping him.

It was heaven. Ashley hadn't shared such a romantic experience like this with anyone, and it felt even better than she had hoped or imagined. He made love to her with a sweet intensity that set her on fire and made her never want to burn out. Caught up in him, she cried out his name.

Afterward, they lay on the couch for a long time, embers cracking low in the fireplace. Aidan softly caressed her, whispering stories about places they would see together. Things they would do, the life they could have.

She loved this—the bubble the two of them were creating together.

"Are you as happy as I am?" she whispered.

He nodded, but rubbed his back. "I will be completely happy once we go upstairs." He laughed self-consciously. "I've been sleeping on a cot for weeks. Honestly, my fantasy has been to get you into bed. A real bed, where we can stretch out and not get up for days."

She sighed. "That sounds like heaven."

"I know," he agreed.

AIDAN WOKE SOMETIME during the night. A light was shining into their bedroom, and when he moved to the window, he saw that there was a full moon over the lake, beaming a path across the water.

He glanced back at Ashley, sleeping on her back with her auburn hair spread over her pillow. She looked so content, so satisfied. He smiled to himself. He wouldn't wake her to see the beauty outside. They had plenty of time ahead of them for that. Years, he hoped.

He'd fallen for this woman, and there was no going back. He'd put a lot of thought into her situation, and he'd decided that he wanted to make her and Brandon permanent fixtures in his life.

She'd been good for him. When he'd told her that he loved her, he'd meant it. He still believed that she felt the same way, even if she hadn't told him yet. She had more at stake than he did; she made decisions for two people, not just one. At the moment, he was rootless, but he hoped that would change. For now, he would just continue being with her as long as they could.

He went back to bed.

In fact, they spent a good part of the weekend in bed, laughing and getting to know each other more intimately. Even sleeping.

He hadn't slept so well in years. The dreams had stopped—he hadn't experienced one in weeks. The nightmares that he'd thought would haunt him forever had finally stopped.

Loving Ashley had a good deal to do with it.

ON SUNDAY, ASHLEY woke up and stretched, her second morning waking up with Aidan. He was on his stomach beside her, breathing deeply. She smiled to herself and reached over, rubbing his back. Sleeping with him would never grow old for her.

Lazily, he opened one eye. "Good morning, Cinderella."

"Good morning, Prince Charming."

"What would you like to do today?" he asked, drawing himself up on one elbow.

He made her dare to believe. Dare to believe she could have the relationship she had always longed for but never quite thought she deserved.

"I think I'd like to start with one last walk by the lake this morning," she said.

He laughed and tickled her nose. "I'm glad to see that I've converted you to becoming a great outdoorsperson."

"It's true you've converted me in many things." She scooted closer to him, cuddling into his arms. "You know what I was wondering?"

"What?" he asked indulgently.

"What about your hike on the Appalachian Trail? Is that still in your plans?"

He gazed into her eyes as he smoothed her hair back. Ashley found herself holding her breath, waiting for his answer.

"I've decided it's not something I *need* to do anymore," he said.

"Oh!"

"I'm perfectly content being with you. I've found peace right here."

She laughed softly and laced her fingers through his. "I'm glad," she said. She was more than glad—she was ecstatic.

An hour later, they walked farther than they had before, to a spot on high ground with a view of the whole lake. Ashley had packed a surprise lunch and put it in her backpack. She munched on an apple while she leaned against

Aidan's chest. She felt his phone starting to ring in his jacket pocket.

She frowned. It was the first reminder they'd had of the outside world since they'd arrived yesterday.

"I'd love to shut the phone off," he said. "But my condo is on the market. It might be the real estate agent calling."

"Where are you going to live when it sells?" she asked.

He smiled at her. "Maybe that's something we can talk about over dinner."

She felt herself blushing with pleasure.

He fumbled for his phone, which was still ringing, and then glanced at it. "I don't recognize the number. Then again, I didn't program in my real estate agent's number."

Ashley leaned close to his ear as he answered. "Hello?" he said.

"Dr. Lowe?" Ashley heard the familiar voice on the other end. "This is Dr. Elizabeth LaValley. Do you by any chance know where my sister, Ashley, is?"

CHAPTER FIFTEEN

"IT'S YOUR SISTER," Aidan mouthed to Ashley, holding his phone against his chest so that Elizabeth couldn't hear them. "But she says not to worry, Brandon is okay."

Ashley's eyes were huge. Aidan realized with a sinking heart that their peaceful weekend was officially over.

"Ask her what's wrong!" Ashley hissed to him. "But I don't want her to know that I'm... I'm..."

"With me?" he asked quietly.

"Not because of you personally!" she said hurriedly, still whispering. "It's that I'm...I don't know. She'll think I'm indulging myself and neglecting Brandon, or something. Oh, my gosh." She put her hands to her head. "Where's my phone? Why didn't it ring?"

She rummaged in her backpack while Aidan cleared his throat and returned to her sister.

"Sorry," he said to Elizabeth as he held the phone to his ear. "My reception isn't that great at the moment. But yes, I'm due to see your sister this afternoon."

He glanced at Ashley, wanting to do what was best for her. He really did love this woman. He would sacrifice his pride if he had to, let her have her secrecy from her sister for a little while longer. That couldn't last forever, but for the moment, he would cut her some slack.

"Will you ask my sister to call me, please, when you do see her?" Elizabeth asked over the phone.

"Yes," he said to Elizabeth. "I'll let her know you're looking for her and I'll have her call you right away. May I ask why? Is it something about Brandon?"

"It is," Elizabeth said calmly, though her voice sounded faint over the line. Their reception here really was spotty. "The school called me because I'm the alternate emergency number. It seems one of the chaperones slipped and broke his leg, so they decided to send everybody home early, because there weren't enough adults to watch the kids. This was about four hours ago, by the way."

"So...let me repeat this to be sure I've got this straight," he said, looking at Ashley as he spoke. She hung on his every word.

"Brandon is fine," he repeated into the

phone, for Ashley's sake. "A chaperone hurt himself, so the bus returned to the school about four hours ago. Where is Brandon now?"

"He's with his friend Douglas's grandparents," Elizabeth said.

"Okay. He's with Douglas's grandparents. I'm, uh, writing this down." He glanced at Ashley, who was pale. She was still hanging on his every word. "Should I have Ashley call Brandon there?"

"No, evidently he doesn't have his phone with him. The school said that Ashley has his friend's home number, though. But have her call me before she calls them. All right?"

"Okay," Aidan said. "Will do."

"Thank you, Aidan." Elizabeth didn't seem angry or suspicious, and that was something. She hung up.

He glanced at Ashley. "Did you get that?"

"I can't believe this happened! I'm usually so careful!"

"It's all right," he said calmly. "He's not in danger. You know it could have been a lot worse."

"I did a terrible job! I wasn't thinking about him at all! It's my responsibility to have my phone on, and with me, and I didn't!"

"Ashley, it's okay. You don't have to be perfect all the time—"

"Yes, I do. When it comes to Brandon, I do." She turned and ran without waiting for a response. It appeared she was already running back to the cabin.

He picked up the backpack she'd left, and then descended the pathway. His heart sinking, he met her in the cabin a few minutes later. She'd found her cell phone charger and was frantically plugging it into the wall. "I can't believe I didn't notice the battery was dead," she said. "I thought I plugged it into the bathroom outlet last night."

"Sometimes plugs don't work if the light switch isn't on."

"I've never heard of that before! That's ridiculous!" Ashley was white-faced. "And the school explicitly told us that we wouldn't be able to reach the kids by phone during the trip. In fact, they told us to keep their phones at home, because they didn't want them damaged."

"Brandon must have memorized my number and given it to his aunt," Aidan realized. He glanced at Ashley. "You can't blame yourself. You couldn't have known they'd come back early. Maybe we should just be grateful that Brandon is okay. He's safe and with his friend's grandparents."

"Right. Of course I'm grateful." She rushed

around the cottage, picking up their things. "We have to get back to Boston, Aidan. I'm sorry."

"I know. I'm with you."

Once she'd finished packing, he carried her suitcase out to the trunk of the rental car.

"How about if I run down and return the key to the cabin?" he suggested. "By then your phone should be charged enough to call your sister. We'll start driving, and you can phone her on the way."

She nodded, but she was still pale and trembling.

"He's obviously safe," Aidan said logically. "He's being taken care of—the school would never leave him somewhere without permission. He's probably having the time of his life. Maybe he even finally got his chance to be a boarder for a little while."

Ashley blinked at him. "I need to talk to my son."

"Of course," he said. "Wait here for your phone to charge. I'll be back in a few minutes."

He took the rental car, and made the quick run to the management office in town. Then he sped back to the cabin.

He'd only been gone about twenty minutes. He hoped she was okay.

When he pulled up to the cabin, the rest of their stuff was sitting on the gravel driveway. Ashley ran outside when she saw the car pull up.

"The phone is charged enough," she said. "We need to go, please. I'm sure I have voice-mail messages. I'll listen to those first, then I'll call Lisbeth."

"Sounds like a good plan." He took the car keys from her and popped open the trunk, while she helped him load their suitcases and gear.

Then she climbed into the car.

"Let's go," she said, even paler, if that were possible. "Please just drive." Then she took out her phone and held it in her hands, intently studying the battery bar.

"If you're worried about the battery not lasting, we can stop at a store and pick up a car charger," he suggested.

She gave a slight nod. "Yes, that would be good. Thank you. Roaming sucks up a lot of battery power."

He wanted her to know that he was on her side. He was here to help. They were a team now.

As he drove down the gravel road, away from the cabin, he put his hand on hers, still resting on her phone. "Ash, we'll figure it out together. Please don't worry. Taking care of Brandon is our top priority. For both of us."

"It has to be," she said, her voice shaky. "It's my job not to screw up."

ASHLEY'S HANDS TREMBLED as she logged in to her voice mail.

Ten messages in just one short afternoon. While she'd been enjoying herself, romping in bed and outside with Aidan, the unimaginable had happened. Not the chaperone's accident, though that would have been stressful enough. There was more in her sister's messages that Lisbeth hadn't passed on to Aidan.

Ashley closed her eyes, feeling sick. Not only had her son been unable to reach her, but, according to Lisbeth, he'd called her back to let her know that he had found his father's family.

"He said he found a newspaper clipping in a tin on your kitchen shelf. Do you know anything about that, Ashley?"

How could this even be happening? *How* could he have found out?

She really did feel like throwing up. This was her worst nightmare. Nothing worse could happen now. Nothing. And Brandon was making this discovery without her there. She really was going to lose him. She felt it.

Panic filled her body. Leaving Brandon for the weekend like this, having him possibly talking to strangers claiming that they were his family, was worse than anything her mother had ever done to her and Lisbeth. Ashley was a horrible mother. Just horrible.

She'd worried about and prepared for this moment Brandon's entire life, and then, when it had come, she'd been indulging in romantic fantasies that...just did not fit with her reality.

She'd been so foolish. She'd wanted Aidan—so badly—to be a partner who made *her* happy. The person who let her be more than Brandon's mom.

But in being with Aidan, she'd slipped. In being with Aidan, she'd been irresponsible again, just as her mother had been. Being Brandon's mom was her job. Her fulltime job. He came first and she just couldn't do both together.

"Ash?" Aidan said, interrupting her thoughts. "There's a superstore on this exit. Do you want me to run inside and find that car charger?"

"Thank you," she mumbled. "Please." It broke her heart, because he really was good to her. She believed that he loved her. He'd said he did, and his actions proved his sincerity.

But if he did love her, he would understand.

He had to know how her past had shaped her and where her priorities for the future must be.

He pulled into the parking lot. "I'll be right back."

Five minutes later, he emerged from the store with charger in hand and gave it to Ashley as he got back behind the wheel.

"Thank you." She plugged it in and attached it to her cell phone. "I'm going to call Brandon now," she said, her voice unsteady. "He doesn't know I'm with you, remember."

"Right." But Aidan's voice sounded pained. He took his hand off hers and concentrated on driving.

She just needed to deal with Brandon's issues right now. But that was a conversation she couldn't have until she talked with her son and found out exactly what was going on.

She waited until they were on the highway again and there was relatively little road noise.

With trembling hands, she dialed the phone number that James and Maria had left her.

It rang for longer than made her comfortable.

"Hello?" This was Maria's voice. "Is this Ashley?"

"Yes," she said, her voice shaking. "I understand that my son is with you. May I speak with him, please?"

"Certainly," Maria said.

"Mom!" Brandon said when he came on the line. "Where are you?"

She tried to keep her voice light for him. She didn't want him to panic, too. "I'm fine— don't worry. It's just that I went for a hike, too, and I was out of range for a few hours. How are you?"

"Okay. Where are you now, Mom?"

"I'm on Route Ninety-Three, on my way back to Boston. I'll be home in two hours." She cleared her throat. "Can you give me Douglas's grandparents' address so I can come pick you up? I left my copy at home on the table." Ashley paused. In response she heard talking in the background.

"Brandon?" she asked.

"That was Douglas." There was another pause, and Brandon's voice got quieter. She heard something squeak, maybe the sound of a screen door opening and closing.

"Mom?" Brandon was back. "I, um, found that clipping you had in the kitchen cabinet."

She drew in a breath, wondering how best to handle this.

"When?" she murmured. "When did you find it?"

"Thursday night."

She thought back. She'd been on the phone with Aidan then.

"So…can we talk about it?" she asked.

"Well, I saw the picture, and the man looked like me. And I know you wouldn't have saved it if it wasn't important. But the biggest thing is that I knew the people who were listed as being his family. Did you know I have cousins and…relatives and stuff…from my father's side?" His voice sounded shaky, but not as shaky as she felt.

How could she even answer that question?

From her peripheral vision, she noticed Aidan quietly watching her.

Exhaling slowly, she said, "No. I really didn't know that, Brandon. I'm sorry."

"My father is dead."

"Yes. You knew that already." She'd never hidden that fact from him.

"This whole thing is so weird," he said. "I've been talking with Auntie about it just now."

"I know," Ashley said, her heart breaking. "Auntie Lisbeth called me and left me a message, too. And, Brandon, you and I will deal with this when I get home. I was going to wait until you were older to talk to you about it then. But we'll figure it out now."

"I'm still kinda getting used to it." He

paused. "I've been staying with them this afternoon. Douglas's grandparents." His voice shook. "*My* grandparents, I mean."

Her mouth dropped open. She'd had no idea. None. And then fear just sliced through Ashley's heart as she'd never felt it before.

What if Brandon preferred staying with them over her? She was having trouble breathing. Douglas's grandparents seemed so normal—more stable than she was. She could deal with it better if the family were monsters. But she'd met the grandparents—they'd been in her home! James and Maria were lovely people.

She groaned to herself—how had she missed it? The two boys did bear a resemblance. And Brandon's father had also been called Doug.

She started to shake again. This couldn't be happening…

And then a new fear occurred to her—what if they wanted custody of Brandon? What if they tried to take him away?

Their home was surely so much nicer than her dingy apartment. They could offer him so many more advantages.

Ashley closed her eyes and leaned back against her seat.

"Mom? You really didn't know about them?"

"No," she said quietly. "This is the first I've heard of it."

Beside her, Aidan coughed. She glanced at him, remembering where she was. She did feel calmer in his presence. Stronger. She thought of some of the things he'd inadvertently taught her while he was tutoring her son.

She sat up straighter. "You and I will get through this," she told Brandon. "We'll meet with everyone, and we'll talk about it. There's nothing to worry about, okay?" Her voice shook, because honestly, though, she *was* worrying. Even now she was mentally phoning her counselors. Where did a person even start in such a situation?

"Okay, Mom." There was a pause. "I'm just glad you're safe. You're coming to get me now, right?"

"Yes, I am. I love you," she told her son.

"I love you, too, Mom." The connection clicked off.

She sat back again and closed her eyes.

"Everything okay?" Aidan asked.

She could only nod.

AIDAN PARKED THE rental car on the street before Ashley's apartment. She was still on the telephone with her sister, getting the details that she'd missed. She'd spent the entire drive on the telephone, but he didn't blame her for it. He understood that she was gathering all the information she needed in order to deal with the issues that Brandon had uncovered.

From what he could tell from what he'd overheard in the car, Brandon had figured out who his birth father was, and, evidently, it was because his nephew was one of Brandon's friends at school.

It didn't surprise Aidan all that much. The timing, yes. The fact of the discovery, no. Brandon had struck Aidan as being curious and open to it. Aidan hadn't been entirely comfortable that Ashley had put the boy off as she had. She'd always known that her secret would be uncovered. He ached for the pain she was in, but he had every confidence that she could handle the ordeal to come. Besides, he would stand by her. Truth be told, he was a bit hurt that she hadn't included him in her conversation yet, but he understood that she'd been taken off guard. He empathized. He could definitely cut her some slack.

While she continued listening to whatever Elizabeth—Lisbeth—was saying, Aidan got out and unloaded Ashley's suitcase. He accepted her house keys from her, and opened the door to her apartment. Then he brought in her bags as she walked into her bedroom and quickly changed her clothing.

He waited, his car keys in hand. He'd left the rental car parked illegally, with yellow flashers running.

She came out of her bedroom in a dressier outfit and with her hair combed and clipped back. She glanced at him and then ended her call.

"Sorry," she said, pocketing the phone. "I have so much to absorb." She sat on the sofa and placed her head in her hands.

"Would you like me to drive you over to pick up Brandon now?"

She lifted her head, alarm in her eyes. "Oh," she said. "You don't need to do that. I'm calling a taxi."

He jangled the car keys, alarmed himself. "You don't want me to go with you?"

She swallowed, then looked at him pleadingly, with genuine sorrow on her face. "I can't, Aidan. You know I have to deal with Brandon's issues right now."

"Yes." He nodded. "And you know that I want to be here for you. Don't cut me out, Ashley."

"I'm not cutting you out. I just…I just can't *slip* again."

"I don't understand what that means."

Her eyes filled with tears. "I make so many mistakes. This time, I might lose him."

He sat beside her. "You won't. He loves you."

"If I'd been paying attention, it wouldn't have happened this way."

"You think I'm bad for you?"

"I think I need to take care of this without distractions. I know what it looks like. It looks like I prioritized my weekend away with you over being responsible for my son."

"This is about appearances?"

She nodded.

"What does your heart say?" he asked.

Tears were dripping down her face. "Oh, Aidan. My heart wants to be with both of you. But that isn't possible right now."

"Are you asking me to wait?"

She nodded, her lips trembling. "Could you?"

He exhaled. "Until when?"

"Until... I don't know."

They stared at each other for a moment. Ashley's hand went to her mouth. "Oh, God," she murmured. "I understand, Aidan. You want to be a close team. You want to be how we were when you were tutoring Brandon. But this is different. It isn't the same."

At another time, he might have gotten angry

with her for putting words in his mouth, but he really couldn't. She was right. He did want to be a team.

"But I can't give that to you right now. I feel like I have to focus on Brandon above all," Ashley continued, her voice shaking.

"Can't we both focus on Brandon?" Aidan asked.

Slowly she shook her head. "Aidan, I have to ask you—to beg you—please, please just give me some time to work through this."

"A day? A week?"

She shook her head, feeling helpless. "I don't know how long!"

Aidan stared at her. "I wish I could agree to that limbo for you," he said. "But I can't. I just can't."

She nodded, miserable. She completely understood. "I know you love me. You want us to work on things together as a team."

He nodded. He knew she understood. He wanted her to give him what Fleur could never give.

Ashley wanted to give it to him, but she couldn't, either. At least not as long as she had this problem.

And there was nothing either of them could say to change each other's mind.

She knew what came next. She knew it, and she dreaded it.

He took out the car keys. "Please, Ashley," he said, his gaze laid bare. "I love you, and I want to help you through this."

Her heart seemed to rip in two.

But all she could do was shake her head. "Not now," she whispered. "I can't be with you now."

"That makes no sense! What are you afraid of? We've been working together with Brandon for weeks. Have I hurt him? Have I hurt you?"

"You don't understand," she said.

"Tell me!"

A sigh shuddered out of her. "Because now, the truth is out. And I'm being looked at and I'm being judged by a lot of different people, including my son. And I have to be above reproach. And to be above reproach, I can't have a man in my life right now. I was once in Brandon's shoes, and I know what I have to do to make it safe for him."

She squared her shoulders. "I can't risk losing him to have a relationship with you."

THERE WAS NOTHING Aidan could say to that. In his opinion, these weeks of keeping their relationship secret from Brandon had taken its toll. Now it was a wedge between them that couldn't be overcome.

There was nothing left to do but return to his default mode. Escape. What he'd planned to begin with, all those weeks ago when he'd returned to Boston, not sure where his life was headed.

But this time, when Aidan returned to his condo that night, he didn't recognize the place. True, he'd gotten used to the new, gleaming kitchen. The completely updated bathroom. And the rooms fully furnished.

But while he'd been gone, his real estate agent had also staged the place.

She'd also left a message on his voice mail. "Aidan. Gin here. We got two solid offers at the open house this afternoon. Call me when you get in."

He tossed the phone on the counter. Then he went into the bedroom and lay down on the new, hard mattress.

He liked his bed better when he shared it with Ashley, but what could he do?

There was only one thing left to do. He dragged out his laptop and bought a plane ticket. He was hiking the easiest part of the

Appalachian Trail that a beginner like him could hike in October.

He was leaving tomorrow. There was nothing more he could do here.

CHAPTER SIXTEEN

One Month Later

ASHLEY ENTERED THE counseling center, where she met with a family therapist each week. Navigating these confusing waters hadn't been easy for her. She'd sought out the best advice that she could find.

Luckily, James and Maria had been accommodating. Brandon's well-being really did seem to be their top priority. Honestly, they hadn't judged her harshly. All in all, they'd told Ashley they were thrilled to have discovered a grandson they'd never known about. As it turned out, other members of their family had known about Doug and Ashley's brief relationship but hadn't realized that there had been a child. Once they'd met Brandon, they'd immediately accepted him, much to Brandon's delight. He relished having more people in his family than he'd had before.

The hardest thing for Ashley had been to keep her jealousy in check. Brandon wasn't just her son anymore. He wasn't just a LaValley. He was also part of another tribe, and for the first time in nearly thirteen years, he had a family that she wasn't related to.

Ashley drew in a breath and watched her son through the window into the teen rec room. Brandon and his friend—cousin— Douglas were firing Ping-Pong balls at each other, as fast as they could.

Cho had joined them—it was Saturday after all—and the result was chaos. But they were laughing and happy, still kids in most ways, really. They didn't see all the complications that the adults focused on.

Sighing, she pushed herself away from the window.

"Brandon's wrist seems to be doing better," her counselor remarked.

"Yes," she agreed. The black cast had come off several weeks ago. "The doctor doesn't think there will be any lasting effects. Kids' bones are much more resilient than adults'."

"How did his party go with the Captains last night?"

She smiled. "He was disappointed they didn't make the play-offs, of course, but Vivian made a fuss about him and gave him an award for excellence in fundraising, so he was pretty happy about that."

"Wonderful. Are you happy?"

Ashley nodded. She had a newfound belief that the worst was over. She had Brandon, who was happy and healthy. She had more confidence in herself. And she was particularly proud that she hadn't slipped or succumbed to her old temptations with alcohol, despite the stress she'd been under.

But otherwise...

She wasn't truly happy. Something large and all-encompassing, the foundation and the spice to all these other areas of her life, was missing.

She missed Aidan with a fierceness that had stunned her. She knew that she loved him. She'd known it for a long time. What she hadn't realized was how vital his presence had become to her wellbeing. That part she'd only realized once he was gone.

She put her hands in her pockets and walked to the library on the other side of the building. Inside were lounge chairs overlooking the brown park. The trees were bare, now that they were well into November. She took comfort in sitting here, lost in contemplation in the private corner, away from other people.

Her time with Aidan had given her a new perspective. She now saw that while Brandon would always be her son, he would also, as he grew, begin new, healthy relationships with people that didn't necessarily include her. And these people might even judge her, whether she wished it or not.

But did it have any bearing on whether she was a good mother or not?

Tears stung her eyelids. She'd wanted to be a good mom to Brandon. Until recently, she'd defined that as being selfless. And perfect. Maybe too perfect. Too giving. And unable to forgive herself when she made a mistake.

She hadn't been able to see it before. She saw it more clearly now as she'd had to learn to work with Maria and James and their big, unfamiliar brood.

Maria had said something that had triggered her realizations. "You've raised a wonderfully giving, self-sufficient and personable young man. You should be proud of what a good mother you've been."

Ashley had been shaken. It was true. It was also true that Maria's definition of success was much better than her own had been.

Ashley had been at her best—in how she felt, in how Brandon had grown—when she'd been with Aidan. She just hadn't realized it until she'd lost him.

She wanted to be with Aidan again. *And* she wanted to be a good mom. Until recently, she thought they were mutually exclusive states. But having calmed down, and realizing that the new self-sufficiency that Brandon was demonstrating was in part due to Aidan's influence, she no longer thought this was true.

She picked up her phone and dialed his cell number. Her hands were a bit unsteady, but from excitement rather than fear.

She wanted to hear his voice. She wanted to see him, desperately.

A computer-generated voice answered, the standard service recording. She debated whether to leave a message or to try again later, but she didn't want to wait any longer.

"This is Ashley." She hesitated. "Please call me." She hesitated again. "I miss you," she whispered.

Then she bit her lip, wondering whether to admit anything more on the recording.

She did. She wanted to give herself the best possible chance. Taking a deep breath, she said, "I've found that I can be a good mom and still let go of my fears enough to have my own life, too."

She ended the call, then sat still for a long time, watching the wind in the trees. She could only hope that he would call back.

But she had to face facts: what if he didn't want her anymore?

TWO DAYS LATER, Ashley still hadn't heard from Aidan. She took a walk to his condominium on the waterfront and headed over to chat with Bill.

Bill smiled as she approached. "I haven't seen you since Dr. Lowe sold his unit and moved out of Boston."

Her smile threatened to waver. Her knees felt as if they might give out. But she swallowed back her disappointment. She had known this could happen.

"Did Dr. Lowe leave a forwarding address?" Ashley asked.

"Certainly," Bill replied. "Mrs. Sharpe is receiving his mail, as before."

Ashley clasped her hands over her stomach. *He's hiking the Appalachian Trail, just as he'd planned.* She knew it in her bones.

"Thank you," she said to Bill. *Now what?*

Aidan could be in the wilderness anywhere from Georgia to Maine. She had no idea of knowing.

There was one woman who did. Ashley groaned to herself.

She didn't have Vivian Sharpe's private phone number. The best chance she had of finding the elderly lady on short notice was to go to her home and throw herself on her mercy.

Gritting her teeth, she headed for the street.

She would do it. She would do whatever it took to have one more chance with Aidan.

She went outside and caught a taxi to Beacon Hill. Mrs. Sharpe's townhome was located on an exclusive cul-de-sac. She had as much security as the governor.

This was scary, but she would do it for herself. She was worth it.

Ashley presented herself to the guard who answered the door.

"Please tell Mrs. Sharpe that Ashley LaValley is here to see her about her grandson Aidan."

The guard placed a call and in a murmur, relayed her message.

"You may wait here," he informed her.

Ashley sat on a chair in a grand hallway. She fixed her gaze on a curving staircase, wondering if Vivian herself would descend.

"I wondered when you would come see me," Vivian said.

Ashley jumped in her seat. The lady had appeared from a side room.

"Oh!" she said. "Mrs. Sharpe!"

"Are you looking for my grandson or for me?"

"For Aidan," Ashley admitted. She swallowed. "I'd like to go see him."

Vivian looked at her with clear blue eyes.

Then she felt in her sweater pocket and took out a little gold pen. "He has a resupply stop scheduled for next Tuesday in Virginia."

Virginia? Ashley's strength faltered. She would have to leave Brandon with someone else as she flew to meet Aidan.

Swallowing, she thought of everything she stood to gain.

"Very well. Thank you, Mrs. Sharpe." She pocketed the slip of paper.

Vivian nodded. "Will you go to him, dear?"

"Yes."

"Good for you." The woman turned and walked away, her cane thumping softly.

Back home, Ashley borrowed Brandon's laptop to go online and purchase a single airline ticket. Then she picked up her phone and called Maria to see if Brandon could stay with them while Ashley was gone.

AIDAN SAT IN a remote shelter with a group of hikers he'd met on the trail and watched the sun set over the Blue Ridge Mountains. Truly one of the most beautiful sights he'd ever seen.

But try as he might, he hadn't been able to get Ashley out of his mind.

For the hundredth time that day, he wondered what she was doing now. He wondered how Brandon was doing. The baseball season was over, and he'd surely be out of the cast by now. Maybe he'd be preparing for ski season. St. Bartholomew's School had a great beginner's ski program.

The phone rang from another hiker's backpack. Privately, Aidan appreciated the irony. He'd gone on this trip looking for solitude, hoping to be completely alone and cut off from civilization. The thought made him laugh now.

What Aidan had found instead was that he naturally gravitated to people. And people hiked with their cell phones. Even on the trail, they were never long out of cell phone range.

"Yeah," the hiker he'd been sharing the trail with said. Aidan only knew him by his handle, Wanderer. "Sure, Mrs. Sharpe, your grandson is right here."

Aidan chuckled to himself. His wily, meddling "spider" grandmother never gave up, and he'd come to find that he especially loved that about her. She must have even saved this phone number from the one time he'd borrowed Wanderer's phone to call her about his condo closing.

"Yeah, Gram," he said to her when he took the phone. "What's up?"

"Ashley LaValley came here looking for you today."

Aidan jumped from the rock he'd been sitting on and stood at attention. "What did she want?"

"I told you. You."

"Me?" He shook his head in wonderment. "What made her change her mind?"

"Does that matter? I gave her the town and date for your next scheduled stop, and she said she was buying a plane ticket."

"A…" He was so flabbergasted he couldn't get the words out of his mouth. "I have to go." He handed the phone back to Wanderer.

Then he picked up his knapsack. "Goodbye!" he called. "I have to run!"

ASHLEY SHOWED UP for work to find Kylie pinning Christmas decorations on the lobby wall. "Christmas?" she exclaimed. "It's not even Thanksgiving yet!"

"I know." Kylie smiled. "But I asked Ilana, and she agreed. Don't you think it just makes Christmas last longer?" She sighed happily. "It's my favorite holiday."

Ashley wasn't sure. What she most wanted for Christmas was Aidan Lowe, but she wouldn't have a chance to go find him until next week. Even then, she had no idea how he would react to seeing her.

She went back to her workstation and began

to arrange her things for tomorrow. The light outside was fading, and it was getting darker earlier. Almost time to go home and meet Brandon for dinner.

"Um…" Kylie came around the corner, sheepishly shuffling her feet.

"What is it, Kylie?"

"You have a walk-in client. A man is here to see you."

"But we don't take walk-ins."

"I know, Ashley, but he insisted. And his grandmother is a very important client of ours."

Ashley gasped. Kylie broke her acting face and began to giggle.

As if in a dream, Ashley walked to the waiting area.

Aidan was there. He looked thinner than the last time she'd seen him, and his hair was long and wild again. He definitely needed a haircut. But he looked wonderful to her, just as he always had. She ran into his arms, sobbing with happiness. "Aidan, you came!"

"All you had to do was call me when you were ready, Cinderella." He scooped her into his arms and kissed her as if he never wanted to let her go.

"I'm home, Ashley," he murmured, brushing back her hair. "Do you have a place for me in your family?"

"I do. I always will." Tears were running down her face. "I realized so many things after you left. I was my best self when I was with you. Brandon was at his best, too. We both…" She nearly faltered, but gathered her courage.

"I love you, Aidan Lowe. I don't care what anyone else thinks of us, I just care that we're together. Please, I'd like us to be a team. You and me. No matter what."

"You got it," he said, and then he grinned at her. "Whatever crazy thing comes along—and with us, it'll always be something—then you know you can count on me."

EPILOGUE

"Mom, you look beautiful!"

The day that Ashley had never thought would arrive, had. Blinking, she stood in front of the cheval mirror and gazed at her reflection.

Rosy cheeks, a happy smile, if slightly dazed. And wearing the most gorgeous white silk wedding gown she'd ever seen.

This truly was a happy ending.

Lisbeth came up behind her and gave her a gentle squeeze. The sisters smiled into the mirror together. "Who would ever have believed that the LaValley sisters would both be married and happy?" Lisbeth whispered.

"Sometimes I still have to pinch myself," Ashley confided.

Lisbeth laughed. Her six-month-old daughter, Sarah, made happy, gurgling baby noises from the bed were she sat in her cousin Brandon's arms.

Ashley sat down on the bed and took out a tissue.

"Oh, don't cry. You'll mess up your makeup," Lisbeth said.

"Do you ever look back and wonder at how far we've come?" Ashley asked in wonder.

Lisbeth sat beside her. "I'm still getting used to living down the street from you."

Ashley laughed. Aidan had started up his new orthopedics practice at Wellness Hospital, the same hospital that Lisbeth had transferred back to once Jon had been traded from San Francisco to Boston.

Ashley's handsome brother-in-law was off with her husband-to-be in another room at the Cape Cod Inn, where they were soon to be married.

"Brandon, what time are you meeting Aidan and Uncle Jon?"

Brandon grinned at her as he bounced baby Sarah in his lap. Her pink tulle dress stuck out in all directions, and her matching headband looked adorable on her sweet baby face.

"Don't worry, Mom," he said. "We've got it all under control."

"That's good to hear." And she smiled at him, because it really was good. And miraculously, she really didn't need to worry.

Wow. Have I come a long way, she thought. She'd once been a constant worrywart, living her life in fear of the unknown. But now she knew that no matter what happened, she could handle it. As long as she loved and kept her loved ones close in her heart, then she was equipped for whatever surprise twists life might throw her way.

"Soon you'll be Mrs. Lowe," Lisbeth remarked. Ashley nodded. Her sister had chosen to keep her own name after her marriage, but Ashley was looking forward to being Ashley Lowe. She already had her plans drawn up for her own hair salon: Ashley Lowe Creations.

She hoped to open in the fall at home in Boston after they spent summer weekends here on the Cape, where Aidan and she were renovating a weekend cottage a short way down the sandy beach from a vacation home that Jon and Lisbeth had recently purchased.

That left Brandon. Headed back to St. Bart's at the end of the summer for his second year of private school, he still had a big decision to make.

Aidan had offered to adopt him. To give him his last name, as well. Ashley had felt her heart grow big with love—and she'd thought she couldn't feel any bigger—but this was Brandon's decision to make. If he chose not to, then she would respect his wishes. If he decided he wanted to, then that was wonderful.

As she watched him with his baby cousin,

she felt deep pride for her boy. He was gentle and kind with children, just as his stepfather-to-be was.

"You know, Mom?" Brandon said. "I think I'd like Aidan to adopt me. But I think I'm going to keep my own name."

"Oh?" she asked. "And why is that?"

"Because that was your name all those years, and you've been a really good mom to me."

That was the best thing Brandon could have said to her. The very best thing.

* * * * *

LARGER-PRINT BOOKS!

HARLEQUIN

Presents

GET 2 FREE LARGER-PRINT NOVELS PLUS 2 FREE GIFTS!

PASSION GUARANTEED SEDUCTION

LARGER-PRINT BOOKS!
GET 2 FREE LARGER-PRINT NOVELS PLUS
2 FREE GIFTS!

H HARLEQUIN®

INTRIGUE
BREATHTAKING ROMANTIC SUSPENSE